2010

# "CAPTAIN, THIS JUST ISN'T GOOD."

"Their engines are built to travel at about half the speed they're moving. I don't know how it's even holding together with its low-end structural integrity system." Duffy paused as he read more. "They don't have replicators or transporters to speak of. They don't even have inertial dampers; they use acceleration couches when they travel." He shook his head. "If we're not careful, any sudden deceleration will turn these guys into paste."

"*Oy gevalt*," Gold muttered. "Then I suggest you start scouring the computer library for ideas if you have none of your own, Commander."

Duffy turned his attention to the computer's library files on ion storm encounters, hoping that past experiences of Starfleet's finest engineers might spur his thinking. He scanned past more recent entries, dismissing accounts of ships with more advanced shielding than that employed by the Senuta. Before long, the log records began to bear twenty-third-century timestamps and four-digit stardates . . . and the signatures of someone very familiar to him.

"Well, I'll be. . . . Montgomery Scott." Duffy again found himself speaking aloud to no one in particular.

"Captain Scott? Did you call this in?" Abramowitz asked.

"No," said Duffy. "But I have a feeling that Captain Scott is going to help us out of this jam without his even knowing about it."

And voices from the past began ringing in his mind. . . .

# STAR TREK®

## S.C.E.

### BOOK FIVE

# FOUNDATIONS

**DAYTON WARD**
**&**
**KEVIN DILMORE**

Based upon *Star Trek®* and
*Star Trek: The Next Generation®*
created by Gene Roddenberry,
and *Star Trek: Deep Space Nine®*
created by Rick Berman & Michael Piller

**POCKET BOOKS**
New York   London   Toronto   Sydney

POCKET BOOKS, a division of Simon & Schuster, Inc.
1230 Avenue of the Americas, New York, NY 10020

*Star Trek® S.C.E. #17: Foundations, Part One of Three* copyright © 2002 by Paramount Pictures. All Rights Reserved.
*Star Trek® S.C.E. #18: Foundations, Part Two of Three* copyright © 2002 by Paramount Pictures. All Rights Reserved.
*Star Trek® S.C.E. #19: Foundations, Part Three of Three* copyright © 2002 by Paramount Pictures. All Rights Reserved.

STAR TREK is a Registered Trademark of Paramount Pictures.

This book is published by Pocket Books, a division of Simon & Schuster, Inc., under exclusive license from Paramount Pictures.

ISBN: 0-7434-8300-6

First Pocket Books paperback printing March 2004

10  9  8  7  6  5  4  3  2  1

POCKET and colophon are registered trademarks of Simon & Schuster, Inc.

Manufactured in the United States of America

These titles were previously published individually in eBook format by Pocket Books.

For information regarding special discounts for bulk purchases, please contact Simon & Schuster Special Sales at 1-800-456-6798 or business@simonandschuster.com

# FOUNDATIONS

# CHAPTER
# 1

Stardate 53675.1

As he sat in the center seat of the *U.S.S. da Vinci's* bridge, the young officer knew all eyes were on him. The bridge personnel had turned from their flashing consoles and even away from the main viewer to focus their attentions on the "big chair." Their hands were stayed from taking action as they awaited his next words. Silence hung in the air.

The officer smiled. Above all else, Kieran Duffy lived for a captive audience.

"So there we were at the bar, the three of us, and for whatever reason, the Andorian woman's face turns this almost royal blue color . . ."

"It couldn't have been that she was embarrassed," said Ensign Robin Rusconi, seated at the *da Vinci's* conn for her usual gamma-shift duties. "I can't imagine your open speculations about an

Andorian wedding night would have upset her sensibilities."

Duffy looked to the conn officer and knit his brow. "What, you're not curious?" He smiled, letting his eyes drift up to the viewer and the comforting stream of streaking stars it provided as the ship traveled at warp speed. "Ensign, I wasn't trying to pick a fight. I was trying to initiate a cultural exchange."

"You're lucky you didn't get your chronometer cleaned," Bart Faulwell said from his seat at the bridge's communication station. Duffy laughed a bit, knowing that Faulwell had sat through his rendition of this particular encounter maybe a dozen times. While he'd always been indulgent, Duffy was pretty sure that the linguist had not volunteered for a late-night turn of duty on the bridge just to be regaled by tales of the crew's extracurricular antics.

"Okay, okay, forget the Andorian," Duffy said, trying to regain his listeners' focus. "This is where it gets good. In walks this pair of Tellarites, and Fabian perks up in his seat. Don't ask me why, but the guy finds Tellarites endlessly fascinating. You know he can even speak some of their language?"

Faulwell laughed this time. "One of their languages, anyway. Ever since our last trip to Maeglin, I've been giving him lessons. And he makes me listen to him in our quarters, usually when I'm trying to sleep."

A look of understanding spread across Duffy's face as he regarded Faulwell. "Ah *hah!* So that's why you're up here tonight. You're trying to ditch your roomie."

"Not in so many words," said Faulwell. "But I am glad to be here if only so I may report back to Fabian that you succeeded in relaying this story to each member of the *da Vinci* crew."

"I'm goal oriented," Duffy replied as he turned back to his audience. "So Fabe launches from his stool and says, 'Watch this.' He walks up to the pair and, well, grunts out something. Carol, who's next to me, can only sit there stunned at the whole thing. She just can't believe it's not *me* doing something dumb in front of the Tellarites."

Faulwell laughed despite himself and shook his head. "He'll never get the hang of declining his verbs properly. And people ask me why I dislike first contact missions so much."

"So time just freezes. Then the bigger Tellarite—"

A sudden blaring klaxon cut Duffy off, jolting everyone on the bridge. Rusconi's eyes glared wide as she spun toward the console and others on the bridge followed suit. Forgetting all notions of finishing his story, Duffy straightened in the command chair.

"Report!"

Ensign Joanne Piotrowski, the gamma-shift tactical officer, called out over the alarm without looking up from her console. "Long-range sensors have detected a vessel, approaching fast. Estimated speed is warp eight-point-eight and it may be climbing."

Duffy turned to face her. "A ship? What kind?"

"It doesn't match anything in the ship-recognition database. Whatever it is, it's not very big, probably only large enough to carry a few dozen humanoids." Studying her tactical displays for several more seconds, Piotrowski added, "There's no indication they're doing any scanning of their own, or that they've locked onto us as a target. But there's no variance in its heading." She tapped a command into her console. "Its speed is definitely increasing, but minutely."

Duffy saw Faulwell sweep up a Feinberg receiver from the communications console and slip it into his left ear. Though it was a throwback to Starfleet technology almost two centuries old, Faulwell was one of the few Duffy knew who still used the tiny tuner consistently. It seemed to help focus his attention on transmissions intercepted by the *da Vinci* while filtering some of the noise from elsewhere on the bridge.

"I'm picking up a signal from the ship, Commander. It will take the UT a bit to sort this out, though. It's a language I've not heard before."

If Faulwell had never heard this alien tongue, Duffy knew that posed a new set of variables. Given his background as one of Starfleet's premier cryptographers, let alone his linguistic training, Faulwell had been exposed to the languages of countless races across two quadrants. Duffy wouldn't have been surprised if Faulwell doped the language out before the Universal Translator.

"Well, I doubt anyone would announce a sneak attack," Duffy said. "Thanks, Bart." He settled a bit back into his chair. "And would you mind turning off the alarm before it wakes up everyone on the ship?"

Faulwell regarded Duffy with an amused expression. "Isn't that the point of a red alert?"

"Sure, but this isn't anything gamma shift can't handle on its own." The klaxon went quiet, allowing Duffy to once again hear more typical bridge sounds: chirping consoles, the chatter of shipwide communications, the hissing door of the turbolift. "No reason at all to disturb the beauty sleep of our shipmates."

"So the lieutenant commander thinks my appearance would benefit from some shut-eye?"

Duffy snapped up in the center seat, instantly recognizing the voice. He spun to face Captain David Gold, who stood at the entryway of the bridge appearing ready for anything.

Or at least as ready, Duffy thought, as a beige textured-cloth bathrobe and slippers allowed a commanding officer to appear.

"True beauty, Mr. Duffy, is reflected in the soul."

"Captain!" Duffy cleared his throat a bit, hoping to suppress the giggle he so wanted to release. "There's a ship of unknown origin on a course intercepting ours. Sensors recognized nothing about it, so the alert sounded." He tried to talk around that giggle, but failed miserably. "It doesn't appear immediately threatening, sir, if you'd like to head back to bed."

Gold narrowed his eyes at Duffy, a signal that he was there strictly for business and not for a crack at his expense. "Just when will we cross paths with this vessel?"

Duffy looked to Piotrowski, who was ready with the information. "Unless we alter course, about twelve minutes, Captain."

Gold looked to Faulwell next. "And we haven't made contact with the vessel yet?"

"No, sir," Faulwell replied, two fingers helping to keep his ear receiver in place. "I'm still working to sort out its transmissions. Whatever the message might be, it appears to be running on a repeating loop. It may be steadily broadcast or programmed to sound whenever something enters that ship's sensor range."

The captain nodded and smoothed the front of his robe as Duffy rose from the command chair to make room for him. "Oh no, Duffy, keep your seat. It's about time that something interesting took place during one of your quiet gamma shifts. I'd suggest you risk disturbing a few more of your shipmates, though. Abramowitz and Stevens in particular would be helpful." To the rest of the bridge crew he offered, "We may have a first contact situation this evening, folks, so let's put on our best faces. I'll rejoin you in a few."

Duffy's verbal impulses finally got the best of him. "And we can't have our new friends greeting the captain in his . . . um . . . *babushka.*"

"Leave the Yiddish to the experts, *boychik.*" The captain allowed a smile as he reentered the turbolift and let the doors close behind him.

A loud sigh escaped from Faulwell's lips, catching Duffy's attention. The linguist shook his head and turned to the communications console. "Splendid. My favorite. A first contact on the late shift. I thought working gamma was supposed to be relaxing."

As the rest of the bridge officers worked at their various stations, Duffy could do nothing except look to the main viewer and wait for the situation to develop.

"Guess the Tellarite story will have to wait."

It took less than five minutes for Captain Gold to return to the *da Vinci*'s bridge, this time properly groomed and wearing a more familiar Starfleet uniform. Duffy rose from the center seat and the two officers exchanged silent nods as he walked to the bridge's engineering station. From there, he could monitor the *da Vinci*'s propulsion and other systems as events warranted.

While not the ship's chief engineer, Duffy took personal pride in the efficient and smooth operation of the warp drive on the *Saber*-class vessel. Chief Engineer Jil Barnak never got territorial over his habit of wandering into main engineering just to fine-tune intermix ratios or tweak frequencies of fields within the ship's warp core. As he often noted to his fellow crewmembers following his transfer from the *U.S.S. Enterprise,* taking the boy out of engineering rarely translated to taking the engineering out of the boy.

"Duffy," Gold called out from the center seat, "what can you tell us about our friends out there?"

Turning back to face his captain, Duffy replied, "It's not like anything with a Federation registry, that's for sure. Its outer hull appears to be electrically charged, very similar to the way our older ships used to polarize hull plating before we developed shield generators." It was a means of ship protection that recalled for him the twenty-second century and the beginnings of deep-space exploration for the people of his world. "We're not picking up any kind of sensor capabilities, either."

"What about propulsion?"

"Looks to be driven by ion reactions, Captain. Their drive system appears to use magnetic fields and electrically charged gases rather than one fueled by mixes of matter and antimatter." Ion drives in Duffy's experience were connective technologies; ones that races used until finding something superior, as did the Jem'Hadar, if his memory served. Technologically, this race looked to be far inferior to most others encountered by the Federation, he decided.

That didn't change the fact that they were now a few minutes from intercepting what appeared to be one of the fastest space vessels they had ever encountered.

"So how can that thing be traveling so fast?" Duffy had spoken aloud without realizing it, and he looked up sheepishly. Maybe no one had heard him, he thought, until he saw the smiling face of Carol Abramowitz as she worked at the nearby communications station with Faulwell.

"I don't know, Commander. Maybe they got a push?"

Duffy gave her a friendly smirk. "Don't you have a call to make?" He was well aware that Abramowitz had been tasked with contacting the craft once Faulwell and the computer's linguistics banks had cracked the language barrier. The endlessly repeating series of calls had been found to be cries of distress, but few other details were to be had.

"Don't start on me, mister," she said. "I'm not even supposed to be here today." They shared a quiet laugh as she turned back to her console. "They're not responding to our hails, anyway. I'm hoping it's a matter of their communications systems and not because we've been rude."

Considering Abramowitz's expertise as a cultural specialist and the starship's best liaison to other races, it did not surprise Duffy that she would be concerned with the aliens' issues of perception. Abramowitz worked hard at understanding even the subtlest nuances of behavior or voice inflection that might inadvertently belie one's actions and intentions toward others. Her poise and politeness on duty frequently made Duffy smile, though given her usual behavior when he "got her out of the house" as he called it when they laid over at the occasional station or starbase, she tended to be a different person.

*Certainly those Tellarites would agree.*

A rise in Gold's voice drew his attention back to the situation at hand. "Abramowitz? Any luck in contacting the ship?"

"None, Captain," she answered. "Still working on it."

"I know that you are, and I appreciate your persistence." Gold then looked at the second officer. "Duffy, we've plotted the other ship's likely course and I aim to bring us alongside her as she passes. Are the engines up to sustaining the speed we need to do so?"

"Yes, sir," Duffy replied. "It shouldn't pose any problems for us to shadow them. My readings have their speed at just a shade below warp eight-point-nine. We can maintain that level for twenty hours or better."

"Good." Gold nodded firmly as he settled into the center seat. "Let's get moving, then. Rusconi, start along a course parallel to our projections and let's get our speed up to warp eight . . . oh, let's say point three."

Rusconi attended to Gold's orders as Duffy again watched over the fluctuating graphic displays at the engineering station. The *da Vinci* smoothly came to speed and he allowed himself some inner satisfaction as the gauges did not waver from tolerance levels.

A flash from the viewscreen made him snap his attention forward. A blip of speeding light had shot from the viewer's left side, and it now was tracing a path toward the center of its starstreaked image.

Piotrowski indicated the screen with a nod of her head. "Captain, the ship just passed us."

"Then let's catch up," Gold replied. "Match course and speed."

In a matter of moments, the streak of light took shape in the main viewer as the *da Vinci* came alongside the alien vessel. The silvery, wedge-shaped craft sported small, swept-back wings that appeared more aesthetic than functional. Several window ports peppered the outer hull of the ship, and its sleek skin looked to Duffy as though it could almost be cast from liquid mercury. He appreciated their approaching from the ship's aft as the view allowed him a lingering look at its engines, which appeared to be exhaust ports rather than nacelles.

*Whatever is coming from those ports,* he

thought, *has to be more than this ship was built to handle.*

Abramowitz spoke to break the silence on the bridge. "Captain, I'm getting a hail from the ship. It's coming in on a low-frequency audio band. Maybe they couldn't respond to our subspace transmissions."

"Maybe so," Gold said, his eyes not leaving the viewer. "Put them on, Abramowitz."

Speakers on the bridge crackled a bit as static filtered in and out of words translated by the *da Vinci's* computers. "*Greetings, unidentified vessel. This is Daltren. We are of the Senuta. We are in great need of assistance and we hope you are here to help us.*"

Gold tipped his head up to the ceiling of the bridge, as if that might make him better understood. "We certainly are here to help, Daltren. I am Captain Gold from the United Federation of Planets. My crew is ready to assist you with whatever you need. Can you tell us what the trouble is?"

"*We cannot stop.*"

Duffy sat and laced his fingers. *That surely would pose a problem,* he thought, *but one that we should be able to solve without breaking a sweat.* Seeing Gold's questioning glance, he nodded in response. "We're on it, Captain."

Satisfied with that, Gold turned his attention back to the main viewer. "My crew is already examining your situation, Daltren, and we should have a solution in short order. We'll need some information about your ship and its technology. Can you arrange that?"

*"We will have to awaken Bohan, and he has been ill, but it will be done."* The voice paused, but as Gold drew breath to speak, it continued. *"Thank you, Captain. We have needed help for far too long."*

Puzzlement crossed Gold's features. "Just how long have you been unable to stop, Daltren?"

*"We have traveled this way for forty-seven of our cycles, ever since we encountered what we think was some form of electromagnetic storm."*

Duffy swallowed hard at hearing those words. After moving at close to warp nine for that time, he guessed the ship could be a dozen sectors from its homeworld. Such a journey would be of little consequence for a Starfleet vessel with the latest that twenty-fourth-century technology had to offer, but who knew what kind of effect such a trip would have on the Senuta ship?

Daltren continued. *"Our supplies are nearly exhausted, Captain. Our computers have locked us out of many functions. My people are ill from the journey. Three have died. We need your help."*

"Count on it, Daltren," Gold said. "Get us your information as soon as you can."

The bridge crew worked in silence as they awaited the Senuta transmission. Before long, Abramowitz noted its reception and Gold waved a finger to indicate he wanted it all transferred to Duffy's workstation.

Calling the information to his console, Duffy instantly disliked what he saw.

"Captain, this just isn't good. Their engines are built to travel at about half the speed they're moving. I don't know how it's even holding together with its low-end structural integrity system." He paused as he read more. "They don't have replicators or transporters to speak of. They don't even have inertial dampers; they use acceleration couches when they travel. No wonder they're sick. Just moving about the ship during high warp must be hell for them." He shook his head. "If we're not careful, any sudden deceleration will turn these guys into paste."

"*Oy gevalt,*" Gold muttered, and Duffy could tell that his choice of words had been poor when he saw the glowering expression on the captain's face. "Then I suggest you start scouring the computer library for ideas if you have none of your own, Commander." Duffy's own expression must have revealed too much, because Gold added with a wry grin, "Oh come now, Duffy. Gomez tells me you love research."

"Oh, yes, sir. I'm your man." As Duffy began tapping into the ship's library computer, a thought struck him. "Carol, ask Mr. Daltren to send over ship's logs or any sensor readings they have on that storm he mentioned. I've got a hunch about something." As he browsed the library, Duffy let his mind wander.

*Ion-charged engines thrown into hyper-*

*efficiency . . . locked-up computers . . . a lack of shielding on the ship . . . this has to be the result of an ion storm, and a powerful one at that.*

He let that idea roll around in his mind as his console blinked to indicate Abramowitz had sent over the Senuta ship's latest report.

"Their sensors detected ion bombardments at levels that would have wreaked havoc on even a shielded vessel," he said aloud. It was a storm that experienced space travelers would have done their best to avoid. In this case, sheer misfortune had resulted in the Senuta being flung far from home and powerless to do anything about it.

"Give me a few minutes, Captain," Duffy said, not bothering to look up from his console. "I think I'm on to something."

"Good," Gold said as he moved toward the turbolift. "It's time to get Gomez out of bed. Once we get this ship stopped, I'm sure she'll want to beam over and have a look at things for herself. Shall I tell her you'll have your plan ready for us in, say, twenty minutes?"

"Give me fifteen, sir," Duffy said. "These people have been at warp long enough."

"That's the stuff," Gold said, smiling approvingly. "Carry on."

Duffy turned his attention back to the computer's library files on ion storm encounters, hoping that past experiences of Starfleet's finest engineers might spur his thinking. He scanned past more recent entries, dismissing accounts of ships with more advanced shielding than that employed by the Senuta. Before long, the log records began to bear twenty-third-century time-stamps and four-digit stardates . . . and the signatures of someone very familiar to him.

"Well, I'll be . . . Montgomery Scott." Duffy again found himself speaking aloud to no one in particular.

"Captain Scott? Did you call this in?" Abramowitz asked, again tuning in to Duffy's spoken voice. Members of any of the S.C.E. teams welcomed any contact by Scott. As chief liaison officer for the Starfleet Corps of Engineers, he was the man responsible for assigning their missions and keeping them from running afoul of Starfleet brass when their means of accomplishing those missions turned to the unorthodox.

"No, Carol, sorry about that," said Duffy. "But I have a feeling that Captain Scott is going to help us out of this jam without his even knowing about it."

And voices from the past began ringing in his mind. . . .

# CHAPTER
# 2

"*Mayday! Mayday! This is Outpost 5!*"

As the distress signal began to repeat, Commander Alicia Burke touched a control set into the top of the conference room table, silencing the recorded message. Several seconds passed as the group of fifteen Starfleet officers sitting around the table regarded one another silently.

*The plot thickens,* Lieutenant Commander Montgomery Scott mused to himself. It was a mystery that had begun when, instead of receiving official word of his promotion to chief engineer of the *U.S.S. Enterprise,* he'd been given orders to board the first transport bound for Starbase 10. No reason had been given for this abrupt change of assignment, one Scott had been assured was temporary. Only now, after being ushered into this room had everything finally started to become clear.

"There you have it," Commander Burke said, rising from her chair at the head of the table and beginning to pace around the room's outer perimeter as she addressed the group. "The ion storm swept across the Neutral Zone, enveloping several of our outposts stationed along the border." The observation outposts had been placed along the Federation side of the Zone more than a century before in the years following the Earth–Romulan War.

In accordance with the treaty that had been enacted to end that bitter conflict, they had served as the first line of intelligence gathering and warning for Starfleet since then. Drifting silently in the void, the outposts watched and waited for the day when Romulan forces attempted to abrogate the treaty by crossing the Neutral Zone into Federation space. So far, no such attempts had been made and in fact there had been only isolated contact with any Romulan vessels in the decades since the war's end. However, there were those in Starfleet, especially those with relatives who had fought and died in the war, who believed that the Romulans would one day return.

"As tough as those outposts are supposed to be," Scott said, "that storm must've been packin' quite a wallop."

Burke smiled, though there was no humor or

amusement in her expression. "An understatement, Mr. Scott. Six of the outposts have suffered varying degrees of structural damage as well as a wide variety of onboard systems failures. There have been several injuries but no deaths, fortunately. However, those outpost crews aren't really equipped to handle this type of recovery and repair operation." Indicating the assembled group of officers with outspread arms, she added, "That's why we're sending you."

Murmurs of approval greeted Burke's pronouncement, and Scott could feel the air of pride and confidence filtering through the room. Everyone here, he had learned, was a Starfleet engineer just as he was. A few of the faces were familiar; people with whom he had served on other ships or, in one case, hadn't seen since his days at the Academy. Also, like him, these people were accustomed to being given all manner of seemingly impossible tasks to accomplish. With Starfleet sending more ships than ever before farther out into unexplored space, those ships needed crews capable of operating for months and even years without outside assistance.

Engineers, especially those posted aboard long-range exploration vessels, often viewed themselves as the epitome of such talent and self-reliance. Scott would admit, if asked, that such attitudes could be perceived as arrogant, but he knew it was nothing more than assurance in one's own abilities, honed through experience and, on unfortunate occasions, adversity.

"Luckily for us," Burke said, "you in this group were available when we needed you. Most of you will be transported to the various outposts to help carry out repair efforts." She paused, her eyes scanning the engineers for a moment before finally coming to rest on Scott. "However, there is an additional problem requiring our immediate attention."

*Uh-oh,* Scott thought. *Here it comes.*

"Outpost 5 has been hit especially hard by the storm," Burke continued. "Maintaining contact has been next to impossible, but we do know that the station's primary PXK fission reactor has suffered damage. We've since lost communications with them, so we don't know how bad it really is. If the situation is critical, then our problems are only just beginning."

"The subspace relay?" asked another of the engineers, a female Alpha Centauran who had introduced herself to Scott as Lieutenant J'lenn.

Burke nodded. "Correct, Lieutenant. Outpost 5, for those of you who do not know, serves as the subspace communications relay center for that region. Without it, our long-range sensor and intelligence-gathering abilities will be crippled for the entire sector." Looking about the room, the commander's eyes came to rest once more on Scott. "Mr. Scott, as you're the most experienced engineer in this group, you will be on the team going to Outpost 5, along with Lieutenant J'lenn. That reactor must be repaired at all costs."

"Aye, Commander," Scott replied. "That we will."

J'lenn leaned forward in her chair. "I've been to those outposts before, when I was serving aboard a border patrol ship. Outpost 5's reactor is two kilometers beneath the surface. If the station's been as badly damaged as we think, just getting to the reactor might be difficult."

Scott added, "As I recall, the composition of those asteroids interferes with transporters. Ye can't beam more than a few hundred meters down before the signal is corrupted." While there were those who had felt uncomfortable with the notion, the outposts had been deliberately designed with transporter inhibition in mind. At a time when humans were only just becoming used to the idea of having their bodies converted into energy and transmitted across vast distances in the blink of an eye, it was also known that other races were much more accustomed to the process.

More strategically oriented minds in Starfleet saw the tactical advantages transporters could bring, and had therefore decided that any means of defending sensitive installations from attacks by enemy soldiers materializing out of thin air should be employed. This thinking had extended most especially to the isolated and vulnerable observation outposts such as those along the

Neutral Zone, and Scott tended to support such practical planning.

"So we'll have to use turboshafts and access crawlways," J'lenn said. "There may be damage in those areas as well. We could find ourselves digging our way down to the reactor."

"We've thought of that," Burke replied. "In addition to those of you in this room, we're also sending along contingents from the Corps of Engineers. They've got the type of heavy equipment that could be needed."

Scott nodded in approval. "Aye, that's the ticket." Though he had never worked with anyone attached to the organization, he'd heard more than a few stories about the Corps of Engineers. These were the people who usually found themselves in such hazardous situations as providing life-support habitats on otherwise inhospitable worlds, or creating the types of underground facilities found on asteroids and lifeless moons throughout the Federation. In fact, it had been the Corps who had originally devised and constructed the line of outposts that Scott and the other engineers in this room were discussing at this very moment.

Corps engineers also had a reputation for approaching their dangerous duties in a much more relaxed fashion than their more "spit-and-polish" contemporaries who served aboard starships and starbases. It was something Scott found almost completely incongruous with the nature of their dangerous and demanding assignments. Part of him was looking forward to seeing the contrast in styles between the Corps and what he considered to be more traditional Starfleet methods.

"As you can imagine," Burke said, "security on this operation is very tight. If the Romulans find out that we have a potential gap in our communications and sensor network along the Zone, they won't hesitate to exploit it. We haven't heard from them in quite a long time, but you can be sure they're waiting for an opportunity just like this one, and we don't want to simply drop it into their laps."

Scott sighed. *As if we won't have enough to worry about.*

Starbase 10's officers' lounge was a hive of activity, with the changing of duty shifts allowing personnel from all over the station to congregate here and unwind after their workday. Judging by the crowd of people at the bar and those populating the other tables in the room, it was obvious to Scott that this was one of the facility's more popular gathering places.

*And with Scotch such as this,* he thought as he raised his glass to his lips, *it's easy to see why.* The vile brew that had the gall to pass itself off as Scotch on most starships and bases wasn't fit to lubricate the fittings on a shuttlecraft's impulse engine, in his opinion. But the rich, satisfying drink he'd been served here was nothing short of nectar of the gods. In Scott's eyes, whoever was in charge of requisitioning for this station's lounge was deserving of a medal.

In addition to the fine refreshments and cozy, welcoming atmosphere, the lounge also afforded a wondrous view of the surrounding space. Just from where he sat, Scott could see a brilliant, multihued nebula, the storms roiling within it giving the spatial phenomenon a savage beauty that he had rarely seen in his travels.

*That's likely to change, however,* he told himself.

Though he had spent several years in space aboard nine different vessels during his Starfleet career, none of those assignments had offered the opportunities for exploration and discovery that his next post promised. Indeed, the years he would spend aboard the *Enterprise,* if what he'd heard about its proposed mission were true, could potentially bring him into contact with sights and wonders that would make the nebula he was observing now pale in comparison.

Not to mention, it would be his first assignment as a chief engineer.

Unlike many of his friends in Starfleet, including Academy classmates, Scott did not aspire to command a starship. His goals had always pulled him in a different direction. Since his childhood, he had been fascinated with the inner workings of spacefaring vessels, from the earliest fragile craft to leave Earth's atmosphere to those of Vulcans, Andorians, and the other races humans had encountered since first venturing to the stars. Even at a very young age, Montgomery Scott knew that he would never be happy, never be truly fulfilled, until he became the chief engineer of a spaceship.

No, a *starship*. And at last, his lifelong dream was about to come true.

*But,* he reminded himself, *there's one last job to finish.* This emergency at the Neutral Zone had to be secured first, but he knew that the *Enterprise* would still be waiting for him when his work there was done.

"May I join you, Commander?"

The question broke Scott from his reverie, and he turned to see Lieutenant J'lenn standing before him, holding a glass filled with an electric-blue liquid that he did not immediately recognize. He did notice, however, that it possessed the same luster as her eyes, which were at this moment studying him as she waited for an answer to her question.

"Oh," he said, rising quickly to his feet. "Aye, lass, please." He indicated the other chair at the table. "Have a seat. And please, call me Scotty."

As they settled into their chairs, J'lenn indicated the row of windows. "Beautiful view, isn't it?"

"That it is," Scott replied. "I'm not usually one

to spend time starin' at the stars, but it's so peaceful here, I couldna resist."

J'lenn nodded. "It certainly is captivating." She took a sip of her drink before continuing. "It reminds me, oddly enough, of the Neutral Zone. When we were on patrol, we'd go for weeks without seeing another ship. There'd be an occasional run-in with pirate vessels or the odd Klingon ship, but usually it was just one of our own. Other than that, it was just us and the stars." She sighed a bit. "Sometimes I miss that duty."

"Which ship were ye on?" Scott asked.

"The *Chandley*, a frigate. Not the most advanced ship in the fleet, and it didn't have a lot in the way of creature comforts, but it was quite the tough little ship in a fight." She shook her head as if momentarily lost in thought, before adding, "Given what they're sending us to the Neutral Zone with, I'd love to be on the *Chandley* right about now."

Scott chuckled at that. "Oh come now. I dinna think the Corps of Engineers would be usin' the *Lovell* if she wasn't a capable ship."

Thinking about that for a moment, J'lenn finally shrugged. "Maybe, but a *Daedalus*-class? Those have been out of service for seventy years. Why would they opt for something so old when there are newer and faster ships available?"

"Available for things like deep-space exploration and border defense," Scott countered, "but the Corps has never really been a priority when it comes to dolin' out new equipment, especially ships." Scott knew that the Corps of Engineers had been given authorization to retrieve its choice of decommissioned vessels from one of the several storage depots maintained by Starfleet, including the facility at Qualor II, in order to transport its heavy equipment from assignment to assignment.

"It's not surprisin' that they picked three *Daedalus* ships," he said. "In their day, they were Starfleet's workhorses. They were durable and reliable, and given the right bit o' care, there's no reason they couldna all still be in active service today."

"True, and with a shipload of engineers to tend to it," J'lenn replied, "the *Lovell* should be quite the sight to behold."

"*Attention, all personnel,*" the starbase intercom system called out, interrupting Scott's thoughts. "*The* U.S.S. Lovell *will be docking momentarily. Lieutenant Commander Scott and Lieutenant J'lenn, report to Docking Port 7 immediately.*"

Movement beyond the viewports caught Scott's attention, and he turned in time to see a ship, still several dozen kilometers away, slowly approaching the station. Though he had never seen such a vessel outside of textbooks or a museum, his practiced eye immediately recognized the large, spherical primary hull and squat, cylindrical engineering section as that of a

*Daedalus*-class ship. It was moving fast, approaching the starbase at what Scott judged to be full impulse power. As it drew closer, he also noticed other things about the vessel.

"What the . . . ," he began, but the words faded as he rose from his chair, studying the dull, pock-marked paint that only partially covered varying-size areas of otherwise bare metal. Visible dents in the hull plating along with a port warp nacelle that looked as though it might shear away at any moment added to Scott's rapidly escalating sense of dread.

"Well, look on the bright side," J'lenn said, her own expression one of near shock as she too beheld the vessel. "We won't have to worry about the Romulans coming to kill us. That ship will blow apart long before we get to the Neutral Zone."

Scott's only reply was to drain the contents of his glass.

# CHAPTER
# 3

The unease Scott had felt upon first seeing the *Lovell* certainly wasn't helped when he got a close look at the ship. In all his years in Starfleet, he had never seen a vessel in such deplorable condition, save for those that had been in combat.

*Aye, and along with a few that had crashed into planets.*

Eyeing the *Lovell* through the viewing ports near where it had docked with the starbase, Scott could see that the struts supporting the warp nacelles were not even of the type normally used on *Daedalus*-class ships. He wasn't sure, but he thought that the struts could have come from an even older model of vessel, perhaps even one of the first deep-space exploration craft Starfleet had ever deployed.

"It certainly isn't much to look at, is it?" J'lenn asked.

Scott shook his head in disbelief. He could see the weld lines where the sections of hull plating were joined, and Scott could scarcely believe that the ship was capable of withstanding the stresses of interstellar flight.

"What in God's name is holdin' that ship together?"

From behind them, a voice answered, "A little luck, a lot of tender loving care, and the best crew of engineers in the fleet."

Scott and J'lenn turned to see a human male, looking to Scott to be of Middle Eastern descent and sporting a wide, knowing smile. The man's dark hair was an unruly mop, uncombed and definitely longer than regulation. He appeared to carry himself with a relaxed, almost lackadaisical air that seemed out of sorts with his Starfleet uniform.

"I'll admit she's an eyesore," the man continued, "but she gets us where we need to go. Cruising speed of warp seven, and she'll even make warp nine when we really need it."

Unable to conceal an expression of doubt, Scott regarded the newcomer warily. "Warp seven, ye say? That's quite a feat, lad. After all, *Constitution*-class ships are only rated for cruising speeds of warp six or so."

The smile on his face fading not one iota, the other man nodded. "The difference between ships of the line and us is that we have more time to tinker. Idle hands and all that." Extending his hand in greeting, he offered, "Lieutenant Mahmud al-Khaled, Corps of Engineers."

Scott returned the man's firm handshake, making the introductions for himself and J'lenn. With that accomplished, he indicated the *Lovell* with a nod of his head in the direction of the viewport.

"I dinna mean to offend ye, lad. It's just that, well, I hafta admit she's quite a sight compared to what I'm used to."

Waving the apology away, al-Khaled chuckled. "It is forgotten. We're used to the looks she gets, but you'll change your mind when she goes to warp. I'll bet you dinner on that."

"Throw in a bottle of Scotch and Denevan whiskey," J'lenn countered, much to Scott's appreciation, "and it's a wager."

Al-Khaled's smile widened and he nodded enthusiastically. "Agreed. The whiskey might be hard to come by, but I have this feeling it's really not going to matter."

"Three root beers, please, and be sure to put them on Commander Scott's tab."

As the beverage dispenser in the *Lovell*'s mess hall processed his request, al-Khaled directed the latest in what Scott was sure would be an ongoing series of triumphant grins in their direction. Scott could only look at J'lenn as both engineers shook their heads in mock defeat before turning to look through the room's viewport once more.

Beyond the plexisteel barrier protecting the room's occupants from the harsh vacuum of space, stars streaked past, dilating and stretching into multihued arcs of light as the *Lovell* traveled rather effortlessly at warp seven toward the Neutral Zone.

Not that it had been uneventful reaching that speed, of course. The *Lovell* had departed Starbase 10 within moments of Scott and J'lenn's boarding, while al-Khaled was giving them a guided tour of the ship's engineering section. The order to engage the warp engines had come from the bridge, and Scott had felt everything from bulkheads to deck plating rattle and threaten to come apart.

"I thought my bloody teeth were gonna shake themselves outta my head," he declared as he and J'lenn seated themselves at one of the tables near the viewport. "But I must admit, she seems to be runnin' just fine now that she has her second wind."

"She can be a bit grumpy at first," al-Khaled said as he arrived at the table bearing a tray with three tall glasses of root beer, Scott and J'lenn's penance for losing their friendly wager. "But once she gets up to speed, I'd bet against any ship in the fleet catching us." As he took his own seat, he indicated the other occupants of the room with a wave of his hand. "Remember, just about everyone aboard is an engineer of some sort, and we spend a lot of time traveling between assignments."

"Naturally there are plenty of opportunities to refine or enhance your onboard systems," J'lenn said.

Al-Khaled nodded, his smile almost mischievous. "Practically everything from the engines on down to the toilets operates above normal efficiency levels."

Scott could see that al-Khaled was an intense young man who took extreme pride in his work, the hallmark of any Starfleet officer, to say nothing of an engineer. In fact, he had gotten that same feeling watching other members of the *Lovell*'s crew from the moment he and J'lenn had stepped aboard. While such positive attitude and work ethic could be found on any worthwhile ship or station in the fleet, Scott felt that there was another intangible quality permeating the atmosphere here. It was as if these people knew they weren't the garden-variety type of Starfleet crew and relished that fact as they performed their duties in an exemplary, if somewhat unorthodox, manner.

His attention was drawn to the doors leading from the mess hall into the corridor, which parted to admit a short, stocky human wearing the tunic and rank insignia of a Starfleet captain. To Scott's surprise, the officer's arrival was acknowledged by a series of informal greetings by various members of the crew, many of whom did not even bother to rise from their seats at their captain's approach. The casual, almost familial way in which pleasantries were exchanged was in stark contrast to what Scott had grown accustomed during his own career.

When he realized the man was making his way deliberately toward their table, Scott rose quickly to his feet, with J'lenn closely following suit. The captain's response was to smile broadly and wave them back to their seats.

"Please, please, as you were," he said as he stuck out a meaty hand to Scott. "Daniel Okagawa, captain of the *Lovell*." Following introductions, Okagawa took the invitation to join the trio of engineers, dropping into an empty chair next to al-Khaled and asking a passing crewman to kindly bring him a cup of black coffee should he be on his way to the food dispensers.

"So," he began as he turned his attention back to Scott and J'lenn, "you're the lucky ones accompanying Mahmud and his team down to the outpost to help us with our little problem."

"Aye, sir, that's the plan," Scott replied, not sure how to handle Okagawa's apparently easygoing demeanor. The *Lovell*'s captain possessed an almost boyish twinkle in his otherwise dark brown eyes that belied the lines in his weathered face. Unlike many of the crewmembers Scott had encountered since coming aboard, Okagawa looked to be every bit a Starfleet officer, judging by his polished boots, impeccably tailored uniform, and exacting regulation haircut. The liberal peppering of gray in his black hair only contributed to the man's distinguished appearance.

"I've read both of your files," Okagawa continued. "Your expertise will come in handy, Commander Scott." Looking over to J'lenn he added, "And your knowledge of subspace communications systems may well be our ace in the hole if the outpost's relay equipment has damage, Lieutenant."

Nodding appreciatively, J'lenn replied, "Thank you, sir. Let's hope the damage is not as severe as Starfleet thinks it is."

Clapping al-Khaled on the shoulder, Okagawa said, "Well, with the two of you and Mahmud and his team, I imagine that old outpost won't deal out anything you can't handle. Our little team may not be inspection-ready if an admiral drops by, but we'll certainly get the job done."

Looking around the interior of the mess hall, with its variety of mismatched bulkheads, some of which hadn't even been painted, and its unpolished deck plates, Scott couldn't suppress an involuntary chuckle. It had been the same in other areas of the ship, including engineering, of all places. The insides of the *Lovell* most definitely fit in with the ship's disarming, dilapidated exterior.

"I know what you're thinking," Okagawa said, a smile on his face as he read Scott's own expression. "We're not exactly a ship of the line, are we?"

Working to school his features in reaction to the captain's blunt question, Scott stalled for an additional few seconds by clearing his throat, an action that only made Okagawa's smile grow wider.

"Far be it from me to question any ship captain's methods, sir," Scott began, but Okagawa only laughed, dismissing the reply with a playful wave of his hand.

"Don't worry, Commander. Believe me, when I first came aboard this old tub, I was just as stunned as you two probably were. I thought I was going to blow a power coupling when I saw just what Starfleet had handed me."

Making a show of covering his mouth and coughing, al-Khaled cast a sidelong glance at his captain. "That's putting it mildly, sir."

Okagawa ignored the remark. "But it didn't take me long to realize that when it came to the Corps of Engineers, I simply couldn't run this ship like I had my previous commands." He spread his arms, indicating the other patrons of the mess hall. "These people aren't regular Starfleet. Hell, some of them aren't any kind of Starfleet. Half of my crew is comprised of civilian specialists, Commander. They humor us by wearing uniforms, but they're about as regulation as my goldfish. You can't treat them like regular starship personnel. I've learned, through no small number of mistakes and a few occasions where I've made a complete ass of myself, that these people do what's needed, when it's needed, every time they're asked." Shrugging, he added, "The difference between this group and the crew on the science vessel I once commanded is that the scientists didn't blow off steam by rigging the transporter to beam someone up without their clothes."

J'lenn had the misfortune to be taking a long drink from her root beer as Okagawa spoke. The engineer couldn't stifle her own laugh, and instead inhaled a good portion of the beverage, coughing and snorting violently as she blew carbonated liquid through her nose and onto her uniform, the table, and even Scott's sleeve.

"Ah," the captain said, "someone else who appreciates that kind of jocularity. Wonderful." Looking to al-Khaled, he added, "More converts for your flock, Mahmud." Everyone at the table waited until J'lenn got her breathing under control, after which an embarrassed smile crept onto her face.

Seeing that she was all right, Okagawa continued. "So you see, commanding a crew like the Lovell's carries with it an obligation to be flexible, and to see beyond the strict parameters of the so-called rulebook."

The more he thought about it, the more Scott could appreciate the advantages of what Captain Okagawa had provided on the Lovell. "'Tis a fine idea, Captain, and my hat's off to ye. Still, I must admit that I don't see myself thrivin' in such an environment. For better or worse, I suppose I'm regular Starfleet through and through."

"Oh, I don't know, Commander," al-Khaled replied. "You'd be surprised at the types of problems we have to deal with from time to time. No two days are alike, I can tell you that. Sure, some of the jobs we get would be boring to a lot of people, but each new assignment brings its own unique set of challenges."

"It's similar aboard a starship," J'lenn countered, "especially with the push for more exploration into uncharted areas. In fact, I'm surprised they didn't send a starship or two to deal with this problem at the Neutral Zone."

Al-Khaled nodded politely. "Fair enough, but just as there are purely medical and science vessels in the fleet, so too are there dedicated crews specially trained to deal with unusual engineering problems. There are some situations where it's impractical to divert a ship of the line, but for which the *Lovell* is ideally suited."

Wiggling his eyebrows impishly at the pair of engineers, Okagawa added, "Wait until you see them in action, Mr. Scott. You just might change your mind."

# CHAPTER
# 4

As he felt the tingling and even chilling effect of the transporter's reintegration process release him, Montgomery Scott had to wait a few extra seconds as his eyes adjusted to his new surroundings. The lighting here was noticeably dimmer than the standard levels aboard Federation starships and starbases. His ears quickly tuned to what was an uncharacteristic silence for a small, self-contained facility as Outpost 5, nestled as it was within a rocky crevasse of an otherwise barren asteroid.

Then he drew a breath.

Reports from outpost personnel had already notified the *Lovell* crew that the station's life-support systems had been compromised by the ion storm, but he recognized the poor quality of the atmosphere he was breathing. The air felt almost textured in his mouth as his lungs worked to fill themselves with oxygen, and a sticky tang that was the most unpleasant aspect of poorly recycled air swept across his taste buds. Instinct and experience told him that the damage to the outpost's environmental systems was probably more severe than originally reported, and had to be operating at the lowermost limit of humanoid tolerance. The engineers would have to work quickly to get the systems restored.

The chamber they had beamed into was the closest thing to a reception area that Outpost 5 possessed. It was in actuality just a cargo hold that had been converted into an exterior-activity dressing area, dominated by lockers containing environmental suits and other accessories for use by outpost personnel when working out on the surface. At one end of the room was an open hatchway revealing a sparsely lit corridor that led to the rest of the outpost. Scott could see where plastisteel wall panels had been installed at points along the passageway, covering up the bare rock of the asteroid from which the tunnel had been carved. Even in the muted illumination of the room Scott could make out the stout, heavy hatch of the chamber's main airlock at the room's far end, which led to the airless exterior of the asteroid itself.

"Not very homey, is it?" he asked.

Standing next to him, al-Khaled shook his head. "These border outposts are strictly no-frills affairs. This close to the Neutral Zone, you can imagine the day-to-day tension level, even if no one's heard from the Romulans in years. Combine that with a lack of real recreational facilities or the ability to travel to very many places for R&R, and you can see what a hardship posting this is. That's why they rotate personnel out of these stations every six months." Taking another look around the stark chamber, al-Khaled exhaled audibly. "It's not at the top of my dream duty list, that's for sure."

The sound of labored breathing attracted Scott's attention and he turned to see Lieutenant J'lenn bent over at the waist, her hands on her knees as she gasped for breath.

"Are ye all right, lassie?" Along with al-Khaled and the other members of the landing party sent down from the *Lovell*, he moved quickly to the young lieutenant's side.

"Air's . . . thinner than I thought . . . hard to . . . breathe," J'lenn managed to force out between ragged breaths. It didn't take Scott long to realize what was causing the woman's difficulty. On her home planet in the Alpha Centauri system, J'lenn had grown up breathing an atmosphere richer in oxygen than that found on Earth. She and others from her native world could breathe in the somewhat thinner atmosphere found aboard primarily human-dominated ships and starbases. The differences in her physiology, however, also left her more susceptible to the compromised environmental conditions in which the landing party now found themselves.

With that in mind, Scott realized that the last thing J'lenn needed was a crowd of worried comrades competing for the already depleted oxygen around her as they all moved to offer her assistance.

"Let's give her some room, lads," he said. Putting a hand on J'lenn's shoulder he added, "Slow deep breaths, Lieutenant. We'll get ye somethin' to help ye breathe easier."

Footsteps echoed in the corridor and Scott looked up to see a haggard-looking man jogging into the room. He wore a red standard-issue Starfleet utility jumpsuit that was sullied by sweat, grease, and grime. Scott could tell by his gaunt features that it had been days since the man had enjoyed anything even resembling a decent night's sleep. Given the situation here, he was sure that all of the outpost's personnel were feeling the same way.

"You have no idea how great it is to see you," the man said, a smile breaking out onto his tired face. Running a hand through his thick, dirty-blond hair, he said, "I'm Celine . . . Evert Celine, chief of operations. Commander Thompson got trapped below during our last cave-in, so I'm in charge up here for the time being." Noticing J'lenn's difficulty, he asked, "Is she okay?"

"This air's too thin for her," Scott offered. "She's Alpha Centauran, so it's a bit rougher on her than the rest of us. Do ye have a rebreather or some tri-ox compound handy?"

Celine nodded. "The rebreathers we have left are being used by other station personnel, but I can get the doc up here with some tri-ox." Retrieving a portable communicator from a pocket of his jumpsuit, he opened the unit's antenna grid and adjusted the frequency knob. "Celine to Dr. Hoyt. Doc, I'm in the main EA prep room and I need some tri-ox compound for one of our guests. Can you get up here?"

A gravelly voice, sounding every bit as exhausted as Celine's, answered seconds later. *"On my way, Chief. Have the patient lie down and try to relax until I get there."*

"Roger that. Celine out." Returning the communicator to his pocket, Celine regarded the landing party. "Main communications are down, so we're stuck using portable comm until we can get it fixed. One of the many items on our things-to-do list, I'm afraid."

Scott nodded in understanding. "I can only imagine how hard it's been to hold this place together since the storm."

Letting a small laugh slip out, Celine smiled wearily. "There isn't a system on this entire rock that isn't compromised, jury-rigged, cross-connected, or just plain fried. We've been running between circuit panels and crawling through access tubes for days."

They were interrupted as another man entered the room. Noticeably older, he was bald except for gray stubble on the sides and back of his head. He wore a blue jumpsuit and carried what Scott recognized to be a field medical pouch. The man's shoulders were slumped as he walked, and whether it was due to age, fatigue, or both was anyone's guess.

"Somebody call a doctor?" Hoyt asked, a tired smile crossing his weathered features.

"Over here," Scott said, waving the other man over to where he had made J'lenn lie down on a bench near the prep room's dressing area.

Moving over to kneel beside the young engineer, Hoyt gave her a quick look as he drew a hypospray from his medical pouch and affixed a liquid-filled ampule to one end. Pressing the hypospray to her shoulder, he said, "This will help you. Just give it a second to kick in."

At the hiss of the injection, J'lenn closed her eyes and bit down on her lower lip as she focused on inhaling deeply through her flared nostrils. After a moment she nodded as her breathing slowly began to return to normal. "That's much better now." Smiling up at Scott she added, "I'm okay now, Scotty. Thank you." She made an attempt to raise herself to a sitting position, but Hoyt restrained her, placing a hand on her shoulder.

"You just stay right there for a few more minutes, young lady," the doctor said, his voice gentle yet firm like that of a trusted grandfather. "That tri-ox compound will help you for a few hours, but you'll need booster shots. Between the two of us, what say we keep track of the time, all right? I know you engineering types like to run yourselves ragged, but try to call me *before* you pass out, okay?"

J'lenn laughed a bit, nodding in agreement. "No problem, Doctor. Thanks."

Scott sighed in momentary relief. It was tempting to hope that all of the problems they would face in restoring the station to normal operations would be solved so easily, but he knew that such hope was misplaced.

Turning back to Celine, he said, "Chief, ye know best where ye need us first." Indicating the rest of the landing party with a nod of his head, he added, "The sooner we get to work, the faster we can get this place back up and runnin'. So, where do we start?"

In response, Celine reached for the tricorder hanging from his shoulder. Activating the unit, he adjusted its controls before passing it to Scott. "Our first priorities are life support and the main reactor. The life-support system repairs are pretty straightforward, but we have no way to get to our maintenance section for the replacement parts we need."

"We'll get whatever we need from the *Lovell*," al-Khaled replied. "No problem there."

Celine nodded in appreciation before continuing. "The reactor is the major concern, though. That ion storm showered the fuel core with energy spikes that were off the scale. Fission balances are completely out of line, and unchecked power surges are overloading systems all over the outpost as fast as we can repair them. All in all it's a great big mess."

Almost on cue, a resonating hum filled the air and the room's lighting grew brighter. One overhead fixture popped and sparked, sending wafts of smoke across the room's ceiling. Rushing to a wall control, Celine slapped it with the palm of his hand and the entire room was plunged into darkness for several seconds until emergency backup lighting was activated.

Scott closed the tricorder's flip-top cover as the hum of the power surge subsided. Turning to al-Khaled, he said, "We should split up, Mahmud, and go after the reactor and life support at the same time." He looked over at J'lenn, who by now had pulled herself to a sitting position. "You know your way around these outposts. Think ye can find your way to the reactor core?"

"Just follow the glow, right?" J'lenn offered with a wry grin.

"Not exactly," Celine replied as he activated the room's main lighting again. When the lights came back on, they were even dimmer than they had been when the landing party had first arrived. "We can't get to the reactor chamber from up here. The passageway on that level between that area and the turbolift is partially collapsed from a cave-in. If we're going to get to it, we're going to have to dig."

Scott nodded in understanding. The asteroid's

mineral composition, featuring huge amounts of elmyracite, idrenium, and other trace elements all combined to make transporters and sensors useless beyond a few hundred meters.

"We have a whole host of portable drilling equipment aboard the *Lovell,* including a few Mark III laser-drilling packs," al-Khaled said. "They should handle this job quite nicely."

Scotty nodded his approval. Those drills were used to create the very type of subterranean networks common to outposts like these, to say nothing of facilities and colonies on otherwise inhospitable planets.

"And guess who got herself rated on that particular model just last month?" J'lenn replied.

Al-Khaled smiled. "Excellent. You're hired." Indicating one of the engineers who had beamed down with them from the *Lovell,* he added, "I'm sending Kellerman with you. Those are his babies." Looking to the remaining members of his team he said, "Anderson, O'Halloran, you're on the life-support detail."

"I'll send one of my people with them," Celine said.

Scott nodded his concurrence with the plan of action. Al-Khaled was certainly demonstrating his mettle as both an engineer and a leader, he decided. The younger man had analyzed the situation confronting them, and he had quickly and decisively issued orders and gotten his people to work. Within the ranks of the Corps of Engineers, opportunity for taking charge presented itself at every turn, Scott was discovering. These creative and resourceful minds rarely waited to fly ideas past their commanding officers, a function of the necessary speed of their work. An axiom for any engineer, Scott had learned, was that oftentimes it was easier to request forgiveness than to obtain permission. That line of thinking was proving to be quite applicable in the Corps as well.

"And what about you three?" J'lenn asked, a teasing smile on her face. "It's nowhere near happy hour yet."

Scott could not suppress a chuckle, relieved to see that the young engineer was obviously feeling better and had regained her sense of humor. "The drinks'll be on me when ye cut us a path to the reactor."

"Is it possible to get a report on the reactor's current status?" al-Khaled asked. "I want to make sure it's stable before I send anyone down there, and I want to see the path they'll have to take."

Celine nodded. "The main operations center was heavily damaged during the storm, but we've converted the environmental-control room to work out as a substitute."

"Then that's where the party is," al-Khaled replied.

*On the grand scale of control rooms,* Scott thought as he looked around the one governing

Outpost 5's environmental systems, *this one ranks just above my dear mother's tinkering shack back in Aberdeen.*

In fairness, Scott could see that the small room had been hastily reconfigured in order to function as the outpost's nerve center. At least a dozen extra display monitors and computer workstations had been added to the room's already cramped array of consoles. Wiring and exposed circuitry littered the room and there was very little in the way of floor space.

"We've spent hours routing network paths to this place, so it's not the most tidy of working environments," Celine said almost apologetically as he stepped over a bundle of cables taped to the floor. "But you'll be able to access just about any information you might need. We've transferred the entire workload to a backup power supply, so even if the reactor goes down we'll still have some control over most systems for a time."

Scott nodded as he surveyed the cramped quarters housing cobbled-together control panels. Many of the stations were dominated by older models of monochromatic display screens, the same type of nearly obsolete models supported by telescoping rods from the ceiling and the slightly slanting bulkheads that were likely being replaced aboard his new posting, the Starship *Enterprise*, at this very moment. "No, Chief, this place'll do nicely. I daresay ye couldna done better with a week's notice."

Al-Khaled found a place in front of one set of display screens and turned one of the monitors toward him for a look. "Are these the readings for the reactor?"

Celine stepped beside him to see the viewer for himself, reaching across al-Khaled and toggling a few switches. "They are now. We've set things up so that we can monitor every system from each seat."

"Aye, lad, that's mighty convenient." Scott seated himself at another station and peered at the bank of displays. Mimicking what he had seen Celine do, he scrolled through a series of data images until he found what he was looking for. "And this'd be a map of the corridors to this place, yes?"

Seeing what the engineer had called up, Celine nodded. "Yes, sir. The highlighted paths indicate clear passageways."

Scott surveyed the map before him. The criss-cross of red lines showed a number of dark gaps preventing them from connecting. He knew that each gap represented clots of rock and debris that blocked portions of various passages. Whole sections of living quarters and work areas were darkened, as was a stretch of the outpost's main corridor that must have represented a collapsed area hundreds of meters long. It was that section of the station that was keeping them from reaching the now failing fission reactor, a failure that soon could spell death for them all if left unchecked.

"We've definitely got our work cut out for us," he said, shaking his head. J'lenn and Kellerman had already been dispatched into the outpost's lower levels. There, with the portable drilling equipment transported down from the *Lovell,* they would confront the collapsed passageway separating the reactor room from the rest of the station.

Al-Khaled shifted in his seat. "According to these readings, it doesn't appear that the reactor has been damaged so much as it seems to be overheating. The readings in the last two hours in particular show a massive rise in internal operating temperature. If I had to guess, I'd say that the coolant regulator system was damaged. We might get away easy after all."

Scott wasn't so sure. "There's an awful lot of rock separatin' us from that room, lad. It won't matter what's ailin' that beastie if we canna get to it."

# CHAPTER
# 5

With a sigh of resignation, J'lenn pulled the hood of her full-body protective garment over her head, sealing herself inside. She had always detested wearing the things. Even though they were lighter and less cumbersome than regular environmental suits used in space, they were still confining and did a magnificent job of retaining the wearer's body heat.

"Okay, Scotty, we're all bagged and ready to drill." Introduced into general use a little more than a year ago, no one she knew liked wearing the garments. They had quickly earned the uncomplimentary nickname of "space bags" from engineers across Starfleet. However, the suits would protect her and Kellerman from the worst of the heat discharged by the laser drilling packs they would be using.

"Orange is really not my color, you know," she added, looking down at herself.

She heard laughter from over her communicator. It was al-Khaled. *"It brings out your eyes."* A few seconds later, the engineer's voice was all business. *"Keep this channel open, J'lenn. We'll be monitoring your progress and I want reports every few minutes."*

"Aye, sir," J'lenn replied. In order to help her do that, Kellerman had provided a minor yet surprisingly effective demonstration of the type of field-expedient ingenuity for which engineers were well-known. He had rigged their communicators inside the headpieces of their protective garments, leaving their hands free to work with the laser drills.

*"Ye get a dram of Scotch for that one, lad,"* Scott said over the channel. *"We're ready here when you are, J'lenn."*

"Affirmative," J'lenn replied as she adjusted the straps on her laser drill's backpack rig. "Kellerman, I don't remember these things being so heavy during training."

Kellerman grinned and bobbed his eyebrows mischievously. "You're right. These are carrying a heavier battery pack than normal. I cannibalized a couple from a pair of old Mark IX artillery cannons."

J'lenn nodded in understanding. The bulky Mark IXs had been carried aboard starships for years and had proven their reliability in a variety of situations, though as far as she knew they had never been used in the types of combat operations for which they were originally designed. In addition to their own self-contained battery packs, the weapons could also receive and reconfigure power transmitted directly from an orbiting ship. The cannons were in the process of being phased out in favor of lighter, self-propelled models, though, so J'lenn wasn't surprised that engineers like Kellerman would seize the opportunity to salvage any useful parts.

"It's like Lieutenant al-Khaled has been trying to tell you," Kellerman began.

She smiled as she waved the rest of his statement away. "I know, there's plenty of time for you and your team to tinker aboard the *Lovell*. I'm beginning to understand the magnitude of that statement, Ensign." Taking hold of the drill itself, she hefted the tool in her hands and tested its weight. "I'm qualified to operate this thing, Kellerman, but that doesn't mean I'm an expert in drilling. How do you think we should proceed?"

Nodding, Kellerman indicated the rock wall that formed the recently created barrier in the tunnel before them. "No problem, Lieutenant. I'll make the first cut on my side, and then you just mirror what I do. Just watch out that we don't cross our beams." He smiled knowingly. "That would be bad."

Choosing a point on the upper part of the rock barrier, Kellerman took aim with his own drill and pressed the firing stud. The tunnel was soon filled with a high-pitched whine as the laser drill ramped up to its full power. Rock immediately began to disintegrate under the beam's power as the ensign carved into the wall.

Taking her cue from Kellerman, J'lenn activated her own drill and began to cut a similar path through the rock on her own side of the tunnel. It only took a few seconds for the pair of engineers to fall into a rhythm, working in tandem as they began to push their way forward. Even though the insulated material of her protective suit blocked most of the noise, it was still loud enough that she had to strain to hear the voices coming across the communicator channel.

*"Aye, that's the ticket, lass,"* Scott's voice sounded near her ear. *"Yer makin' some headway already."*

"This is great," J'lenn said to no one in particular as she watched the effect of the drills on the tunnel wall. "I'll admit to being a bit more optimistic about this now that we've started."

*"That's fair to say, Lieutenant,"* al-Khaled's voice said over the communicator, *"but we may not have as much time as we thought. The reactor's temperature is continuing to rise. You're going to have to speed things up a bit. No points for neatness."*

J'lenn grimaced as she continued to work. "I don't suppose you have any good news for us?"

*"Actually, we do,"* Scott's voice replied. *"Ander-*

son and O'Halloran must have connected the right two wires, because the life-support system is operatin' normally again. No more tri-ox compound for you, I'm afraid."

"Excellent," J'lenn replied, never taking her eyes from where her drill's beam continued to cut into the rock wall. "And the showers? I'm sweating enough to make a Tellarite jealous."

Scott chuckled at that. *"Let's walk before we run, lass. What's your status?"*

Releasing her drill's firing stud, J'lenn looked down at her tricorder, which she had left activated in order to keep track of their progress. "Everything looks stable. We've cleared about fifteen meters, and Mr. Kellerman has almost convinced me that he's not deliberately holding back to avoid embarrassing me as he leaves me in his tracks."

She didn't really need to keep a close watch on the readings her tricorder was gathering as they worked. Back in the control center, al-Khaled and Scott were receiving all of the data the unit was collecting. With many of the outpost's internal sensor systems off-line, the tricorder was providing the only truly reliable information about the area of tunnel they were working in and, as they drew closer to it, the reactor chamber itself.

In the environmental-control center, Scott saw that al-Khaled was engrossed in one of the moni-rs at his console.

"Mahmud?" he said, crossing the small room to join his companion. "What have ye got, lad?"

Not answering immediately, al-Khaled continued to study the display for several more seconds before he turned toward Celine. "Chief, are these the most detailed schematics for the outpost that we can get from these workstations?"

Rising from his own chair, the outpost operations chief shook his head. "We've got everything mapped. What do you want to see?"

"The conduit system for the reactor coolant," al-Khaled replied. "Something's not right here. There has to be a leak somewhere. Maybe we can find the breach and patch it. Then we could direct some more coolant to the reactor and maybe avoid having to dig through to the chamber after all."

Celine leaned closer to the console and tapped a series of switches, calling up a more detailed schematic that showed the system of conduits directing the flow of coolant to and from the reactor. Areas of bright red highlighted several areas along the conduit lines, illustrating where the breaks were.

"We may have to rig a bypass for some of these damaged sections," Scott said as he pointed to various areas on the screen. "It'll take some time, though." Shaking his head, he added, "More time than we might have. We dinna have any choice but to keep diggin' for the reactor."

An alarm suddenly sounded in the cramped

confines of the control room. Scott's head whipped toward the source and he saw that it was coming from the console he had been overseeing a few moments before.

It was the monitor that displayed the scan data from J'lenn's tricorder.

"Stop the—!"

But then the control room rocked like a shuttlecraft struck by a photon torpedo.

The deck abruptly disappeared from beneath Scott's feet. With no time to break his fall as he was dumped onto the grimy floor, the impact drove the air from his lungs and he felt a sharp pain in his back as he fell onto something hard and unyielding. From the corner of his eye he could see al-Khaled thrown from his chair to the deck and Celine barely able to hold on to the console. Dust shook from the walls and ceiling, creating a fine shroud that choked the very air from the room.

Still lying on the littered deck, Scott groped for his own communicator, which had been tossed to the floor by the explosion. It was still open and active.

"J'lenn! Come in, J'lenn! Kellerman? Is anyone there?" His shouting drowned out the plethora of buzzers and alarms now sounding in the control room. It did not, however, drown out the pounding sound of his heart.

"J'Lenn!"

*      *      *

They raced through the winding subterranean corridors of the outpost, their steps echoing off the walls of the passageways. Their headlong flight came to an abrupt end, though, before a small mountain of rocks, shattered thermoconcrete, and twisted metal beams clogging the tunnel ahead of them.

Scott and Celine were forced to halt momentarily, hunching over to gasp for breath in the still-thin air, but al-Khaled continued to sprint ahead to the newly created barrier of wreckage. He began to dig furiously with his hands, whipping stones and dirt away in all directions, oblivious to the fact that he was flinging some of the rubble back toward his comrades.

Managing to sidestep most of the barrage, Scott approached the muttering and obviously enraged engineer. He could hear the words carried by al-Khaled's panting breaths as he stepped closer.

" . . . son of a bitch . . . son of a bitch . . ."

He placed one hand on the frantic man's shoulder, but al-Khaled spun away from the mound to face him, his eyes red with both anger and pain.

*"Son of a bitch!"*

Scott reeled back a step, as much from the volume of al-Khaled's voice as from the rage in his eyes. "We do *not* lose people in the Corps! I have *never* lost anyone before, and I'm not starting here on this damn godforsaken rock!"

Having lost friends on hazardous missions before, Scott could understand the rampant emotions threatening to run unchecked through the lieutenant's mind. This was no time, however, to lose all self-control, even in the face of tragedy. With that in mind, he tried to temper his voice from reflecting the emotion that he, too, felt burning in his blood.

"Mahmud, lad. There was no way to know this would happen. We all knew this was going to be a risky job. You canna blame yourself for this."

"Unacceptable! It's unacceptable!" Al-Khaled's breathing had begun to deepen and slow, his voice still harsh but losing a bit of the anger that had consumed it only seconds before. Instead, he simply let his head hang in despair. "It's . . . dammit, Scotty."

The two men stood there, their panting and the gentle whine of Celine's tricorder the only noise in the tunnel. When he heard the chief turn the unit off, he looked over to see the man standing silently a few paces away. Celine comprehended the questioning look in Scott's eyes and nodded grimly in response.

After a few additional moments the chief finally said, "There're no life readings. Even with the elemental interference, I'm sure we'd pick up something this close to where they were digging." Looking to al-Khaled, his expression softened. "I'm sorry, Lieutenant."

Al-Khaled nodded, and Celine informed Scott

that he wanted to return to the control room and make sure that the outpost had not suffered any other damage.

The chief jogged back up the passageway toward the turbolift, leaving Scott to wait silently as al-Khaled stood before the mound of rubble blocking the passageway. Somewhere beyond the mass of rock and debris, Scott knew, the bodies of the two doomed engineers were buried. For the moment, retrieving them would be potentially hazardous. More air pockets almost certainly existed along the length of the collapsed tunnel, and any or all of them could be filled with leaked coolant, waiting for something to ignite them as J'lenn and Kellerman had unfortunately done.

"Engineers aren't supposed to die like that," al-Khaled said after several moments.

"No one is supposed to die like that, Mahmud," Scott replied. "Engineers are supposed to make sure of it. But accidents happen, and sometimes even we are helpless to do anything about it." He was only partially aware of how incongruous the words sounded, coming from him. They were words that should have come from the mouth of someone with more wisdom and life experience than he possessed at this point in his life. Had his relatively short career in Starfleet and the things he had encountered in that brief span of time aged him that quickly?

The words, however, seemed to be sinking in

as al-Khaled narrowed his eyes at Scott. "This is too dangerous. We can't keep boring along this passageway. We'll just hit more coolant pockets, and there's no way to detect them with all of these minerals fouling up our scans."

"Aye, that's likely." But Scott was at a loss as to how else they might get to the reactor core. A curse of technology, Scott reminded himself, was that it furtively invited dependence, almost an addiction to its developers and users. When the forces of nature stripped away the ability to use such devices as a transporter or a warp drive or a phaser or a scanner, Scott knew, dependence became the enemy of imagination.

It was time for them to think, and think fast.

The chirping of his communicator interrupted his thoughts. Flipping open the unit's antenna grid, he was greeted by the voice of the *Lovell*'s captain.

*"Okagawa to landing party. Our sensor readings up here just showed a large power spike in that reactor of yours. What's happening?"*

Scott paused to look to al-Khaled, whose face showed some regret at what he would have to tell his captain. He offered the communicator to the younger man, who Scott knew was the appropriate bearer of their grim report.

"Captain, this is al-Khaled. We've had an explosion and tunnel collapse. Lieutenant J'lenn and Ensign Kellerman have been lost." Pausing to swallow a large lump in his throat, he added,

"They're dead, sir." He squeezed his eyes closed and pressed his lips tight as he delivered that last part, fighting to keep his emotions in check. Scott refused to rub his own eyes, allowing the sting to burn into them as they awaited a response from the *Lovell.*

Okagawa's words were a few moments in coming. *"I'm sorry, Mahmud. I'm sure there was nothing you could have done to prevent that."* After pausing for several seconds he said, *"I hate to sound cold about this, but I think they'd understand that we have other concerns now. How quickly can you fix the reactor?"*

"It will take me a minute to estimate that for you, Captain," al-Khaled replied.

*"More than two hours?"*

"To reach it and repair it?" Al-Khaled looked to Scott as if to pose the question to him as well as to the captain. Scott shook his head no. If that was the team's time frame, they might as well write off the outpost and its subspace communications relay. Their only hope would be that the Romulans were busy enough with other matters on their side of the Neutral Zone that they didn't notice anything untoward until such time as the outpost could be repaired or replaced.

Nodding in silent agreement with Scott, al-Khaled raised the communicator to his mouth once more. "I'm sorry, sir, but we'll need more time than that."

*"You haven't got it,"* Okagawa replied. There

was no mistaking the quiet confidence in the captain's voice. He had weighed the situation and made a command decision. *"Let's start evacuating the outpost. Pass my order to Chief Celine and the rest of the outpost crew. I'll send more personnel to start salvaging key equipment and copying computer data. That's the best we can do, son."*

Scott allowed himself a sigh. Sometimes, retreat was the only option left in battle, and they had waged war against the reactor, the outpost, and the asteroid itself long enough to know a losing fight when it confronted them. Though he refused to consider the deaths of J'lenn and Kellerman as losses in vain, he was certain he would carry the lessons of Outpost 5 for the rest of his Starfleet career.

"No, sir."

The tone of voice startled Scott. It was still al-Khaled's voice, but now it sounded older. No, not exactly older, but there was definitely an edge to the man's voice that it had not possessed earlier.

"Give us one more shot at this, sir. I can't leave this outpost and watch it destroy itself, not with so much at stake. The relay is too important, and we've already got blood on our hands."

The two merely stared at one another, waiting through what seemed to Scott to be the longest, quietest moment of the entire mission. He was certain that any captain in his right mind would simply tell al-Khaled that while his intentions were well-placed and his passion was heartening, time was simply no longer on their side.

Daniel Okagawa, however, was either not in his right mind or else he was accustomed to engineers and the crazy plans they tended to hatch when under pressure to succeed in the face of overwhelming odds.

*"All right, Lieutenant. What have you got in mind?"*

# CHAPTER
# 6

"I'm not sure if this qualifies under Occam's razor, but it might just be our only chance."

Scott said nothing as al-Khaled tapped a keypad next to the control center's main viewscreen. In response to his command, the screen's image shifted to show a computer-generated schematic of Outpost 5 and the asteroid playing host to it. The station's damaged PXK fission reactor, buried in its own control room beneath tons of solid rock, was highlighted in bright red. A pair of parallel lines colored a brilliant green hue traced a straight path from the surface of the asteroid to the reactor's location.

"Drill down through solid rock?" Scott asked. Contrary to al-Khaled's comment, the idea itself did indeed seem to be as simple as it sounded. It was well in keeping with the centuries-old axiom the younger engineer had referenced, or at least the most common interpretation of the principle widely attributed to William of Occam, a human philosopher who had lived on fourteenth-century Earth: "The simplest solution is often the correct one." Translations and contextual application of the notion had evolved almost continuously to the point that nearly every engineer who heard or invoked the age-old theory simply referred to it in the spirit of "Keep it simple, stupid."

*Aye, a fine idea,* Scott mused, *but will it really work?* Given the dire nature of their current situation, he still needed convincing.

At another workstation, Chief Celine tapped a series of switches on his console and the image changed again, this time zooming in on the drilling path al-Khaled had proposed. "The limited scans we've been able to perform show more coolant leaks in several of the tunnels leading from the upper levels down to the engineering spaces. There's sure to be more that we can't detect farther down. If you take this route, you can avoid that hazard altogether."

When al-Khaled didn't say anything after several seconds, Scott turned to look in his direction and saw by the expression on the younger engineer's face that his mind was not entirely focused on the problem at hand. It was obvious that he was still haunted by the tragic deaths of J'lenn and Kellerman less than an hour before.

Scott felt the loss as well, even though he'd only first met J'lenn at the briefing on Starbase

10 and he hadn't known Kellerman at all. The immediacy of their mission simply had not allowed him the luxury of getting to know too many of the *Lovell*'s crew.

In some ways that was fortunate, for it allowed him to push away the feelings of anger and despair over the engineers' deaths, to isolate them to a certain extent. Still, two people had died, and they deserved to be mourned and remembered.

But not here, and not now. Now, there was a job to do.

Placing a comforting hand on al-Khaled's shoulder, he said, "Easy lad. I know what you're feelin', believe me. But right now, the best thing we can do for them is see this mission through; otherwise their deaths'll have no meanin'."

On another of the control center's viewscreens, Captain Okagawa watched the exchange via the communications channel linking the two engineers with the *Lovell*. "*He's right, Mahmud. There will be time for remembering later, but only if you give us that opportunity.*"

Nodding at the comforting words provided by Scott and his captain, al-Khaled took a few deep breaths before returning his full attention to the task at hand. "The actual procedure shouldn't be terribly complicated. We have heavy drilling equipment on the *Lovell* that will make fairly short work of it. Once we get down there, if we can't shut the reactor down or repair the cooling system, then we'll have to remove it outright. The drilling rig has its own tractor beam, so we can pull or push the reactor right back up the tunnel, at least far enough for the *Lovell* to latch on with its own and pull it the rest of the way."

"That's a mighty bold plan, lad," Scott said, with no small amount of admiration for the tenacity al-Khaled was displaying. The plan was indeed audacious, but the younger engineer had proposed it with an almost matter-of-fact demeanor, as if the risk and the potential consequences were simply factors to be considered in the equation and nothing more. "We'll have our work cut out for us, that's for sure."

Celine said, "Even with the risk, though, this is the fastest way given the time constraints you'll be working under." Captain Okagawa had ordered the evacuation of the station's personnel to the *Lovell*, but only thirty-two of the outpost's fifty crewmembers had been able to get out. Most of the others, including the outpost's commander, were still trapped in the facility's lower levels beyond the range of the ship's transporter, given the interference from the asteroid's mineral composition. Of those, three had been assigned to the reactor area and had not been heard from since the storm had first hit the outpost, and the worst had already been assumed.

As for the remaining fifteen people, no one involved in the current operation had to say aloud what was already known. If the reactor could not be repaired or removed, those people would die.

*"We can transport anything you need to you in ten minutes,"* Okagawa offered over the comm link. *"And I can put a crew to work getting the heavier equipment down to you as soon as you give the word."*

Al-Khaled studied the series of calculations he had requested from the station's computer. "According to this, it will take us nearly two hours to drill down through the rock to the reactor chamber. We won't be able to scan the room or the reactor itself until we're within a few hundred meters of it. It's very possible the room will be flooded with coolant."

Shrugging, Scott countered. "If we do nothing, we'll lose the reactor and most of this asteroid. Seems to me we dinna have much choice, lad."

*Och, how I hate wearin' these blasted contraptions.*

Scott tried to ignore the sound of his own breathing, echoed as it was within the confines of the environmental suit he wore. Instead, he concentrated on keeping himself safely behind one of the protective shields protruding from each side of "the Mole," as the aptly nicknamed drilling vehicle chewed its way through the dense rock of the asteroid.

A squat, bulky piece of machinery, the Mole's most prominent feature was the large, intimidating phased-energy drilling array mounted on the rig's forward section. In addition to the pair of multiterrain treads that helped propel the Mole over ground, the vehicle also had a series of maneuvering thrusters and magnetic plates that would allow it to work in low-gravity environments or even totally exposed in space. Scott had encountered such a rig before, early in his career when his ship had ferried a group of dilithium miners to the newly established colony on Rigel XII. He had taken advantage of the long voyage to acquaint himself with the mechanics who saw to the mining vehicles' maintenance. With an unmatched construction and operational record, drilling rigs like the Mole were a preferred favorite, used at mining establishments throughout the Federation. Upon first seeing this particular unit, however, Scott had not been able to suppress a chuckle when he saw a yawning mouth complete with large, irregularly sharpened teeth painted on its frame just behind the drilling array.

For what could probably have been the hundredth time, he glanced down at the compact control panel mounted to his left wrist. A series of small displays communicated information about his suit's operation to him, continuously updating the status of his oxygen, internal temperature, and other annoying data such as his heart rate, which the suit dutifully informed him was accelerated. Catching himself in the mostly involuntary action, Scott forced his hand down to his sides and returned his full attention to the task at hand.

True to his word, Captain Okagawa had seen to the transfer of environmental suits for him and al-Khaled only moments after severing communication with them, along with the standard tool kit that the younger man had requested. While the pair of engineers had busied themselves preparing for their sojourn out onto the asteroid's surface, a team of two additional crewmembers had been dispatched from the *Lovell* in a shuttlecraft, towing the Mole down from the larger ship with a tractor beam.

Displaying yet another quality Scott admired in officers of any rank or position, al-Khaled had notified the captain that he himself would be overseeing the drilling. Scott could hear the confidence in the man's voice when he had relayed that, noting the determination that he would not stand idly by as another member of his team risked potential injury or death while digging down to the reactor. Okagawa must have heard it, too, for he said nothing except to acknowledge the report his lieutenant had given him and to wish the team luck.

*"Okagawa to landing party,"* the captain's voice abruptly called out through Scott's suit communicator. *"We've beamed everyone that we can reach with transporters up to the ship. That still leaves the eighteen down there that we couldn't get to.*

*Everyone else from our team is back up here, as well, so that just leaves you four."* There was a significant pause before Okagawa added, *"I expect that head count to be the same when you're done down there, Mahmud."*

With about ninety minutes left to them before the outpost reactor was predicted to reach overload, the team was making excellent time. A tunnel more than six meters in diameter was being excavated most efficiently thanks to the firing sequence programmed into the onboard computer controlling the Mole's drilling array. Eight individual drilling lasers, working in rapid alternating succession, were boring and disintegrating the rock so quickly that Scott and al-Khaled were able to walk at an almost normal pace alongside the rig. Inside the vehicle's compact cab, the two engineers who had flown the shuttlecraft down from the *Lovell* were at the Mole's controls.

"How are we doing, Ghrex?" al-Khaled asked.

At the Mole's piloting controls, the female Denobulan ensign responded, "All systems are nominal, sir. We are proceeding on schedule."

Sitting next to Ghrex, Lieutenant Paul LeGere was monitoring the rig's drilling apparatus. "At this rate, Mahmud, we should be able to break through into the reactor room inside of thirty minutes."

Nodding in satisfaction, Scott consulted his tricorder. Though the dense mineral deposits scattered throughout the asteroid were still disrupting scans, he could already see a marked improvement in the unit's sensor returns since they had started drilling.

"I've got a faint readin' on the reactor room," he reported. "No sign of any coolant leaks that I can find. We might be in luck, at least as far as that's concerned." Checking the tricorder's display again, he added, "Reactor temperature is continuin' to rise, though. The damage to the coolin' system is too much for it to keep up. Even if we get down there in time to fix the bloody thing, there canna be enough coolant left to do any good." Without the necessary amount of coolant to assuage the unchecked heat put out by the reactor, there would be no stopping the building overload.

Grasping one of the handholds mounted along the side of the Mole's frame, Scott could feel the powerful vibrations generated by the machine as it continued to excavate the solid rock ahead of it. The reverberations allowed him to feel the variety of sounds of the Mole rolling across the uneven path it was creating as it moved forward. He could also make out the hum of the drilling lasers' synchronized firing sequence and even the pulses of maneuvering thrusters as Ensign Ghrex kept the rig on a straight, precise course down through the interior of the asteroid.

Then the asteroid moved.

It was a sudden jarring movement, nearly throwing Scott off his feet and overriding the series of attitude thrusters built into his suit and which had been giving him a limited ability to walk even in this low-gravity environment. Throwing his arms out instinctively was the only thing that saved him from being thrown headlong into the wall of the tunnel.

"What the devil—?"

Almost immediately another shock wave slammed him into the unyielding rock wall, forcing the air from his lungs. He rebounded off the wall and was tossed back in the direction of the Mole, flailing for something to grab onto as his suit's thrusters fought to bring his momentum under control.

The drilling rig wasn't faring much better, bouncing off the sides of the tunnel despite the best efforts of Ghrex to compensate with the vehicle's own maneuvering thrusters. As Scott managed to get his own body under control, he realized that there was a very real danger of his being crushed between the walls and the Mole itself.

"Mahmud!" he shouted into his helmet communicator as he saw his companion encountering similar difficulty on the other side of the vehicle. "Be careful of the rig!" He breathed a sigh of relief as he saw al-Khaled maneuver safely out of the Mole's way.

"Lovell *to landing party*," Captain Okagawa

called out. *"We're registering explosions from within the outpost. Are you all right?"*

Scott was too busy scrambling away from the Mole to respond. Even as he managed to put distance between himself and the rig he could see Ghrex bringing it under some semblance of control. Instead of bouncing off the sides of the tunnel the Mole was now hovering in place, its treads only a handful of centimeters above the rock floor as the ensign at the controls finally managed to stabilize the rig.

"Are ye all right, lad?" Scott called to al-Khaled as he tried to bring his breathing under control.

Nodding inside his helmet, al-Khaled responded shakily. "Fine. You?" Scott indicated the same, and a quick check with Ghrex and LeGere revealed that they too had avoided injury, strapped as they were into the pilots' seats of the Mole's cockpit. Al-Khaled reported as such to the *Lovell*.

*"From what our sensors are telling us,"* Okagawa said, *"it sounds as though you were luckier than other parts of the outpost. We're reading other tunnel cave-ins and some of the compartments have suffered hull breaches. Contact with the remaining station personnel has been cut off, Mahmud, so we have no idea whether or not they've suffered any casualties."*

"Do ye have any idea what caused the explosion, sir?" Scott asked.

*"We think it may have been an overloaded power*

*distribution relay in a compartment that suffered a ruptured coolant conduit,"* the captain replied. *"There's no way to be certain at this point, and we won't have time to investigate the matter if you don't complete your mission. What is your status?"* According to Ghrex and LeGere, the rig hadn't suffered any appreciable damage.

"Less than a hundred meters remain before we reach the reactor chamber," al-Khaled reported. "We are recommencing drilling now, Captain."

*"Excellent,"* Okagawa replied. *"Keep me informed, Mahmud. You haven't much time left to pull off this minor miracle."*

Though his own tricorder had not survived their ordeal, Scott had retrieved another one from a storage compartment built into the side of the Mole's hull. Adjusting the unit's sensors, he felt a sudden knot form in his stomach as he reviewed the scan results. "He's putting it mildly, laddie. According to these readings, our problems have just gotten worse."

"Don't tell me," al-Khaled replied. "The cooling system?"

Scott could only nod grimly. "Aye. It's given up the ghost, I'm afraid. It's totally off-line." No coolant whatsoever was flowing through the system and compensating, even in a limited fashion, for the reactor's rapidly building heat. "The buildup is increasing," he added. "It'll reach overload long before we can hope to have the cooling system repaired."

\*          \*          \*

Once the Mole had finished drilling the remaining distance through the rock and succeeded in breaking through into the reactor chamber, a visual inspection of the damaged coolant system only confirmed the cold facts relayed by Scott's tricorder. What had once been a finely tuned, efficiently functioning series of components was now nothing more than a useless, mangled heap.

It was very much in keeping with the rest of the room, which had suffered no small amount of damage from the ion storm and its effects. Basically nothing more than a large hollowed-out cavern within the belly of the asteroid, the entire room was enshrouded in a green haze, coolant that had billowed from ruptures all along the vast network of conduits running from the reactor to the cooling system. Explosions had ripped through both sets of machinery, to Scott looking not all that different from the type of damage a starship's hull might encounter during a fierce battle.

"The master control console," al-Khaled called out to Scott, the younger man wasting no time mourning the loss of the critical system and instead moving for the small room at the far end of the chamber. "Ghrex, LeGere, check out the reactor's manual overrides. If I can't execute a controlled power-down, then you're going to have to throw the emergency shutoff." Intended for use only in situations where there were no other options and the reactor's continued operation was a danger to the outpost, the emergency override would instantly deactivate the massive generator. Doing so, however, would almost certainly result in widespread internal systems damage requiring extensive repair work if not outright replacement.

*But it's better than lettin' the damned thing blow up*, Scott thought.

He and al-Khaled reached the sealed door to the control room, and al-Khaled tapped a control set into the wall, allowing the door to slide open. As he moved to enter the room, though, he stopped short.

"My Lord," he whispered.

Moving alongside his companion, Scott felt a lump form in his throat as he beheld the gruesome sight of three bodies lying on the floor of the room.

"The reactor detail," al-Khaled said quietly. As feared, the two men and one woman assigned to this section had been trapped down here when the storm hit, cut off from the outpost's upper levels. When the coolant ruptures had started, the engineers had sought refuge in the small control room, but there had been no escaping the coolant's lethal effects.

Allowing al-Khaled a moment to gather his emotions, Scott then placed a reassuring hand on the man's shoulder. "C'mon, lad, we have work to do."

Nodding inside his suit's helmet, al-Khaled resolutely led the way into the room, focusing his attention on the bank of consoles and deliberately keeping the bodies of the three engineers from his line of sight. He took a few moments to familiarize himself with the controls before tapping a series of commands into one keypad. Watching the results of his actions on one set of display monitors, he shook his head.

"No response from the control computer," he said. "I can't access the deactivation protocols."

Moving to an adjacent console, Scott attempted to coax cooperation out of the computer terminal but received similar results. "There's probably been some damage to the system between the computer and here," he offered. "We'll have to find where the connection's been severed and repair it."

"No time for that," al-Khaled replied. Activating his suit's communicator he called out, "Al-Khaled to Ghrex. What have you found?"

The Denobulan's reply was quick and clipped, as though she were talking while engaged in work requiring more attention than she wanted to devote to conversation. *"We've found the manual overrides, Lieutenant, but they've been fused. It appears they were hit by debris from an explosion. We're preparing to open the panel now and see if we can repair the controls."*

Scott shook his head as he stole a look at the chronometer built into his suit's wrist control panel. "We dinna have time for that. At this rate the reactor will go in about seventeen minutes. All that's left is to pull the beastie out of here before she blows."

*Occam's razor, indeed.*

# CHAPTER
## 7

Removing the damaged reactor from its mounting frame was an easy enough task, as was using the Mole's tractor beam to maneuver the unwieldy PXK unit out of the chamber and into the tunnel created by the rig just for this purpose. The near absence of gravity in the asteroid's interior made the task of pushing the reactor back up the tunnel far easier than the team of engineers had any right to expect, given the luck they had experienced to this point.

They had cut it close. Because of the scattering effects of the asteroid's dense mineral deposits, it had been necessary to push the reactor more than halfway back the way they had originally descended from the surface before the *Lovell*'s tractor beam could lock on and pull it the remaining distance. Scott had been unnerved the entire time, able to feel the oppressive heat being cast off by the reactor in spite of his suit's heavy insulation. Though the chronometer on his tricorder told him they had plenty of time, he couldn't help but worry that the damaged power unit's output would continue to escalate at a rate that would ultimately find the engineers without the time needed to remove it.

With barely more than three minutes remaining to them before overload, the *Lovell* was able to direct its tractor beam far enough into the tunnel to latch onto the reactor. Drawing the doomed unit from the depths of the asteroid, the ship pulled it far enough from the outpost that when it finally exploded, it did so at a safe distance.

*Too bad we canna call it a day after all that,* Scott mused.

Instead, he was standing with al-Khaled and his engineering team in Outpost 5's control center, consulting the master system's displays and debating a new course of action.

"Battery backup systems are functioning normally," al-Khaled reported as he reviewed one monitor, "the ones that weren't damaged, that is." He shook his head in frustration. "Even if we cut all unnecessary expenditures, the available power will only last eighteen hours or so."

"And a replacement reactor that can handle the outpost's power requirements is weeks away," Scott said. Without sufficient power, the station and its vital subspace communications relay equipment would be effectively dead in less than a day, and the worst-case scenario first postulated by Commander Burke at their initial briefing would come to fruition. There would be no way to effectively communicate sensor and intelligence information gathered by the Federation outposts back to Starfleet. The entire region of space would be open to exploitation, not only by the Romulans but also by anyone with the resources to take advantage of the situation.

*"Our only alternative is to create a substitute power source that can meet the outpost's requirements until a replacement reactor arrives,"* Captain Okagawa said over the control center's communications circuit. *"Surely there's something on the station that you can make use of?"*

"We've got the shuttlecraft we brought down from the *Lovell,*" Ensign Ghrex said. "Could its engines be used somehow?"

Scott shook his head. "It can't produce the amount of power we'd need." Then a thought struck the engineer. "Mahmud, how many shuttles does the *Lovell* carry?"

"Three," al-Khaled replied, already smiling at the rest of Scott's unspoken thought. "If we remove the engines from all of them, we could string them together and hook them right into the outpost's power distribution network."

Scott wasn't convinced, though. "The outpost's power requirements would be more than even the engines from three shuttles could produce."

Considering the problem for a moment, he added, "Still, perhaps we can scrounge some additional power out of them."

His smile growing wider at the unconventional idea taking shape before them, al-Khaled said, "Scrounge? Remember who you're talking to, Scotty. The Corps of Engineers are masters of that particular art form."

Montgomery Scott had encountered more than a few unorthodox and rapidly improvised schemes designed to solve various problems he had faced as a Starfleet engineer. Therefore, it was easy for him to accept the idea of a fellow engineer adopting an unusual solution for an unusual challenge.

But working with Lieutenant Mahmud al-Khaled and his team was something else entirely.

Donning their environmental suits once more, they had put their irregular plan into motion, with al-Khaled ordering the two other shuttlecraft brought down from the *Lovell*. That accomplished, he and his team of engineers had expeditiously carried out the task of removing the engines from each of the three small ships. The assistance of the Mole and its tractor beam had made transporting the engine components to the outpost's reactor chamber a simple operation. Now, with nearly six hours remaining before the station's battery power was exhausted, all that was left was to reconfigure the engines' power flow to be compatible with the station's distribution network.

"What the devil have ye done here, lad?" Looking inside an access panel on one of the engine components, Scott could see that the entire inner workings of the power regulation system appeared to have been completely rebuilt from the ground up. The original network of internal circuitry, what was left of it, had been augmented, enhanced, and in some ways reconstructed in schemes he had never seen or even imagined before. It amazed him that the shuttlecraft engine didn't blow apart the instant it was activated, much less actually allow the vessel it powered to fly.

"It's like I keep telling you," al-Khaled told him as he inspected the power settings on another of the power plant components. "We have a lot of time to tinker between assignments. Not to mention that when something breaks, we're usually in a spot where we can't put in to a starbase for replacement supplies. Sometimes we have to adapt to the environment, whatever it might be." Opening one of the engine shell's larger access panels, he indicated for Scott to look.

Doing as he was asked, Scott peered into the opening and saw a plethora of wiring running to and from what should have been a flow regulator, responsible for channeling deuterium within a shuttle's engine core and warp nacelles. But what he was looking at was most definitely not Federation issue.

"That almost looks . . . ," he began uncertainly.

"Klingon," al-Khaled finished for him. "We salvaged it from a crashed scout ship we found about a year ago. We've taken it apart, documented its specifications, and sent the information to Starfleet Research and Development. The thing works better than the one that originally came with this engine. I wish I had half a dozen more just like it." He couldn't suppress the playful grin that was forcing itself onto his face. "Maybe some of its features will make their way into future engine designs. Wouldn't that be something?"

The younger man's enthusiasm was infectious, very similar to what Scott had felt when he was confronted with a challenging technical problem. Having watched the man and his team in action, Scott was now convinced that the Corps of Engineers, with its oftentimes nonconformist methods, was just the arena where a man of al-Khaled's talents could flourish.

"The engines on these shuttles operate around twelve to fifteen percent above normal standards," al-Khaled explained. "And we have a few tricks that can squeeze even more out of them. It still won't replace the station's normal reactor, but it should be more than enough to power most of the outpost's primary systems. We can reconfigure the power distribution to bypass nonessential expenditures, and that should be enough to get them by until the replacement reactor arrives."

"Lovell *to landing party*," Okagawa's voice sounded in their helmets. "*How is everything going down there, Mahmud?*"

Tapping his suit's external communicator control, al-Khaled replied, "We've just about finished here, Captain. Give us five more minutes." He turned to see Ensign Ghrex stepping out of the reactor chamber's master control room as the Denobulan gave him a thumbs-up sign, confirming his report.

"*Excellent. I have no doubt this will work, Lieutenant. You and your team are to be commended.*"

Frowning at the praise, al-Khaled tried to keep the doubt from his voice as he said, "Thank you, sir. However, perhaps it is unwise to congratulate us before we've had a chance to test our theory."

"*No need, Lieutenant,*" the *Lovell*'s captain responded, the tone of his speech adopting a paternal yet almost teasing quality that Scott suspected had been employed against the engineers on more than one occasion. "*After all, if this doesn't work, then the entire Federation intelligence-gathering apparatus in this region of space will be effectively neutralized. You certainly wouldn't allow me to make such a report to Starfleet Command now, would you?*"

Unable to stifle the laugh provoked by that, al-

Khaled shook his head in mock defeat. "Well, when you put it that way, Captain, I cannot disagree. Stand by." Severing the connection, he turned his attention back to Scott. "Well, I suppose there's only one thing left to do. Ghrex? LeGere? Are you ready?"

From the control room, LeGere replied, *"Aye, sir. Ready when you are."*

Indicating the trio of salvaged shuttlecraft engines with a nod of his head, he said to Scott, "Let's see what happens."

While Ghrex and LeGere monitored the proceedings from the control center and stood ready to sever the power connections at a moment's notice, Scott and al-Khaled activated the three engines. Scott could feel the rock floor of the reactor chamber begin to vibrate in concert with the units' increasing power levels.

*"Readings are steady,"* Ghrex reported from the control room. *"Power levels are within normal levels, sir."*

Scott was the first to detect it, though, a tremor in the protective shell encasing the third of the three shuttle engines that was almost imperceptible through the thick layers of his suit glove. Had he not had a hand on the control panel built into one side of the unit, he most likely would never have detected it.

At nearly the same instant, Ensign LeGere shouted from the control room, *"I'm picking up a power fluctuation in engine three!"*

"Shut it down!" Scott called even as an alarm sounded from a status display on the engine's control panel. Reaching out, he stabbed the emergency shutdown switch and the suddenly ailing power unit immediately began to deactivate itself.

"We overloaded the internal flow regulator," al-Khaled reported, consulting his tricorder. Casting a wry look at Scott, he added, "I told you I wish we had more of those Klingon parts."

Ignoring the attempt at humor, Scott was already opening the panel that would give him access to the engine's internal systems. Looking inside, he realized that he would not need a tricorder to determine the extent of their latest problem. "Aye," he said, "it's had it, all right." Without the flow regulator, the power generated by the engine would be unchecked, creating a potentially dangerous situation when trying to channel that energy through the outpost's distribution network.

"Let's get it out of there," al-Khaled said, moving to help. "We've got less than six hours to repair it and get this engine back up and running before we lose the station's battery power." Without its battery backup system, the outpost would lose everything, including life support to the fifteen personnel still trapped within the facility's lower levels.

"Can ye not simply replace it?" Scott asked. "Surely ye've got another one aboard ship?" With the *Lovell*'s transporters all but useless after only a few hundred meters below the surface, they would need the Mole to travel back up the tunnel and retrieve any replacement components the ship could provide.

But the look on al-Khaled's face told him that things were not going to go according to that plan.

"We don't have a replacement regulator," the younger engineer said, grimacing as if in pain at having to admit that. "We were overdue for resupply before we took on this mission, and besides, we're never exactly first priority when it comes to replacement parts. That's another reason we end up improvising so much."

Scott shook his head. It disgusted him to think that, with all the talent possessed by the members of the *Lovell*'s crew of engineering specialists and with the efficiency and practicality with which Starfleet normally operated, any one of its ships should find itself in such a situation. Something as ridiculous as not being considered important enough to obtain proper supplies might actually end up defeating them here, especially after all they'd had to deal with so far.

Not if he could help it, though.

Looking about the reactor chamber, it didn't take Scott long to zero in on the Mole, sitting unattended near the mouth of the tunnel it had created mere hours before. After all, it was the only thing in the room that could even begin to serve their present needs.

"We'll pull the flow regulator from the drilling rig," he said simply as he set off in the direction of the vehicle.

"It's not strong enough to handle the power put out by a shuttle's engine," al-Khaled countered. "There's no way it'll hold together."

Casting a knowing smile at his companion, Scott said. "Trust me, laddie. You've done a fine bit o' miracle workin' here today. Now it's my turn."

"I don't believe it," al-Khaled said, making no effort to hide the stunned expression on his face.

No sooner did Scott activate the repaired shuttle engine than the unit immediately began its power-up sequence. After only a handful of seconds it had begun to generate power at a level equal to its two counterparts. In fact, as Scott scanned the engine with his tricorder, he was pleased to note that the unit's output was actually a few percentage points more than the other engines.

"It's a simple thing, lad," Scott said. "These drilling rigs are tough little beasties, designed to handle a lot more punishment than most engineers are willin' to expose 'em to. In fact, the flow sensors in this particular model work on a wee bit more than the conservative side, if ye ask me. Ye can almost bypass the bloody thing entirely."

Which was exactly what he had done when he had removed the flow regulator from the Mole and hastily installed it into the shuttle engine. Now more than ever, he was thankful for that group of dilithium miners and the patience they had demonstrated all those years ago, obliging young Ensign Montgomery Scott and his endless stream of questions and burning desire to learn about just one more facet of engineering.

"Power levels are steady," Ensign Ghrex called out from the reactor control room. "All primary outpost systems are on-line and functioning. Captain Okagawa reports that full capacity has been restored to the main control center."

Scott nodded in approval. They had already received a report from the *Lovell*'s captain that another team from the ship had successfully reached the remaining outpost crewmembers who had been trapped during the storm. The better news was that all fifteen people had been recovered with no further casualties.

"I guess our work here is done," Scott said to al-Khaled as they made their final preparations to leave the reactor room behind. "There's no reason why these wee bairns willna run just fine until that replacement reactor gets here." Of course he knew that a team from the *Lovell* would be brought down to assist the outpost engineers until the reactor actually arrived, but there was no reason to expect any more problems.

"Just another day at the office, I suppose," al-

Khaled replied. Smiling wryly at Scott, the younger man asked, "So, Scotty, ready to chuck that pampered life aboard a starship and join a group of real engineers? I think you'd fit in just fine with the Corps."

Laughing, Scott shook his head. "I dinna think so, lad. I've been looking forward to my next assignment for quite some time." He wasn't about to give up his upcoming posting to the *Enterprise*, at least not without a fight. Still, he had to admit to himself that were circumstances different, he might very well find life with the Corps of Engineers exciting enough.

With any luck, though, life aboard the *Enterprise* would provide its own set of challenges.

"One thing I intend to do when we get back for our after-action briefing, though," he said, "is file a report to Starfleet Command with recommendations for the Corps. I know that your group was originally established to handle more routine assignments that don't always make the Federation News Network. But this wasna some underground colony ye dug outta the rock, lads. This type of work is a wee bit more specialized, and dangerous. If they mean to send ye out on more missions like this, then they'll hafta do a better job of supportin' ye."

This assignment may not have enticed Scott to transfer over to this branch of Starfleet, but it had convinced him that a dedicated group of engineers, separate from the demands of regular ships of the line, could be a valuable resource. Not simply for performing the regular, mundane, even boring types of assignments for which the Corps had been created, he saw the potential to utilize the obviously unique talents and experience that a group of such highly specialized professional technicians could bring to the table. What was needed was for Starfleet Command to provide the necessary logistical and administrative elements to support such an initiative, just as they would for other departments and ships in the fleet.

"You're talking about changing the minds of bureaucrats, Commander," al-Khaled countered. "That's going to take some serious report writing."

Scott indicated the tunnel leading from the reactor room to the asteroid's surface with a nod of his head. With the turboshafts and access crawlways leading to the outpost's upper levels still blocked off due to damage from the ion storm, it was still the only way for the engineers to effect their departure. However, not even the Mole was at their service for the return trip back up the tunnel. All that was left were the engineers' own feet.

"Well, considerin' that I basically broke our only means of gettin' outta here, I figure I have plenty of time to come up with a first draft. Come along, lad."

And with that, the engineers began their long walk home.

# CHAPTER
# 8

Stardate 53675.4

Montgomery Scott.

*If ever there were an engineer's engineer,* thought Kieran Duffy, *it's Scotty.*

As he started to settle back in his seat at the engineering station, the sound of someone clearing his throat shook him back to the twenty-fourth century and the issues at hand. "Sorry, Captain, are my fifteen minutes up?"

"Promote me to admiral and I'll buy you another fifteen minutes," said Fabian Stevens, who had silently made his way to Duffy's post without interrupting the reading engineer. "I'd look good with a boxed pip or two."

"Good like a Medusan," Duffy quipped, "because if I ever see you sporting one of those, I'd better have a visor on. What are you doing up at this hour?"

"As soon as Bart got back from the bridge, griping about our heading into a first contact situation, how could I go back to sleep?" Stevens turned to look at the Senuta ship in the main viewer. "Any ideas?"

"I'm kicking stuff around," Duffy said as he let out a heavy breath. "You know me. Something's bound to fall out of my head at any minute."

"Out of your head and right onto the deck. Well, I'm ready to help." Stevens leaned on the console and moved a bit closer to speak to his friend. "Bart tells me that you did some morale-building from the big chair at my expense."

"I was just telling the Tellarite story to the night shift."

Stevens groaned. "I hate the Tellarite story."

"I loooove the Tellarite story. I even told Core-Breach the Tellarite story."

"I know. She mentioned it."

Duffy did not mask his surprise that Domenica Corsi, the ship's security chief and one of his prime foils, had talked with Stevens about such matters. "She mentioned it?"

"Yeah. We do converse, you know." Duffy watched Stevens pause a bit as if collecting or tempering his thoughts before speaking. "She's not all business and regulations, Duff. You'd enjoy her, too, if you weren't a smart-ass with her all the time."

"So you're telling me you enjoy her?"

"It's not what you think," Stevens countered.

"We eat together sometimes, or talk in the corridors, just in passing." Duffy refused to suppress the smirk that was spreading across his face. Stevens saw it and knew precisely what Duffy was thinking. The rumors had been flying around the ship since Empok Nor. "Okay, so you know about the one time. She needed someone and I was there. No apologies, no regrets."

"Hey, you two are grown-ups," Duffy said, at once happy to have the rumor finally confirmed and confused as to his feelings about what that confirmation meant. "I'm not anybody you need to justify your flings to."

Stevens nodded. "But truthfully, I think that night helped her remember how to build a friendship, and she's trying that out on me."

"Friends are good. Sonnie and I were friends," Duffy said of his dating relationship with Sonya Gomez, the *da Vinci*'s first officer. "I mean, we still are friends, but we were friends first back on the *Enterprise*." He paused, looking about the bridge and seeing that work continued as usual. "So, what, you think maybe you and Core-Breach are friends?"

"As close as she's willing to have me be one, sure."

"And you'd be open to more than that?"

Stevens paused again, mulling his words. "I'm thinking so, yes."

"And you think she might be, too?"

"That I don't know."

Duffy lost his interest in mincing words. "I know, and I just don't see it."

"Be open to her, Duff," Stevens said. "Don't crack wise next time you talk to her and maybe you'll see it. She told me that she respects you, and that you earned that during the run-in with the Tholians. Maybe someday we can all sit down together. Eat, drink, find some common ground."

"What, you, me, Sonnie, and Core-Breach on a double date? Having a drink and some laughs?" Duffy figured that the chances of that happening were about as likely as a wormhole opening up in his cabin.

Stevens shrugged. "Well, sure."

"Not in my lifetime, pal," Duffy replied as he returned his attention to the bank of engineering displays and began to reconsider the problem of how to slow down the Senuta ship. The alien vessel's ion drive was not like anything he was used to, but the principles behind its method of propulsion were fairly straightforward. It all centered around the flow of ions through the engine's series of intermix chambers. In reality it was a simpler theory to grasp than even the most rudimentary Starfleet warp drive design.

When he noticed that Stevens was still leaning on the nearby console, Duffy looked up and saw the slightly withered expression on his friend's face. "Look, Fabe, I just don't want to see you shot down here. I know Corsi's type. I think what you need more than a meal and a talk is a cold shower."

"Sage advice, Duff. I'll consi—"

"Wait!" And just like that, the answer was there. It was so simple, sitting right in front of him the entire time while he had been so engrossed in searching for a complex solution that he had missed the easier approach. "That's it! A cold shower!"

Stevens was rattled. "Huh?"

Duffy jumped from his seat and put a hand on each of Stevens's shoulders, smiling as he regarded the shocked expression on his friend's face. "You're a brilliant man, Fabe! Brilliant!" Duffy freed a hand from Stevens and used it to tap his combadge. "Duffy to Gold. Captain, I think I have an idea."

"You want to give the Senuta a cold shower?"

Gold looked no less incredulous at the idea than anyone else seated at the table in the *da Vinci*'s observation lounge. Duffy smiled as his eyes moved from Gold to Sonya Gomez, then to Stevens and finally to Abramowitz. "You know that's not exactly what I mean, but in theory, yes."

Gomez nodded back toward Duffy and smiled. "Then please enlighten us."

"As I understand it, their ion engines work on principles very similar to those employed by other races in our experience. What happened, as far as I can tell, is that their ion engine reactions became hyperstimulated in an exchange with whatever charged particles passed through their ship during that storm forty-seven days ago." Duffy paused to take a sip from a glass of quinine water. "Something happened to really heat things up over there. I propose we cool things off."

Gold smiled in approval. Though the captain himself was not an engineer, Duffy knew that his commanding officer had taken advantage of leading a crew of engineers and acquired knowledge in a wide variety of engineering principles. "And your proposal?"

Leaning forward in his seat, Duffy replied, "We use our deflector dish to fire a stream of ions of alternating charges. The goal is to slow the reactions within the engines without disrupting other systems on the ship. And, we do it in a gradual process so the folks inside don't end up more liquid than solid."

"That's a laudable goal," Gold said. Turning to Gomez, he asked, "Does that sound reasonable to you, Gomez?"

"Very, Captain." To Duffy she smiled and said, "I knew you had it in you."

"Thank Captain Scott and Fabian over there," Duffy replied, indicating his friend across the table with a nod of his head. "They're the ones who helped me sort it all out." The assembled group shared puzzled glances for a second time, but Duffy moved on. "What might make this operation less risky would be to evacuate the Senuta ship before slowing it down."

"Great plan," Gold said. "So why don't we?"

Abramowitz shook her head. "They won't hear of it. I've spoken to Daltren twice to suggest it but some of the Senuta refuse to leave the ship. Some of them claim to be too ill or just not completely trusting of us. Daltren said those willing to come aboard are respecting the beliefs of the rest of the crew and refuse to abandon them." She paused as the others took in her words. "I'd like us to honor their wishes and their solidarity. It's not just an issue with the people on the ship. We're representatives of the Federation, and the Senuta are a race new to us. This may determine whether we make friends or enemies of an entire civilization."

Gold nodded. "Abramowitz is right on the mark. We know the dangers here and so do the Senuta. If they want to stay on their ship, then we won't make an issue of it. What else, people?"

"As soon as we get their ship stopped," Gomez replied, "I'd like a team ready to beam aboard her. I'm going, and I'm taking Elizabeth, Soloman, and Bart with me." Duffy shifted in his seat noisily enough to draw Gomez's attention, making her smile. "Kieran, I'll invite you to take a look at the Senuta's systems as soon as we're ready."

"Oh . . . okay," he said, feigning disappointment. "Give me a couple more minutes to double-check my frequencies for the ion shower, and I'll be ready."

Rising from his chair, Gold regarded his officers. "Then we're through here. Fine work as always, people. Let's get this done."

Duffy hurried his step so he could walk through the door to the bridge just behind Gomez. He tugged on her uniform sleeve with two fingers just hard enough to draw her attention, and then he motioned with a nod of his head for her to follow him to his workstation. As the two neared the engineering console, Duffy spoke first. "Quick question. After we get all of this settled, could we set up a dinner or something with Fabian?"

"So I can watch him squirm through yet another retelling of the Tellarite story?" Gomez asked. "It's really not that funny, you know."

Duffy laughed harder than he expected at the jab. "Nope. I just owe him some time, and some open-minded attention." As she nodded assent he added, "And, um, let's invite Corsi, too."

"What?" Gomez's jaw dropped, and then she broke into a huge smile. "Am I actually hearing you acknowledge Domenica Corsi as a real human being?"

He sighed and let slip one more laugh. "Sonnie, I'm happy. Aren't you?"

Gomez's features softened. "Yeah. Yeah, I am, Kieran."

"Fabe is my best friend, and we talk about

everything. Everything but Corsi," Duffy said. "It's time I lightened up, I think, and figured out what makes my friend happy."

"You big softie." Gomez scuffed her fist against his arm. "I'll work it out and make sure she's there."

"Just don't tell her I'm coming."

"Precisely." Gomez smiled as she walked away, taking the opportunity to stroll about the bridge's outer stations and review their status. Satisfied that everything and everyone was where they needed to be, she turned back to Gold, who had taken his place in the *da Vinci*'s command chair. "Captain, we can begin at your discretion."

Gold nodded. "This is an S.C.E. operation now, Gomez. Lead away."

Gomez turned to Abramowitz at the communications station. "Alert the Senuta that we're ready to bring them out of warp. They need to be in their acceleration couches and expecting a bumpy ride." As the cultural liaison tapped at her console, Gomez looked to Duffy's station. "How close are you, Kieran?"

Running a final check of his calculations, Duffy looked up at Gomez and gave her a short nod. "Ready when you are."

On the main viewer, the stars streaked past and the silver Senuta ship was growing in size as the *da Vinci* continued to close the distance. Duffy could feel his pulse beginning to quicken as the time approached to put his bold plan into motion. He was confident in the preparations he had made to this point, and he trusted the *da Vinci*'s computer to carry out the required actions with the necessary precision that no living being could possibly match. With a touch on his console, he expected their problems would be over and then he could get a look at those ion engines. So why was he feeling such a sense of dread?

*Because you're paranoid,* he scolded himself. *But isn't this the point where something usually goes wrong?*

Forcing the errant thoughts from his mind, Duffy returned his attention to the task at hand, his finger hovering over the panel as he awaited Gomez's order. Finally, after what seemed like a century, the words came.

"Mr. Duffy, engage the deflector beam."

# CHAPTER
# 9

*Here we go*, Duffy told himself as his finger pressed the control.

Though his computer simulations had told him that the effects of the varying streams of ions would be fast acting, he was still unprepared for what happened next.

"Reading a fluctuation in their ion drive, Duff," Fabian Stevens reported from the science station. "And a disruption in their warp field." Smiling, he added, "Looks like this crazy idea of yours is working."

From his command chair, Captain Gold said, "Stevens, isn't it a bit early to be inflating the lieutenant commander's ego?"

The witty response that had already formed on Duffy's tongue vanished as an alarm sounded at his station. Turning his attention back to his console, it took only seconds for him to determine the cause of the problem.

"It's the ion stream," he reported, his fingers stabbing at controls as he spoke. "Their warp field is collapsing faster than I wanted it to." He shook his head in mounting frustration. "The damage to their ion drive must be more extensive than we thought. Dammit! We're tearing them out of subspace. I'm disengaging the deflector."

On the main viewer, the effects of the ion stream were plainly visible even as it dissipated in response to Duffy's commands. The Senuta ship was shuddering and bucking wildly as its engines struggled against the unexpected assault.

*What the hell did I do wrong?*

There would be plenty of time later to figure out where he had so obviously screwed up, however. Right now there were more important things that needed his attention, such as how to keep the Senuta vessel from tearing itself apart.

"Their speed is dropping radically," he reported, his eyes glued to the console before him.

Still seated in his command chair and possessing an outward calm that Duffy envied, especially now, Gold called out, "Rusconi, match their speed. Stay with them."

"Fabian," Gomez said as she jumped from the command well and made her way to the science station, "get me a damage report."

"Already on it," Stevens replied, all business once more as he worked. "There's some hull plate buckling, and I'm detecting internal space frame damage." Shaking his head, he added, "They're not built for that kind of punishment."

"What about a tractor beam?" Gomez asked. "We could use it to steady them."

Duffy's fingers were already entering the necessary commands, moving as if free of his conscious control. "Yes! That just might do the trick!"

From his own station, Stevens frowned. "Maybe, but with the damage they've already suffered, it might just make things worse, Duff."

Nodding, Duffy replied, "I know. As small as that ship is, a half-strength tractor should still do the job while being gentle about it." He made no effort to hide the doubt in his voice, concentrating instead on entering commands to make the proper adjustments. That completed, he turned back to Gomez. "It's ready."

"Activate tractor beam."

All eyes on the bridge turned to the main viewer as the *da Vinci*'s tractor beam reached out across the void and enveloped the Senuta vessel. The alien ship's violent gyrations continued for a moment before beginning to subside under the beam's influence.

"It's working," Duffy said, remembering to breathe as the ship's tumbling was arrested. Only a few more seconds passed before the craft was once again traveling on a steady course.

*Congratulations*, Duffy told himself with a sigh

of relief. *But you shouldn't have had to do it in the first place.*

Rising from the center seat, Gold nodded in approval. "Excellent work, people. Open a channel to the Senuta ship, and let's see how bad off our new friends really are over there."

It didn't take long for Abramowitz to respond, however. "They're not answering, Captain."

"There could be damage to their communications system," Stevens said.

Gold said, "Well, since we were planning to beam over anyway, now seems as good a time as any." Looking to Gomez, he asked, "What do you say, Gomez?"

Nodding, Gomez replied, "Duffy and his team will have their hands full with the engines, and I'd like Soloman to take a look at their computer. Maybe he can figure out why it won't let the Senuta engineers in. Bart will be helpful over there, too, since we'll need to communicate with their computer techs. I'd like Dr. Lense to beam over and check out the medical situation."

"Good," Gold said. "Proceed at your own discretion." To the rest of the bridge crew he added, "It looks as though we've still got plenty of work ahead of us, people, so let's snap to it."

Personnel set about their various tasks, and at his own station Duffy began composing the lists of equipment and people he would need to transport with him to the alien ship when he felt a tap on his shoulder. He turned to see Gold, hands clasped behind his back, regarding him with the fatherly air that the captain affected so very well.

"I'm sensing a bit of tension with you, Duffy," Gold said. "Anything you'd like to share?" Though the question was offered in a gentle manner, Duffy knew from experience that the captain would not settle for his declining the offer to say what was on his mind.

"I screwed up, Captain," he said simply. "I missed something in my calculations and I could have destroyed that ship."

Gold frowned. "But you didn't, and you managed to overcome the error and create a solution that salvaged the operation. I also suspect that once this is all over, you'll spend however long it takes to find what it was you overlooked. Am I correct?"

A sheepish expression formed on Duffy's face. "Yes, sir."

"I don't expect my people to be perfect, Duffy," Gold said calmly, "but I do expect them to give their best effort. I've seen nothing to indicate that you've done anything less than that, on this or any other occasion. I also expect my people to learn from their mistakes and use that knowledge to better themselves. I've seen everything to indicate that you will do so in this instance, as well. But right now there's a ship full of people over there who need you to focus on the problem at hand, so my advice to you is to concentrate on that."

Somewhat relieved by the captain's words, Duffy nodded. "Understood, Captain. Thank you."

Gold smiled and his eyes narrowed as he added, "Besides, look on the bright side. Once you get over there, you'll have a whole new audience for that Tellarite story of yours."

*"Aye, it sounds as though ye've got things under control, Captain."*

From the main viewer in the *da Vinci's* conference lounge, Captain Montgomery Scott regarded Gold, Gomez, Abramowitz, and the captain of the Senuta ship, Daltren.

Basically humanoid in appearance, Daltren and Nirsrose, who had been introduced as the Senuta ship's second in command, possessed physiques and stature comparable to that of Soloman and other Bynars. Daltren stood no more than 1.5 meters tall, while Nirsrose was slightly shorter. Both Senuta were slight of build, with pale skin and hair that contrasted sharply with the dark, loose-fitting clothing they wore. Gomez had found herself drawn almost immediately to their eyes. They were colored an iridescent blue, conveying intelligence and intense curiosity that became evident the moment the Senuta began talking.

The questions were seemingly endless, with the Senuta inquiring about anything they happened to see as they moved through the ship.

Their enthusiasm was infectious, prompting Domenica Corsi to express her customary concern about providing too much information to these all-but-unknown aliens. Gomez, however, had convinced her to relent in her desire to have a security team present in the conference lounge while the Senuta were there.

"Commander Gomez and her people are handling all of the hard work," Gold said, smiling affably in the direction of the viewer from his seat at the head of the conference table. The viewer itself had been segmented into two sections. One half displayed the wizened visage of Captain Scott, while the other featured Duffy, who with several members of the S.C.E. team had transported to the Senuta ship more than an hour before. "I just get to sit back and take all the credit," the captain continued. "Judging by the initial reports we've received from the away team, they should have everything repaired in less than a day."

"That's right," Duffy said. "The engines themselves are actually in pretty good shape. There's some structural damage along with those systems taken out by the storm. We've got Senuta engineers helping us to identify the functionality of certain components so we can fashion replacements for the parts they don't have. There's plenty of work to be done and it'll take some time, but nothing too complex, sir."

Gomez noted a renewed confidence in Duffy's

voice, a quality that had not been there when he had first beamed over to the Senuta ship. She knew that he still hadn't forgiven himself for whatever error he may have made while putting his plan to decelerate the alien vessel into motion. She had offered her own encouragement to him prior to his departure, but if there was one thing that she knew about Kieran Duffy, it was that he would continue to feel guilty until he alone had resolved the question over what had gone wrong. That sense of responsibility and obligation was one of the qualities she loved about Kieran, of that she was sure.

It was also one of those things that could make her want to smack him silly.

"Sounds good, Commander," she said. "Keep us informed of your progress." On the viewer, Duffy nodded and severed his connection, leaving only the image of Captain Scott.

"What about our computer, Captain?" Daltren asked. "It controls nearly every system aboard our ship. Many of those same systems are beyond our ability to control without its assistance. The engineering area of our vessel is especially dependent on a number of integrated systems that are fully automated."

"Soloman is making some progress," Gomez reported. "But we may have to come up with some sort of alternative in the short term, at least until my people can learn the ins and outs of your computer system." Faulwell and Soloman had reported that they could be busy for quite a while, as two of the three Senuta crewmembers who had been killed during the ion storm were the ones assigned to oversee the ship's computer. None of the other Senuta possessed the necessary knowledge to really dig in and understand the operating system at a purely technical level, so Gomez knew that her people had their work cut out for them.

"I appreciate the effort your crew is expending on our behalf, Captain," Daltren said. "You must understand, ours is a society that places a great deal of respect and trust in computers. On our world, they autonomously oversee countless routine and mundane tasks, completely removing the need for our people to handle or even to think about them."

Leaning forward in her chair, Abramowitz added, "Mr. Daltren tells me that on his planet, all forms of public transportation, even most orbital and interplanetary travel, are run almost exclusively via automated computer control. It's been that way for generations, with nearly flawless performance and safety records. Their society isn't as reliant on computers as, say, the Bynars, but it is similar to Earth's dependence on them during their equivalent level of technology at the start of the twenty-third century. At the rate they're progressing, however, they could rival the Bynars in a century or so."

*"Quite impressive, if ye ask me,"* Scott said.

*"However, I'd be remiss if I dinna point out that in my experience, such dependence on automation isn't always a good thing."*

"You speak wisely, Captain," Daltren said. "For all the wonders our computers are capable of, the one aboard my ship could not have foreseen what happened to us, nor could it have predicted that the specialists charged with its care would be killed." Pausing a moment, he cast a downward glance to the conference table, and Gomez saw the pain at the loss of his companions in the Senuta's eyes. Shaking his head, he continued. "I sincerely hope that unfortunate instances such as this, rare though they may be, will serve to remind my people of the potential folly for entrusting ourselves so completely to the power of the machines."

Gold nodded soberly. "We've seen our fair share of societies that got themselves into trouble by relying too much on computers. I can certainly sympathize with your sentiments, Daltren."

Gomez agreed as well. "We've encountered two in the past few months alone." The chaos that had ensued when Ganitriul, the mammoth computer system that had overseen for millennia every facet of life on the planet Eerlik, began to malfunction remained a particularly powerful memory.

"I appreciate your insight," the Senuta captain replied. "But you must understand that my people have relied on automation for so long that I fear we may forever be enraptured by its spell. Adopting any kind of philosophy that lessened that dependence would undoubtedly be met with stark resistance."

From the viewscreen, Scott said, *"Take heart, sir. You at least have the presence of mind to know the dangers and limitations of allowing computers to have so much control. There have been numerous societies that dinna have that luxury."*

Smiling, Gold said, "If anyone here would know about that, it's you, Captain Scott. How many planetary supercomputers did Captain Kirk end up convincing to turn themselves off, anyway?"

*"More than his share, I'm afraid,"* Scott replied, chuckling. *"And of course ye know about one of them, that blasted contraption they called Landru."*

Gomez could not help smiling as she remembered the *da Vinci*'s recent encounter with a group of Ferengi who had managed to acquire components from the world computer that Captain Kirk and the *Enterprise* had encountered more than a century before.

"That was one of Captain Kirk's earlier missions," she said, a playful grin on her face, "so he hadn't quite polished his computer deactivation skills yet. If your mission to Beta III had come a few years later, there would have been nothing left for us." Of course, Gomez knew that the *Enterprise*'s original encounter with the Landru computer had been at least indirectly responsible for the evolution of the S.C.E. into the organization it was today.

*"We only thought we were finished with Landru when Captain Kirk turned the beastie off,"* Scott replied. *"But it was really just the beginning."*

# CHAPTER
# 10

Stardate 3176.9

*Will this never end?*

Lieutenant Commander Montgomery Scott leaned into his stride as he slogged through watery muck that rose above his knees. A work-light attached to the hood of his orange environmental suit helped guide him through the tunnel, its illumination reflecting off the water's brackish surface and the damp slime coating the walls around him. Sloshing sounds marked his progress and echoed up and down the sewer pipe, all but drowning out the crinkling and crunching of his suit's protective material. In an effort to fight the oppressive heat in the tunnel, Scott had shrugged off the upper half of the suit and tied the sleeves around his waist, leaving him clad in a standard Starfleet undershirt.

*But the headgear stays on, lest this ungodly smell make me lose my breakfast.*

*"So, how's the view down there?"* said a voice from the communicator Scott carried in his other hand. The voice belonged to his friend and fellow engineer, Lieutenant Commander Mahmud al-Khaled.

"Oh, it's quite the visual treat," Scott replied as he trudged onward. "Ye'll hafta let me give ye the tour before we go."

Laughter came through the communicator's speaker grid. *"Well, you know that you could put a merciful end to this."*

"Don't I know it." With a simple call to the *U.S.S. Lovell*, orbiting somewhere above the surface of Beta III, this sweaty, smelly, dirty walk could be swapped for an almost-instant journey to where he was already headed. However, skipping a naked eye tour of this main sewer connection might have meant his overlooking a fouled pump or a cracked seam or anything else that would lead to a malfunction of the village's wastewater treatment system.

*Besides, if ye'd not taken the easy ride yesterday,* he chided himself, *maybe ye'd not find yourself back in this stinkin' place.*

Scott continued through the pipe, the tricorder in his hand adding a smaller measure of illumination as it outlined the engineer's course.

On its miniature display a blinking dot indicated his goal: a broken proton pump inhibitor located just a few meters ahead. From his review of the sewer system, he knew that the inhibitor played a rather minor role in the overall scheme of things. However, experience had taught him with hard-learned lessons that even a simple problem could quickly escalate into a major crisis if left unattended.

*"You should be getting close to the inhibitor assembly's access panel,"* al-Khaled said over the communicator.

Sloshing a few more steps through the muck, Scott spied the slightest swelling in the left side of the tunnel, the outline of what looked to be a panel perhaps a meter square.

"Aye, I've found it."

Donning the pair of gloves that came with his sullied environmental suit, he traced a finger through the film on the tunnel wall, further distinguishing the panel from the metal surrounding it. He wiped the surface of the panel until he found the recessed pull handle that had been buried under years of accumulated slime and grime. Gripping the handle, Scott tugged the panel free from the wall.

A torrent of cold black water exploded outward, striking the engineer square in the chest and instantly dousing him in more of the same filthy mess that he had been wading through for the past hour.

"Oh, for the love of . . ."

Only the voice of al-Khaled kept him from unleashing a particularly vile string of Scottish oaths.

*"Scotty? Is everything all right?"*

Even as the sludge began to soak through his shirt, Scott raised his communicator to his mouth. "Oh, never better, thank ye very much." Sighing, he added, "Well, ye wanted payback after gettin' shocked by that power converter I sent ye to fix yesterday. I dare say ye've gotten it, lad."

*"That bad, is it?"*

"Let me just say that I'm glad I decided to keep my hood on."

*"Spare me the details until I can really enjoy them. Can you see the inhibitor?"*

Peering into the access panel, it took Scott several seconds to spy the pump inhibitor, tucked away as it was beneath a layer of wiring and other components. There was no mistaking the heavy layer of corrosion coating the gadget's exterior, which itself looked to be brittle and cracked. A quick scan with his tricorder showed what a visual inspection had already told him: The inhibitor definitely needed to be replaced.

"Aye, the wee beastie has given up the ghost, all right," he said, speaking more into the compartment than his communicator. "I'll have it replaced and tested within half an hour."

*"So what you're telling me is that you'll be ready*

*to beam out in about ten minutes. I've worked with you long enough to understand your repair estimate methodology."*

Scott smiled. Only a few short years had passed since his first meeting with Mahmud al-Khaled on Starbase 10. Despite their differing career paths, with al-Khaled remaining on the *Lovell* and Scott continuing with his assignment aboard the *Enterprise*, fate had conspired to bring the two friends together here, overseeing the operation to help the people of Beta III get back on their feet again.

"When a system works for me, Commander, I stick with it." Setting the communicator on the edge of the access compartment opening, Scott dug around in his bag again until he produced a tool to assist him in removing the useless pump inhibitor. Leaning forward, he craned his head for a better view. The environmental suit's hood was not designed to facilitate easy viewing of one's workspace, though. Sighing in resignation, Scott took a final breath of clean air before pushing the hood over and off his head. The unfiltered stench of the sewer pipe wasted no time wafting up his nostrils.

"Och."

*"Something amiss, Commander?"* came al-Khaled's mildly taunting voice over the communicator. Scott glared at the unit, sorely tempted to toss it into the dark sewage.

"Nothing I canna handle. As nasty as it might

be down here, it still beats bein' in the captain's chair of the *Enterprise* right about now."

Al-Khaled laughed. *"I heard rumors that Captain Kirk got his aft shields chewed up rather severely."*

"You dinna know the half of it, lad." Suppressing a gag, Scott leaned into the access panel once more.

As friendly as he had become with al-Khaled in the past few years, it still would not do to discuss what had transpired in the wake of Captain Kirk's decision to disable Landru, the mammoth computer that had ruled the people of Beta III for more than six thousand years. Memories of the post-mission briefing, held with the *Enterprise* senior officers, remained very clear in his mind, as did the urgent call from Starfleet that had interrupted it. He also remembered the one very important lesson of command he had learned that day.

*Never take an admiral's call in front of your crew.*

After reviewing how Captain Kirk had convinced the Landru computer to deactivate itself upon realizing that its programming and actions had stifled the growth of the Betan people, Admiral Nogura had not been a happy man. His comments on the subject were both succinct and memorable.

*"You pulled the rug out from under an entire civilization . . . and then you just left?"*

*Not exactly, of course,* Scott conceded as he pulled the broken proton pump inhibitor from its recess and stuffed it in his satchel, only to snatch up its replacement.

Though Kirk had left behind a team of cultural and sociological experts to aid the Betan people in transitioning away from life under the rule of Landru, it had become apparent that more assistance in a wide variety of areas would be required. The *Enterprise* was ordered to return to Beta III in order to provide engineering assistance in assessing the technology and its usefulness in the wake of Landru's deactivation. More important, however, they were tasked with determining just how much influence the supercomputer had actually held over day-to-day operations of "the Body" of Betan society.

To their relief, Landru's grip had not been as tight as they had originally feared. While the computer had controlled their actions, the Betan people were more skilled technically than their architecture, dress, and mannerisms might lead a casual observer to presume. They were capable of operating electrical generating plants, waste water systems, food distribution centers, and the like. What they lacked was the ability to determine on their own when and how tasks ranging from the mundane to the critical needed to be accomplished. Without "the will of Landru," the people of Beta III simply had no direction.

Therefore, it had become the job of Scott and other engineers, to say nothing of the team of sociologists and cultural scientists the *Enterprise* had provided, to teach the Betans about "the will of the people." Since beaming down from the ship, he and a dozen of his engineers had quickly become mother ducks to the suddenly "orphaned" Betan citizens.

It took less than two days for the assignment to gnaw at Scott's patience.

Thankfully, it had also taken less than two days for reinforcements to arrive. To assist the *Enterprise*, Starfleet had also assigned a crew of crack problem solvers already known to Scott: the *Lovell*. Once they had established orbit, wave after wave of technical and mechanical experts appeared to help the now-leaderless people begin to make their own way.

"That's got it," Scott said as he felt the satisfying click of the inhibitor snapping into place. Picking up his communicator he added, "She's in. Now I just need to run a diagnostic before we reactivate this section."

*"Excellent,"* al-Khaled said. *"You just may make a decent engineer one day, Commander. Sure you don't want to stay on with the* Lovell?*"*

Scott laughed. "It's only a temporary assignment, lad, just until the *Enterprise* comes back to get me. I figure they're about halfway to the rendezvous with the *Lexington* by now."

Despite the proverbial can of worms that Captain Kirk may have opened here, it did nothing to alleviate his other responsibilities. Indeed, at this very moment the *Enterprise* was on its way to pick up an ambassador en route to the starship's next assignment.

"*That's right,*" al-Khaled said. "*You're going to ferry Ambassador Fox to his diplomatic mission in that star system with the two warring planets. I hear that he's a hard man to get along with.*"

Scott had heard the same thing, mostly from colleagues on the *Lexington* who had informed him that life with the ambassador was something akin to being consigned to the Third Concentric Circle of Hell. Faced with two weeks in the volatile company of Ambassador Robert Fox, slogging through the sewers of Beta III did not seem all that bad.

*Is it too much to hope that the captain might forget to pick me up on the way to NGC 321?*

His work with the inhibitor finished, Scott mopped sweat and grime from his forehead with the back of his sleeve, then closed the access door.

"All right, Mahmud, I'm ready to reactivate the inhibitor assembly."

"*What? Has it been thirty minutes already?*" Scott smiled as al-Khaled paused for a moment. "*Stand by, Scotty. We're setting it up now.*" Several moments passed before Scott heard the telltale vibrations and groans of ancient machinery, much of it embedded in the concrete all around him, returning to life. After the initial few seconds, the hum of the equipment settled into a comfortable rhythm.

*"Sensors show the pump inhibitor is working perfectly,"* al-Khaled reported. *"A job like that should earn you a beam-out, unless you'd rather hike back to base."*

For a fleeting moment Scott pictured himself hurling his friend headfirst into the depths of the murky water, followed closely by the communicator in his hand.

"Energize."

Mahmud al-Khaled closed the flap on his communicator and returned the device to his belt, chuckling at the expense of his friend. That minor yet welcome distraction completed, he drew a breath before returning to his own apparently unending task. Looking up from his desk and the pile of status reports that seemed to multiply every time his attention was drawn elsewhere, al-Khaled saw that the line of engineers and other specialists waiting to see him had grown as well.

"And I traded Scotty's job for this one?" The question was voiced just low enough that none of the crewmen waiting to see him had heard it. Looking up, he waved the first man, an ensign he recognized as a member of the *Enterprise* crew, to step forward.

The ensign offered an electronic clipboard

containing his status report. "We're finished checking the water treatment systems with the new automation computers and everything is working fine, sir. Actually, the system's working a bit above specifications, if I may say so."

"You may," al-Khaled replied. "And great work there, too." Quickly signing the report and returning it to the ensign, he looked up at the line of men and women still waiting to see him. "Now, who's next?"

The process was repeated, with al-Khaled reviewing and approving report after report from the engineers who had come to him, watching as even more of them filled in the ranks of those who left the room with new assignments. As he worked he listened to the voices of crewmembers from the *Enterprise* and his own ship rise above the ambient noise within the makeshift command center that he and his team had established here in the first hours after arriving on Beta III.

*It almost sounds like the bridge of a starship*, al-Khaled thought, *except busier.*

In the wake of Landru's deactivation, there had been an atmosphere of confusion and uncertainty as automated systems working behind the scenes of this normally tranquil city and others like it across the planet had suddenly found themselves operating without the guidance of the master computer. Power, water, sanitary systems, food distribution, all of these processes were controlled by some means of mechanization, their systems overseen by the all-encompassing presence of Landru as it had been for more than six thousand years.

Without that influence, Betan citizens found themselves in the position of having to quickly learn how to issue instructions and see to the management of these processes on their own. Al-Khaled and his engineers had been tasked with assisting in that transition, teaching the Betan people to be self-sufficient while at the same time working to reconfigure and reactivate the master control system, this time without the vast network of software that had comprised Landru's "personality."

Finishing his review of one final report, an update from his *Lovell* shipmates O'Halloran and Anderson on their installation of a new computer monitoring station, al-Khaled put the paperwork aside and leaned back in his chair. He was not used to jockeying a desk, but coordination of the considerable effort under way here had made it necessary for him to assume a more managerial role than was typical for him on other missions.

*This is starting to feel too much like a real Starfleet outfit,* he mused, with no small amount of disappointment. It would be good to finish this assignment and get back to the *Lovell* and to being just a regular engineer for a while.

At the sound of a set of tentative footfalls

behind him, he smiled. He had no need to check the chronometer on his desk to know what time it was or who was approaching. Sitting up in his chair, al-Khaled turned to see Bilar, a young Betan male who had volunteered to assist him with various duties around the command center. He was dressed in a formal gray suit, complete with tie and bowler hat, and carrying a tray of food.

*Yes*, al-Khaled thought, *right on time*.

"Needing a break, Mahmud, ayeh?" Bilar said in the almost lyrical dialect that many Betans used. "I am sure this will be to your liking."

Al-Khaled surveyed the tray's contents: typical Starfleet cuisine of a tuna salad sandwich, a mix of raw vegetables, and hot tea. Ration Pack #47, and one of the better offerings, truth be told. Nodding his thanks to Bilar, al-Khaled scooped a wedge of sandwich from the tray and ate.

Removing his hat, Bilar asked, "What is your will for me now, Mahmud?"

The engineer knit his brow, uncomfortable with the man's choice of words yet knowing that the Betans could not help themselves from speaking in such a subservient manner. "Just watch and learn, Bilar. The Elders tell me that you'll be the person who manages these systems once we leave, so you'll need to know how to keep an eye on things."

"It is an honor to serve as best I can, Mahmud." Bilar paused as al-Khaled chewed. "Marplon and the others should be coming at any moment. Might I wait for them outside?"

Al-Khaled rose, grabbing the rest of his sandwich in one hand and swigging from his tea with the other. "We'll both go. I need to get an update on how the reprogramming efforts are proceeding, anyway."

"It helps much that the Elders are so learned," Bilar said as they left the command center.

"That it does, Bilar, but don't sell yourself short." Seeing by the look on the man's face that he did not comprehend his words, al-Khaled added, "Everyone in the city has proven useful and willing to help get things going again. You all have reason to be proud."

"It is for the good of the Body," Bilar said. Then, catching himself, he smiled and amended with, "I mean, it is good for us all. Yes, Mahmud, it is a time of change."

"And it is a welcome change!"

The voice from behind him startled al-Khaled for a moment, as he turned to see the men he awaited.

"Greetings, gentlemen," al-Khaled called to the approaching pair. Reger and Marplon, formerly Elders in the society Landru had once overseen, had covertly participated in an active resistance to the computer's rule before its ultimate deactivation at the hands of Captain Kirk. Marplon in particular had quickly earned al-

Khaled's trust and confidence through his knowledge of Landru's operating systems. Along with Reger, Marplon had been working with several of al-Khaled's engineers to eliminate any trace of pseudo-consciousness from Landru's master computer network.

Marplon extended a hand and when al-Khaled returned the gesture, he grasped it in both his hands. "This is a time long in coming, and one I did not think I would see. But it is here." He paused, barely containing his joy. "Landru is no more. With the assistance of your technicians, we have gone through the data banks, as you call them, and have removed all that supplied the will of Landru."

"Your men now are seeking to locate any of what they called subroutines, but we agree that the task is almost completed," Reger added.

Al-Khaled smiled in satisfaction. By far this had been the most difficult task that had presented itself to his engineering team since arriving on Beta III, given the extensive nature of the software that comprised the vast entity once known as Landru. "Excellent. Once we reconnect the master computer to the remainder of the network, your systems will be running just as they used to, only now without Landru making all of the decisions."

"My people owe you a great deal, Mahmud," Reger said. "We have lived in the grip of Landru for far too long."

"We still have some work to do, and you will need to help," al-Khaled replied. "But once we are gone, Beta III will be in your hands. You will be able to live as you see fit."

Marplon nodded. "We are ready, of that you can be sure." Turning to Reger, he placed a hand on his companion's arm. "Come, my friend. We still have many matters to attend to this day."

As the Elders turned and departed the command center, Bilar turned to al-Khaled. "And where are we off to next? Meeting with our Mr. Scott, ayeh?"

"Not until he hits the sonic showers. He probably smells worse than a platter of haggis."

"Haggis, Mahmud?"

Al-Khaled could not help but laugh at the quizzical expression on his protégé's face. "Be sure to ask him about it the next time you see him."

# CHAPTER
# 11

The people of Beta III moved differently these days.

Christopher Lindstrom noticed it more and more as he walked through the streets of the city, greeting passersby while threads of the afternoon sun peeked between buildings that looked to him as if they had sprung from history tapes of the late nineteenth or early twentieth century Earth.

The residents of the city had put him off when he had first arrived a little more than a week ago, but that had not daunted him. His training as a Starfleet sociologist helped him keep an open mind to all differences in manner of speech, dress, custom, and interaction he might observe in sentient races inhabiting worlds far from his home on Earth. He thrilled to the idea of meeting representatives of new civilizations, and dreamed of one day leading his own first contact mission.

Yet his gut had given him an odd feeling about the Betans from the moment he materialized on the planet's surface as part of Captain Kirk's landing party. In reflection, he attributed his initial unease to one thing. It had been their gait; a slow, methodical stepping that gave them the appearance of being more automated than human. They had moved as if every action, from tipping a hat to holding a door, had been programmed or dictated to them by an unseen source.

*Of course, we learned just how right that observation was, didn't we?*

When not driven by inner voices from Landru, the citizens had taken some direction from the Elders. This select group of senior residents of the village had been groomed by Landru to lend some of their insight and experience to the others in context with the computer's grand plan for peace and life on Beta III. They had also been charged with the secrets of Landru's maintenance and operation, possessing closely guarded knowledge that had been passed quietly from generation to generation of Elders.

Continuing his casual stroll down the street, Lindstrom noticed a young woman emerging from one of the buildings that had been converted into a temporary supply warehouse. Dark-haired and fair-skinned, she was dressed in a black skirt and cream-colored blouse, fastened at the neck with an ornate lace collar. It took only a moment to recognize her. Catching sight of him, she smiled brightly as she waited for him to approach her.

"Good morning, Tula," he offered as he drew abreast of her. Noting the parcel she carried, with the familiar logo of the Starfleet Medical Service emblazoned on it, he asked, "Still helping out at the hospital?"

"Yes, Mr. Lindstrom. I was bringing these to Dr. Hamilton right now. Are you headed that way yourself?"

"Eventually, yes," he answered as she began to walk beside him. "And please, I know I've told you that my name is Chris."

Tula's face flushed slightly and she turned away from him. "I know you have. This is more . . . comfortable for me, at least for the moment. I hope that doesn't upset you."

Shaking his head, Lindstrom said, "Not at all. I'd never want you to be uncomfortable with me, Tula." Once again he found himself drawn to the young woman, just as he had the first time he had laid eyes on her, on a street much like this one mere moments after beaming down with Captain Kirk. He felt more than a little protective toward her, and he knew the feeling arose from the chaotic scene that had unfolded minutes after the landing party's arrival from the *Enterprise*.

They had found themselves in the midst of "the Festival," a period of wanton violence and decadence that had abruptly gripped the entire city. The landing party soon discovered that the Festival was a manifestation of Landru, just another way that the mammoth computer entity had exerted its control over the populace. Tula had been swept up in the bedlam that had ensued when the "Red Hour" had struck and the Festival had commenced.

Fearing for their safety, Lindstrom and the rest of the landing party had sought a place to hide and found it in the home of Reger, a man they would quickly come to know as an Elder and, to Lindstrom's surprise, the father of Tula. Lindstrom had initially expressed shock at her father's lack of concern for the safety of his daughter, but it had worn off when he and the other *Enterprise* officers learned just how powerful Landru's influence had been.

"Thank you for understanding," Tula replied. "Understanding is the will . . ." She brought herself up short, and Lindstrom turned to look at her, concern etching his features. Seeing his expression, she attempted a small smile. "I am fine," she said after several awkward seconds. "I meant that understanding each other is good for us all."

Lindstrom nodded uncertainly as they resumed their walk to the hospital. Originally run under the auspices of several Elders who possessed all the medical training that Landru could provide, the hospital had been augmented with Starfleet medical equipment and supplies, to say nothing of a full contingent of doctors and assistants. It was yet another way the Federation had found to assist these people in the wake of Landru's deactivation.

The people, he had learned, were quick studies when it came to technical training, something for which the Starfleet engineers and scientists had expressed a great deal of gratitude. They knew how to operate the mechanical systems of the village, and they could perform the basic functions of running their own lives at home. While they did not possess the understanding of social interaction and subtle nuances of emotions that came into play during such situations, these too could be taught. It would be Lindstrom's job, and the task of other sociological experts like him, to shepherd these people through the obstacles of simply living in harmony without the assistance of a machine to make the decisions for them.

If only they could get a jump start of their initiative.

"Tula," Lindstrom said. "What are you going to do after you give your supplies to Dr. Hamilton?"

He watched as the young woman knit her brow and mulled his question. "Well, Dr. Hamilton asked me to bring her these bandages and cloths from the supply area. So I gathered them and am doing that."

"But, Tula, what will you do afterward?"

Her look showed she was becoming more perplexed as she seemed to grapple with what would be a simple question for someone with practice at exercising free will. "I . . . these bandages. I need to give them to . . ."

Lindstrom put his hand on her forearm and they paused. Tula looked into his eyes as she sought some direction from the Starfleet sociologist, and he ached a little inside for the Betan woman, who in many ways was but a child. "It's all right, Tula. You're doing fine."

"I still have much to learn, don't I?"

Nodding, he offered what he hoped was a reassuring smile. "We all do, I think. I . . ."

His attention was drawn to a sudden disturbance up the street, where a woman wearing a Starfleet engineering jumpsuit was working with a Betan man. The man was holding his head in his hands and shouting in pain as he staggered away from his companion. Sinking to his knees, the man rolled into a fetal position as he continued to groan in agony. The female engineer rushed to his side in an attempt to help.

Running to the scene, Lindstrom saw that the woman was Lieutenant Vanessa Masters, another of the *Enterprise* engineers. He could not help but notice the circles under the woman's eyes and that her dark skin was smudged with dirt and grime, testament to the hard work and long hours she had been putting in since arriving on Beta III. "Vanessa," he called out as he sprinted to join her. "What's going on?"

Masters shook her head as she knelt beside the fallen man. "I don't know." She placed her hands on his arm, trying to reassure him. "We need a doctor."

Reaching for his communicator, Lindstrom flipped the unit open. "Lindstrom to Dr. Hamilton. We have a medical emergency and could use your help." Looking up to verify his location, he added, "We're just to the south of the hospital."

The doctor's response was immediate. *"I'm on my way, Lieutenant."*

As the connection went dead, Lindstrom noted that the Betan had fallen into unconsciousness. He checked for a pulse and to ensure that the man was breathing.

"We were running some scans on the gas lines beneath the street," Masters said, "when Dorin was gripped by this seizure."

Tula, who had run up behind Lindstrom yet remained silent to this point, said suddenly, "He is a Lawgiver."

"What does that have to do with anything?" Masters asked, her eyes narrowing in confusion.

Ignoring the question, Lindstrom gently reached around the back of the man's head, his fingers seeking out the area just beneath the bottom edge of the hairline at the neck. There, just where Dr. Hamilton told him he would find it, his fingers traced the telltale bump beneath the surface of the skin.

"What is it?" Masters asked.

His suspicions confirmed, Lindstrom replied, "Tula's right. Dorin was once a Lawgiver."

The Lawgivers had been Landru's version of a police force, and, until the computer's deactivation, the chief method of maintaining order in the city. Where the Elders had led by example and sincerity of purpose, the Lawgivers had struck fear in the souls of the people. In their long flowing robes and concealing hoods, the Lawgivers had usually appeared at the first sign of trouble or discord. In addition to their intimidating appearance, they alone had carried the only weapons allowed in the city: long cylindrical staffs that projected a type of forced energy pulse. Despite a week of continuous study, the construction and operation of the staffs still baffled Starfleet engineers.

The sounds of running footsteps caught his attention and he looked up to see a woman in a blue Starfleet uniform running toward them. Her fair skin and long locks of fiery red hair, to say nothing of the medical kit she carried under her left arm, immediately identified her as Dr. Jane Hamilton.

"What happened?" she asked as she dropped

to a knee beside Dorin, simultaneously reaching into her kit for her medical tricorder.

"He's a Lawgiver, Doctor," Lindstrom answered. "I think the scans they were conducting induced a neural shock."

Frowning as she activated her tricorder and accompanying diagnostic scanner, Hamilton asked, "You found the chip?"

"Just above his neck, where you told me to look."

"What are you two talking about?" Masters said, making no attempt to hide her confusion.

Waving her scanner over Dorin's forehead, Hamilton glanced up at the engineer. "Sorry, Lieutenant. I haven't been able to brief the engineering staff on what our medical research has learned about these people." Noting Tula, who was standing just behind Lindstrom with a worried look on her face, she amended, "Some of these people, that is."

Turning off her scanner, she returned the device to her kit. "The shock has induced a light coma, but I'm not detecting any neural damage. We should get him to the hospital." Swapping her tricorder for a communicator, Hamilton contacted the hospital with instructions for medics to bring a stretcher.

Lindstrom rose to his feet and, noting the still-puzzled look on Masters's face, indicated Tula with a nod of his head. "Landru controlled the bulk of the populace with sonic and light waves to literally reprogram parts of the brain. When it came to the Lawgivers, his hold was even tighter."

Putting away her medical instruments, Dr. Hamilton ran a hand through her long hair, the bangs of which were matted across her forehead with perspiration. "The Lawgivers all have a computer chip implanted at the base of their brains. Landru used the chip to control them, even more so than he did the rest of the people. Electronic signals sent to the chip carried instructions directly into the Lawgivers' brains. They had no choice but to obey."

"Are the chips malfunctioning?" Masters asked. "Is that what caused Dorin's seizure?"

Shaking her head, Hamilton replied, "Some of our equipment operates on frequencies similar to those used by Landru, including ones he apparently used for punishing individual Lawgivers when discipline was needed."

Pointing to the tricorder Masters had slung from her shoulder, she added, "If you were running a high-intensity scan, it was probably enough to trigger the chip. We haven't figured out the complete range of frequencies that were utilized yet. We have learned, though, that the chips can't be removed without extreme risk to the patient, at least not here. Once the *Hippocrates* arrives, we'll have the facilities we need for further research and even delicate surgery." Starfleet had already dispatched the medical ship to Beta III, but it was not scheduled to arrive for at least another week. For now, Dr. Hamilton and her staff were on their own.

During the past week Lindstrom and the physician had spent long hours, when time permitted, discussing the situation here, and had found their specialties overlapping in their quest to better understand the Betan people. They had used each other as sounding boards several times already as they each strove to peel away one more layer of mystery surrounding the people of Landru.

Hamilton said, "If I didn't already have orders to the *Defiant*, I'd be tempted to stay here. There's enough research potential to last several years." Nevertheless, Lindstrom knew, the doctor would soon be leaving Beta III to assume her posting as chief medical officer of the *Enterprise*'s sister ship. She had already confided to him how the compelling nature of both this assignment and the one that awaited her had given her pause to consider a change of orders, even though she had already admitted that the *Defiant* was where she truly wanted to be. This mission, however, had already proven to be as challenging as anything she was likely to encounter during her upcoming deep space assignment.

"It's amazing," she said. "An entire race mentally controlled by some computer implant. If, somewhere in this universe, a race ever set to using such technology to conquer and subjugate its enemies, that race might be unstoppable."

"Well," Lindstrom replied, the visions conjured by the doctor's words causing a small shiver to run down his spine, "let's hope that never happens."

# CHAPTER
## 12

Reger stepped up his pace through the darkness as he neared Marplon's residence. Although the two Elders had worked together for years within the secret resistance to Landru, this would be his first visit to his friend's home. After all, he hadn't even known Marplon's name until a week ago, the organization of the resistance cells having been such that, although he had worked with the man, he had been unaware of his identity.

*All of that nonsense can be forgotten now,* Reger reminded himself.

He ascended the several steps to the stoop of Marplon's modest home and reached for the front door's handle. It flew from his grasp, however, as the door was opened from the other side to reveal Marplon standing in the doorway, a worried expression clouding his aged, distinguished features.

"Joy be with you, friend," Marplon said.

*Without Landru to guide us,* Reger thought, *even old habits such as a traditional greeting seem out of place now.*

"Thank you for coming so quickly, Reger," Marplon continued. "I fear we may have a problem."

Marplon ushered Reger into his home and as he stepped forward into a simple yet warmly furnished sitting room, he saw his friend Hacom sitting on a couch with his face in his hands. The man was visibly distraught, dressed in wrinkled bedclothes and a robe. His gray hair, normally groomed impeccably, was tousled.

Casting a questioning look at Marplon, Reger crossed the room to his friend. As he drew closer, he could hear the man sobbing quietly. "Hacom," he said, putting a hand on the old man's shoulder, "what troubles you so?"

Hacom looked up, and Reger saw a measure of calm ease the deep lines of his face. "You are strong," he said. "You are much stronger than I. The will of Landru is so great, and I can resist it no longer."

Reger's eyes narrowed in confusion. "Hacom, Landru is no more. You have no reason to fear his wrath."

"But I do," Hacom replied, watching as Marplon entered the room and seated himself in one of two overstuffed chairs situated near the fireplace. "He will not let me sleep. He troubles my every thought. I have abandoned him in his hour of greatest need!" Tears ran from the old man's eyes as he looked at Reger.

"Why do you say that, Hacom? Landru is powerless against you."

Marplon said, "I believe Hacom is the Guardian."

Feeling a shiver run down his spine at the words, Reger's eyes widened in momentary shock. He brought his hand to his mouth, his finger rubbing his lips. It was an almost unconscious gesture, one that he performed whenever he was nervous or uncertain.

*The Guardian? Does he truly exist?*

"Surely you jest," he whispered. Looking at Hacom, his friend for uncounted years, Reger found it difficult to speak for several moments. Then, "We have heard the stories, certainly, but . . . Hacom, can it be true?"

"I do not know!" He shouted with a force of voice that Reger hardly expected from the slight-framed man. "I have never been called that, neither by man nor by Landru. I know only that he calls to me with a voice distant and yet powerful. He tells me what I must do."

Stepping forward, Marplon placed a comforting hand on his friend's shoulder. "Hacom, let me get you something warm to drink. Settle yourself, and let us help you seek peace."

"There can be no peace without Landru! It is he who brings us peace and tranquility." Sinking back into the couch, Hacom began to sob once more.

Rising from the couch, Reger guided Marplon by the arm into the small kitchen just beyond the sitting room. As Marplon busied himself warming a kettle on the stovetop, Reger could see that, despite trying to project an outward appearance of calm by involving himself in the mundane act of preparing tea, his friend was anything but relaxed. Taking a moment to look back to where Hacom was still sitting on the couch, Reger asked in a low voice, "What has he told you?"

"Hacom has told me nothing," Marplon said as he gathered three mugs from a cabinet. "I found him and led him here just before I summoned you. He was in the Hall of Audiences, screaming for Landru and asking for his guidance."

Confusion returned to Reger's face. "Why would he go down there?" The Hall of Audiences had been the main auditorium where Elders and other trusted advisors could go to seek Landru's counsel. With the computer's deactivation, there seemed no need to return to that once-hallowed chamber.

"I asked him a few questions when I found him there," Marplon replied, "and his responses made all very clear to me." Looking up from his tea preparations, he fixed Reger with a solemn stare. "He is the Guardian."

"The Guardian is a myth," Reger countered. "A tale of the prophets, is it not?"

Marplon shook his head. "Was not the prophesied return of the Archons just another tale to you not ten days ago? 'And at my darkest hour, when the winds of change are upon us all, from among you shall come the Guardian to champion the will of Landru and restore all as it once was.' Those are the words of the prophets, Reger. I think it best that we heed them."

"Hacom is overwrought," Reger said. He too knew the words, but that did not change one unalterable fact. "He has simply not been able to come to grips with the fact that Landru is gone and that a new life lies before us, one that Landru does not control." Even as he spoke the words, though, Reger knew that he had at least to acknowledge the possibility that Marplon could be right.

"We have always known that the Guardian was among us," Marplon replied, "but we could never imagine what events would come to pass that might require him to come forward. Surely what has happened to Landru at the hands of Starfleet is just such an event."

"But if Hacom is the Guardian," Reger said, "he is not strong enough, neither mentally nor physically, to fulfill this prophecy on his own. Is the power of Landru so great that it can act on Hacom despite that fact?"

Reger began to move about the small kitchen, somewhat frustrated that the confined space did not allow him the freedom of movement he craved when he wanted to pace and think. "If what you say is true, Marplon, then the mind of

Hacom must be more deeply affected by the will of Landru than any of us, anywhere in all of this world. Landru is strong, my friend, but we must be stronger if we are to succeed in our dream to live as free people."

"What shall we do?" Marplon asked.

"If we calm him and keep watch over him this night, Starfleet will finish their work and we will have our world as our own." On the stove, the kettle started to whistle and boil. "He trusts me, Marplon. Let me speak with him. I may be able to reason with him."

"Yes," Marplon replied as he moved the kettle from the hot burner. "You have known him far longer than I. Perhaps you can . . ."

The thud of a closing door cut Marplon off in midsentence. The two men rushed from the kitchen into the sitting room only to find it empty.

"Oh, no," Marplon whispered as Reger ran to the front door and flung it open. Looking into the dark street, illuminated only by the faint glow of the gaslights lining the street, he saw no sign of his friend.

"Hacom? Hacom!"

But he was gone.

It was hardly a celebration feast, but Montgomery Scott looked upon his tray of Canopian spiced salad, lasagna, and steamed vegetables as if it were food fit for a king rather than a meal processed in a field kitchen. Not only was this his first hot meal in two days, but tonight would be the first time he had actually relaxed since arriving at Beta III. It was a sure sign that their assignment here was more than likely drawing to a conclusion.

Taking a seat at the table already occupied by Lindstrom and al-Khaled, Scott offered the men a greeting before turning to his meal. As he took his first bite, he glanced down at Lindstrom's plate and thought he recognized the orange contents of the lieutenant's soup bowl.

"Is that *plomeek* soup yer eatin' there, lad?"

Lindstrom nodded. "I'm in a Vulcan phase, I guess. I go through the dietary cards of all the races I can stomach. I guess you could say that it helps me to understand them as separate peoples, at least in some fashion. I've been doing it since I got my first sociologist's posting after graduating from the Academy."

"And has Beta III proven to be an interesting case study for you?" al-Khaled asked.

"It has," Lindstrom said. "I would bet that there are plenty of assignments given to the Corps of Engineers team that would be of great interest to Starfleet sociologists. Have you ever given any thought to creating such a post onboard your ship?"

Shaking his head, al-Khaled replied as he reached for a piece of bread, "You have to remember that this is hardly a typical mission for us. We're usually out making emergency repairs to subspace relay stations or catching up with starships that have matter/antimatter drive problems or digging tunnels through asteroids. Situations like this do not come along all the time, Mr. Lindstrom, and we're not the type of team that gets first contact missions."

"Granted," the sociologist answered. "But should this type of situation arise again, you don't necessarily want a group of engineers handling things."

Al-Khaled said, "I'm no sociologist, but even as an engineer I can appreciate how this situation has hobbled the Betans as a race. I don't know how I'd react if someone told me my god was dead."

"You've just underscored my point, Commander," Lindstrom said, smiling. "The Betans did not view Landru as their god. They didn't worship him in churches, nor do they even have any churches that we've been able to find. The Betans talk of a few prophecies but they read no scripture. There are no dogmatic beliefs that we can find stemming from the will of Landru, other than that he is to be obeyed and feared. He told them what to do and dictated almost every decision they made."

Scott and al-Khaled exchanged looks, the full weight of the sociologist's words beginning to sink in for the first time since they had set foot on this world. "So, they really are lost," al-Kahled said.

"Yes, Commander," Lindstrom replied. "But these people do not miss their god. Instead, they miss, some of them desperately, being told what to do. Keep in mind that sometimes the need to be led is stronger than the need to lead. People seeking that kind of direction have done unexpected things to get it."

Scott nodded, realizing for the first time in several minutes that he had left his meal untouched while Lindstrom was speaking. "You raise good points, lad."

Smiling, Lindstrom shrugged and offered his hands in mock surrender. "I'm not trying to be full of myself here. Just an observation that long after the machines have been fixed, the people will still need tending to."

The conversation paused as the men finished their meals. Scott looked at a chronometer on the mess hall wall as he stood from his chair. "What needs tending to right now, gentlemen, is my body, in the form of sleep. This is the earliest we've knocked off for the day since we got here. If there are no objections, I think I'll be honorin' that request."

"Barring any unforeseen weirdness," al-Khaled said, "I do not see that as a problem, Commander."

Scott smiled at that.

*Now wouldn't a break from weirdness be nice?*

Hacom shielded his eyes from the cloud of displaced dust rising up to enshroud him as the wall panel before him slid through the floor. The musty smell that escaped from the room beyond the doorway was distasteful and stale, but he didn't dare hesitate. As the door mechanism's grinding ceased, he crossed the threshold into the hidden chamber.

Though he had never even known of this room's existence before tonight, Hacom had arrived here as though he'd known the route his entire life. How had he known about the concealed street-level entrance and the elevator that descended hundreds of meters beneath the city to this chamber? And the correct procedure to open the sealed door? The knowledge had come to him as easily as any fact he had ever committed to memory.

There was, of course, only one explanation.

"Landru!"

His words echoed in the Spartan chamber. Lighting panels set in the walls reacted to his presence, glowing even brighter as Hacom stepped farther into the room.

"Landru?" After the torment he had been experiencing these last days, would his calls go unanswered?

The centerpiece of the room was a single waist-high railing, constructed of ornately carved wood and highlighted with sections of polished metal. Hacom listened carefully, but he did not hear the comforting hum that he typically had sensed whenever he had come to any of Landru's halls.

"Landru! Where are you?"

His cries unanswered, Hacom walked to the rail and kneeled before it, bowing his head and supplicating himself before a blank wall. "Guide me, Landru."

Opening his eyes after a moment, Hacom noticed a small, hinged plate set nearly flush within the center metal section of the railing. He worked a fingernail under its seam and raised it. Underneath was a single button, blinking with ruby light. He ran a finger over the button, feeling the warmth that pulsed in rhythm to the light. For no other reason than it seemed the proper thing to do, Hacom pressed the button.

Immediately a low rumbling began somewhere beneath his feet. No, it was in the walls. It was everywhere, surrounding him as it grew in intensity before evolving into the hum of power, no, of life, that had always signaled the presence of . . .

The wall before him began to glow brighter than even the lighting panels as an image took form before him. Hacom gasped as the blurry image came into crisp focus, that of a man wearing a gown and draped with a golden sash. The man's head, made larger in appearance by upward streaming hair, seemed almost to levitate above his shoulders. His eyes were piercing yet friendly. The edges of his mouth carried the hint of a smile.

"Landru!"

*"Guardian, you have carried out my will,"* the image said. *"You have rescued the Body when all seemed lost. Landru is grateful for your service."*

"I am your humble servant, Landru," Hacom said, drinking in the image of his protector, of the one who had guided him throughout his entire life. "I want only peace and tranquility as there was before."

The image nodded, its thin smile unwavering. *"Soon, all will be as it was."*

Hacom smiled, reveling in the bliss that only moments ago he feared had been taken from him forever.

# CHAPTER
## 13

"Mr. Scott! Mr. al-Khaled!"

As he exited the building that housed the Starfleet contingent's temporary mess hall with al-Khaled and Lindstrom, Scott caught sight of three men running toward them. Actually, Scott realized, two of the men, Reger and Marplon, seemed to be assisting the third man, whom the engineer recognized as Hacom, moving as fast as their aged bodies appeared able to carry them.

"Marplon? What's wrong?" Al-Khaled broke away from his companions to meet the approaching Elders. The three men stumbled to a halt, gasping for air, and Reger dropped to his knees.

*What could upset the Elders like this?* Scott wondered. As he crouched beside the fallen Reger, the old man's breaths were coming in ragged wheezes as he fought to speak.

"Lan—uunh!" was all he could force out before the effort overwhelmed him.

Grasping Marplon by the shoulders and trying to steady the man, al-Khaled's face was a mask of concern and confusion. "Marplon, what is it? What's happened?"

The Elder was beginning to catch his breath, nodding in response to al-Khaled's words. Indicating Hacom with a wave of his hand, he managed to say between deep, sucking breaths, "The Guardian has been revealed! Hacom . . . Hacom . . . Landru is returning as it was foretold in prophecy. He is coming to enslave us again."

"What?" The words seemed to Scott at first to be the ramblings of a man lost in hysterics. "That canna be possible. Landru is gone, Marplon. Ye helped to turn him off, remember?"

It was Hacom who answered, his expression one of mild contentment. "I have carried out the will of Landru. He has returned. We will all be of the Body once again."

Scott rose to his feet. "I thought the beastie was completely shut down," he said, "that its memory banks had been wiped."

"Landru is all-powerful," Hacom countered, his voice remaining calm. "He has been here for six thousand years, and he will be here long after our passing."

Al-Khaled's eyes were wide with near shock. "If this is true, then we may be in big trouble. We should get these men to the hospital. Reger doesn't look good at all."

And then the wailing started.

Screaming, shrieking voices filled the outdoor air from all directions at once. Scott saw a pair of passing Betans fall to the ground, writhing and moaning in what must have been intense agony. Another man burst from a nearby building, his hands over his ears while shouting something unintelligible at the top of his lungs. All around the Starfleet officers the sounds of panic and pain from women and men alike were beginning to bleed together in a single unrelenting cacophony.

"This can't be good," Lindstrom said.

Marplon froze, his voice a whisper. "Landruuuu . . ."

The hospital that had once belonged to the Elders now rivaled, thanks to the efforts of Dr. Hamilton and her staff, the sickbays of most active Federation starships. For that Scott was grateful as he observed Reger and Hacom on two of the diagnostic beds. Hamilton was studying the readouts on the medical displays arrayed around the patients' heads.

"How is he?" al-Khaled asked, referring to the unconscious Reger.

"Severe heart palpitations," the doctor replied. "And I don't like the looks of his blood pressure. He's a little too old and out of shape to be running around like he was."

Moving over to Hacom's bed, her frown deepened as she studied the diagnostic monitors. "As for Hacom, scans show unusual brainwave activity. The frontal lobe stimulation is consistent with what we've seen in our research of Landru's neural reprogramming processes."

Only partly listening to the doctor, most of Scott's attention was instead on the report from the security detachment commander over his communicator. When the report was finished he said, "Send a detail to the hospital on the double. I want a man on each door right now."

Lindstrom shook his head. "I've seen this mob mentality at work, Commander. One man on each door won't be enough."

"It'll have to do, Mr. Lindstrom," Scott replied as he flipped the unit shut and returned it to his waist. "Things are beginnin' to get out of hand. Reports are comin' in from all over the city. Mobs are formin' and fights are breakin' out. It seems that some people have fallen back under a kind of trance while others haven't."

"So it's true," al-Khaled said, sighing in exasperation. "Landru has been reactivated somehow. If we let it go unchecked, he could undo everything we've accomplished here."

Scott shook his head. "I dinna think so, lad. The systems we installed are independent of the main computer network. Landru canna tie into them."

"But he can turn the Betans against them and physically tear them apart," al-Khaled argued as he reached for his communicator. "That's not happening on my watch." Activating the unit, he barked out a series of orders. "Al-Khaled to all personnel. Report to your primary duty stations. The Landru computer has somehow been restarted and is in the process of reassuming control over the people. Everyone is to be armed with phasers on stun. Guard your stations and await further instructions. Al-Khaled out."

As the engineer severed the connection, Scott regarded his friend. "So, how do ye propose we shut Landru off again?"

Al-Khaled almost smiled. "I don't know. I'm making this up as I go along."

"Ye remind me of my captain sometimes, do ye know that?" Scott replied, shaking his head. "I suppose the best place to start formulatin' a plan is the command center." Turning, he walked over to where a sagging Marplon sat limp in a nearby chair. "Marplon, we're going to need your help, sir."

Having been administered a vitamin supplement and tri-ox compound by Dr. Hamilton to help ease the discomfort of his earlier exertions, Marplon nodded enthusiastically. "Whatever I can do to assist you, my friend. You have only to ask."

Taking the Elder by the arm, Scott looked to the rest of the group. "Let's get to the command center."

Leaving Hamilton to tend to Reger and Hacom, the four men made their way to one of the hospital's street level exits. Scott was thankful to see that a security guard he recognized from the *Enterprise* but whose name he could not remember was already stationed at the door and was observing the street outside through a small window. At the group's approach the ensign nodded to Scott.

"It was almost a riot out there a few minutes ago, Commander," the security guard reported, "but it seems to have quieted down now."

Moving to the window, Scott peered out and saw dozens of Betans standing motionless in the street. He motioned for Marplon to take a look.

"They are communing with Landru," the Elder said after a few seconds. "We should hurry."

Taking his own look out another window, al-Khaled sighed. "It's a long way to the command center. I wish we had a phaser or two."

"Look at it this way, lad," Scott said. "We'll have plenty of them when we get there."

Chuckling at the deadpan remark, al-Khaled cast a wry glance in Scott's direction. "Is that supposed to make me feel better?"

Scott said nothing as he opened the door and moved out onto the sidewalk. Seeing that the citizens on the street still appeared to be communing, as Marplon had called it, he motioned for the others to follow him as he set off at a brisk jog up the street. As they ran, he tried to inspect every person they passed, looking for some hint that any of them might be about to come out of their trance.

*Don't move,* he willed the crowd of people all around them. *Don't move.*

They began to move.

"Uh-oh," al-Khaled said.

A sharp pain lanced through Scott's shoulder and he felt himself knocked partially off balance. "What the . . . ?" Then he heard al-Khaled cry out in pain from behind him. Turning, he saw that his friend was grabbing the back of his thigh and limping.

"Rocks! They're throwing rocks!" Lindstrom called out as he raced ahead of the running pack, leading Marplon by the arm with the older man struggling to keep pace with the sociologist. "Watch out!"

Scott and al-Khaled both picked up their pace, running even faster up the street as the crowd around them began to react with more urgency to their presence.

"Why is it . . . Scotty?" al-Khaled said between pants, his breathing becoming labored as they continued to run.

Scott was feeling the exertion, too. "What . . . ?"

"When things . . . go to hell . . . they always go . . . so fast. For once . . . why can't something go . . . to hell at a . . . leisurely pace?"

Moving as they did, they were able to avoid most of the objects thrown at them. Rocks, bricks, pieces of wood, and anything else people could heft rained down all around them, bouncing off the sidewalk and the walls of buildings. Scott was beginning to feel his lungs burning in protest to the extended sprint. The group turned a corner, and he saw the familiar entrance to the building housing the Starfleet command center. As they approached, the doors opened and two security officers beckoned to them, phasers in hand to provide cover from the horde of people chasing after them.

"Seal the door!" Scott yelled as he and the others piled through the entryway. Safely inside, they allowed themselves to sag against a nearby wall, each of them doing their his to inhale all of the unused oxygen in the room.

"I haven't run like that since the Academy," Lindstrom spat out between breaths. "And we sure didn't have to run so far for cover when this happened after the Red Hour."

Al-Khaled said, "Sorry I missed that."

"Aye," Scott added. "And I was having my own problems onboard the *Enter*—"

He froze in midsentence as he remembered yet another problem Landru had caused when it was still operating. The computer's influence had not been confined to the planet and the people who lived upon it, after all.

"Oh, dear lord," he breathed as he reached for his communicator and viciously flipped the unit's cover open.

"Scott to *Lovell!*"

\*       \*       \*

On the *Lovell*'s bridge, Captain Daniel Okagawa heard the alarm in Scott's voice as it exploded from the intercom. Swiveling his command chair toward the communications station, he nodded toward the ensign on duty there to open the frequency.

"Okagawa here. Mr. Scott, what's wrong?"

*"Captain! Ye've got to get the hell away from here, now!"*

Feeling the hairs on the back of his neck stand up, Okagawa leaned forward in his seat. "Mr. Scott, what are you talking about?"

The engineer's voice was almost frantic. *"The Landru computer is back online, Captain, and its planetary defenses are sure to follow. It'll drag ye down just as it did the* Archon, *and tried to with the* Enterprise."

Though he had worked with the *Enterprise* engineer only once before, the man's reputation had preceded him, both then and before this current mission. He was not known for irrational or ill-advised courses of action. If Scott believed that something bad was about to happen, Okagawa was obliged to at least consider what he was saying.

Turning to the science station, he said, "Run a scan for any new energy sources down there." Then, returning his attention to Scott he asked, "What are we looking for, Mr. Scott?"

*"It's a series of heat beams that Landru used to*

*defend itself from orbital attack,"* Scott replied. *"If it gets a lock on ye, the* Lovell *will be unable to break orbit or do anything until it's off. Ye've got to leave right away."*

From the science station, the Tellarite lieutenant on duty, Xav, turned to the captain. "Sir, sensors are picking up a large power source coming online, from a location approximately five hundred meters beneath the surface of the city. It's larger than anything that's been running since we arrived here, and it's increasing in intensity."

Okagawa ran the scenario through his mind. With nearly eighty Starfleet personnel on the planet, it would take a good bit of time to transport them all back to the ship, maybe more time than they had before . . . before what?

His course of action, therefore, was simple.

"Raise shields," he ordered. "Helm, prepare to leave orbit." Then to Scott he said, "Mr. Scott, does Mahmud concur with your theory?"

*"Aye, that he does, sir. This is the first he's hearin' of this, too, but he's agreein' with me."*

That was enough for Okagawa. "Break orbit, helm. Put some distance between us and . . ."

Then the ship shuddered around him and nearly threw him from his seat. Personnel at every bridge station flailed for something to hold on to as the deck shifted beneath their feet.

"What the hell is that?" he asked as the shock wave began to intensify.

Xav, still holding on to his console to keep

from being thrown to the floor, replied, "Some type of energy beam from the surface, sir! Shield strength is at seventy-nine percent and dropping rapidly."

"Helm, get us out of here. Full impulse power!"

The very hull of the *Lovell* seemed to voice its objection as the ship's powerful impulse engines, modified and reconfigured over the past few years by its crew of talented engineers, strained and fought against the attack. Okagawa had a vision of the ship in the grip of Landru's orbital defense system, being dragged down through the atmosphere of Beta III.

Then there was the feel of a rubber band snapping and the ship's inertial dampeners groaned in protest as the *Lovell* gathered enough power to break free of the beams' influence and head away from the planet.

"That was a bit too close, thank you very much," Okagawa said to no one in particular, wiping his brow as he sighed in relief. To the ensign at communications he asked, "Can we still contact the landing party?"

The ensign shook his head. "Afraid not, sir. We're out of range."

Nodding, the captain turned his chair to face the main viewer, which now displayed a field of moving stars instead of what he wanted to see, the welcoming curve of Beta III from high orbit. As he settled back into his seat, Okagawa had the sudden feeling that his ship seemed very empty to him, to say nothing of feeling a lot less purposeful.

*It's up to you now, gentlemen,* he mused, directing his thoughts and good wishes to the men and women he had been forced to leave on the planet's surface.

# CHAPTER
## 14

As his connection with the *Lovell* crackled and finally died out altogether, Scott closed his communicator and returned it to his belt. His expression was somber, a fact not lost on his companions.

"Did they make it?" al-Khaled asked. "Have they left orbit?"

"Aye, that they have," Scott replied. "They're out of range now. We're on our own for the time being, lads."

"I don't understand," Lindstrom said, finally bringing his breathing under control. "I thought that you removed Landru's control over everything."

Al-Khaled nodded. "We severed the ties between Landru's central core and the rest of the network that it once oversaw. We also removed any trace of the Landru personality from the databanks we found."

"Landru is all-powerful," Marplon said as he lowered himself into one of the few chairs in the command center. "He foresaw a time when he might face enemies such as you, and provided for that eventuality. The Guardian, Hacom, must have been the instrument of that will."

Shrugging, al-Khaled replied, "Obviously there was some sort of recovery or backup system in place that we missed. That must be what Hacom found."

"Well," Scotty said, "it doesna matter now how it happened. All that matters now is that Landru is active again and is regaining control of its computer systems."

"But his overall influence will be limited, Scotty," al-Khaled countered. "Landru doesn't have the control he once did over the rest of the automated network. We saw to that. None of our modifications tie into the central core yet, so we still retain control over most of the city's automated systems."

"He still has control over the important parts, though," Lindstrom said. "We've already seen that he is reasserting his influence over the people. There's nothing to say he can't order someone to launch physical attacks on those areas we've removed from him."

"Exactly," al-Khaled said. "Landru is like a severed head in search of a body." When his friends looked at him with odd expressions on their faces, he amended, "Sorry. Bad choice of words."

"Actually," Scott said, "that brings up a good question. Landru may have regained control of the systems he used to keep the people under his control, but will the people fall back into his grip that easily?"

Marplon mulled the engineer's question. "We all are vulnerable to some degree, but the indoctrination runs undeniably deep in many. There are those among my people who long for Landru's return."

"You mean like Hacom," al-Khaled said.

Shaking his head, the Elder waved the suggestion away. "You do not understand. Hacom was chosen by Landru to protect his will at all costs. His role as the Guardian was decreed for him long before you came to us."

Hacom was only the cause of their current problem, Scott knew. The effects of the Elder's actions were continuing to reveal themselves with each passing moment. The longer he and his friends waited to act, the harder he knew their task would become.

"We have to find a way to shut down Landru again, for good this time. Not simply deactivate him, but disable him completely." Sighing in resignation, he nodded as the implication of his words became clear even to him. "We may have to destroy the central core completely to do it. Of course, that's easier said than done, isn't it?"

Al-Khaled moved to a supply locker and opened it after keying in the proper security code on the small keypad set into its door. Inside were twelve Type II phasers along with extra power cells. Extracting three of the weapons, he resealed the locker before handing a phaser each to Lindstrom and Scott.

"So, how do we get to the central core?" al-Khaled asked.

Marplon shook his head. "With Landru once again active, approaching it will be all but impossible. Lawgivers will be stationed to protect that area."

"The Lawgivers," Lindstrom echoed. "With the microcircuit chips they each carry, Landru's control over them is sure to be absolute."

"And we don't have the resources to launch any kind of attack," al-Khaled added, "not with the *Lovell* out of communications range." He shook his head. "A few well-placed photon torpedoes and our problems would be solved."

Marplon started at the words, rising from his chair with an excited expression on his face. "Are you saying you require weapons?"

"Possibly," Scott said, holding up his phaser for emphasis. "These willna be enough if we're going to have any chance of stoppin' that contraption."

The Elder nodded. "There may be a way."

Not pausing to explain himself, Marplon instead waved for the trio of Starfleet officers to follow him from the command center, leading them deeper into the building. A curious Scott

followed close behind, with al-Khaled and Lindstrom bringing up the rear. Each of them had
drawn his phaser and was keeping an eye out for
trouble.

"Where are we going?" Scott asked.

"You already know about the underground
tunnels that connect many of Landru's control
centers," Marplon replied. "They were used by
Lawgivers and Elders to better carry out his will.
There are entrances to the tunnels throughout
the city. I believe we can use the one in this building to take us where we need to go."

Rounding a corner, Marplon reached out to
what Scott at first thought was nothing more
than a section of wall, unadorned except for a
coating of drab yellow paint. The engineer was
only mildly surprised when the wall panel swung
open, revealing a concealed doorway and a dark
tunnel beyond.

What he was surprised to see, however, was
the Lawgiver ascending from stairs beyond the
hidden entrance.

"Look out!" he called, reaching to pull the
Elder clear as the Lawgiver, dressed in the now
familiar robe and hood that concealed the
wearer's head and carrying the staff that was the
symbol of their power, moved to stand in the
doorway.

"Stop," it said, pointing its staff at the group.
"You attack the Body. You are enemies of Landru."

Before Scott could react, a blue beam of

energy appeared from over his shoulder, striking the Lawgiver in the center of the chest. The beam held the robed figure for a moment before fading, leaving the Lawgiver to collapse in a heap to the carpeted floor.

Turning, Scott saw Lindstrom, his phaser arm still extended in the direction of the Lawgiver. Seeing the look on Scott's face, the sociologist shrugged. "Sometimes the simplest approach is the best one."

"There are liable to be more of them throughout the tunnels," Marplon said. "We must hurry now!"

As he moved to inspect the opening that led downward into the vast network of tunnels beneath the city, al-Khaled regarded the Elder. "Just where exactly are we going?"

It was a cache the likes of which Montgomery Scott had not seen outside a museum.

The room was filled with Federation technology and Starfleet-issue equipment. An assortment of items, some of which Scott had never seen outside of reference books and historical texts, lay before them. Everything was shrouded with fine dust and tucked away on shelves in accordance with no rhyme or reason as to order or function.

More than a century old, it was all that remained of the *U.S.S. Archon.*

"Landru decreed all of this, even the room in

which we walk, forbidden," Marplon said as he watched the three Starfleet officers assess the room's contents. "No one was to examine the devices, or reveal to anyone that they even existed. Even those who salvaged the artifacts were . . . never heard from again."

Scott ran a finger along the edge of what looked to be the monitoring console for an impulse engine. More than likely, he decided, this panel had come from the *Archon*'s main engineering center, regulating fuel flow and output efficiency levels. He could see that the gunmetal gray surface beneath the layer of dust was smoked with soot. Had this been caused by an onboard fire? Had the ship suffered structural failure as it was dragged from orbit by Landru's defensive systems, allowing the unyielding heat of the planet's atmosphere to roast the interior of the vessel during its plummet to the surface? Shaking off the vision, he looked about the rest of the room.

*That looks like the barrel of an old laser cannon,* he told himself as his eyes fell across the antique weapon. *A Mark II at least, and there's a subspace relay beacon, an interphasic coil.* However, none of it seemed to be operational or even salvageable.

"I have no idea what most of this stuff is," Lindstrom said. "I wouldn't know if there was anything useful in here even if I was looking right at it."

Al-Khaled replied, "I doubt we'd even have the

time to rig up something that clever or involved. Our best bet might be something we can use to subdue the Lawgivers so we can get at Landru and start tearing out circuit boards by the handful."

Scott crouched to floor level to examine what appeared to be a section of scarred plating from the *Archon*'s hull. "I'm not even sure what we could devise from this collection of junk."

Inspecting another section of metal, apparently a door panel from one of the ship's interior hatches, Lindstrom shifted it aside to get a look at what lay underneath. "Scotty, I think I may have something here." Moving the door panel completely out of his way, he added, "Are these what I think they are?"

Their interest piqued, Scott and al-Khaled abandoned their own searches to join the sociologist. Getting a look at what Lindstrom had found, the engineers gasped in surprise.

"My dear mother's mother," Scott said. "Those look like old-style spatial torpedoes." Long and slender, the dull silver casing of the torpedoes appeared to be largely undamaged, possessing few marks other than the standard Starfleet codes and serial numbers stenciled on their exteriors. These weapons were not nearly as powerful as the photon torpedoes carried by modern-day starships like the *Enterprise*, but they had still packed quite a punch in their day.

"That's exactly what they are," al-Khaled

replied, making no effort to contain the rising excitement in his voice. With Scott and the others assisting, the younger engineer directed the movement of the torpedoes to where he could better inspect them. The next several minutes were spent in silence as al-Khaled gave the weapons a fast visual once-over.

"All three look to be fully operational," he announced, "at least as far as I can tell. Amazing, isn't it?"

Scott shook his head in near disbelief. "Aye. Things in those days were built to withstand all sorts of harsh punishment and to last a long time, but this . . . well, this is definitely beyond the warranty period."

"These might be powerful enough to use against Landru," al-Khaled said. "We can set them to detonate either individually or together. It would be no trouble to set them to a timer or to a remote control."

"Landru would never permit you to move such weapons close to the central core," Marplon said. "He would either deactivate them before they detonated or else he would simply send an army of Lawgivers to repel you."

"And we canna launch 'em," Scott added, "nor could we guide them once they were launched."

Shaking his head in frustration, al-Khaled swore under his breath. "Besides, all of those options would likely destroy the central computer, and we'll still need it to keep things running here."

The engineer began to pace the room. "There has to be a way to disable the machine without destroying it." Then he eyed the torpedoes again. "Wait. What about a bomb without the blast?"

Scott looked askance at his friend. "I don't follow ye, lad."

"We tune the torpedoes not to detonate their charges, but to channel their explosive energies into an electromagnetic pulse. That should short out the active Landru routines without causing catastrophic damage to the equipment."

"But," Scott said, "it'd also wipe out the other computer systems we've been working on for a week. That's a lot of effort to sweep away, Mahmud."

Waving the comments aside, al-Khaled shook his head. "Listen. We'd have to coordinate a shutdown of the active power systems that we've established. The pulse won't affect any inactive power sources. We have eighty people in the city, Scotty. That's more than enough people to cover all the bases." Indicating Marplon with a nod of his head, he added, "And we have Elders to help us, as well."

"Getting all of that in order will take some time," Lindstrom said. "Landru may not give it to us."

Nodding, al-Khaled replied, "Then we had better get started."

# CHAPTER
# 15

Chaos reigned supreme.

At least, that was the way it looked to Scott as he stared with a mixture of fascination and horror at the disorder that was quickly descending upon the city. From his vantage point, looking through a basement-level window of the command center, Scott could see citizens fighting and running amok in every direction. Others who had taken up their roles as Lawgivers once again moved slowly yet purposefully through the crowds, assisting in the roundup of those who still retained their free will.

Scott heard footsteps behind him. Turning, he saw that it was Lindstrom.

"Something wrong, Chris?"

The sociologist smiled in response. "I'm something of a fifth wheel until al-Khaled finishes with the torpedoes." He indicated where al-Khaled and Lieutenant Ghrex, the female Denobulan engineer from the *Lovell,* were still working feverishly, all but oblivious to anything going on around them.

After moving the torpedoes from the subterranean cache to the command center, al-Khaled had wasted no time turning to the task of reconfiguring the weapons to emit the electromagnetic pulse needed to disable Landru's central processing core. Though Scott considered himself fairly knowledgeable when it came to ship-based weaponry, the century-old torpedoes were an unfamiliar model to him. The engineers from the *Lovell,* however, with their experience serving aboard a near relic from the same era as the *Archon,* were more than equal to the task. With time being of the essence, Scott had elected to step aside and allow the others to work until they called for him.

*But when I get back to the* Enterprise, he decided, *I've got some catch-up learnin' to do.*

"Well," he said, "there's still plenty for us to do before this is over. Have ye made the other arrangements we need for this crazy plan to work?"

Nodding, Lindstrom replied, "Everything's underway right now." Consulting the chronometer displayed on his tricorder's monitor, he added, "We've got about fifty-seven minutes to go. Reger and Marplon are already coordinating with other former Elders, getting the people we need into the key positions. If anyone knows how to organize this city, it's the Elders. Even Hacom is helping us." Shrugging, he added, "I think he feels guilty over what's happened, even if he had no conscious control over his actions."

"Aye, I hope so, lad." While the timetable they had established for this plan had seemed too rushed at first to Scott, the engineer knew that delaying the operation any longer would seriously jeopardize their chances of succeeding.

Lindstrom held up his tricorder. "They also helped me to pinpoint the best place to position the torpedoes." Turning the unit for Scott to see, he indicated the small display screen with a finger. "Landru's central processing core is almost directly below the center of the city."

Studying the information on the tricorder's display, Scott frowned. "That area's also very heavily shielded, as I recall. From the readings Mr. Spock took with the *Enterprise* sensors, that underground area was built to withstand anything short of an orbital bombardment. We'll have to be almost on top of the bloody thing if this is going to work."

"The Town Square," Lindstrom said. Nodding in the direction of the basement window and the pandemonium ensuing beyond it, he added, "And we'll probably have to fight every step of the way to get there. Reger told me that Landru has already regained control of all Lawgivers and that people who need to be reabsorbed are being rounded up. At the rate they're moving, the entire city could be back under Landru's control by nightfall."

Scott nodded, closing his eyes momentarily as he listened to the sounds of disorder on the streets outside. In addition to the chaos already taking place, reports had come in that Landru had also regained total control of its complex security system. Neither the *Lovell* nor even the *Enterprise*, which was at this moment on its way back to Beta III to retrieve him, would be able to safely assume orbit around the planet until that security grid was disabled.

They turned to see al-Khaled walking over to join them. The engineer was wiping his hands with a towel and was wearing a small smile on his dirty, tired face.

"We're finished, Scotty," he said. "All three torpedoes have been reconfigured and tested. Together, they should produce a pulse more than enough to disable any active power source."

"Nice work, lad," Scott replied, letting his gaze wander over to where Ghrex was reattaching an anti-gravity unit to the trio of torpedoes, which had been bundled together with packing straps Lindstrom had found in one of the tool kits brought down from the *Lovell*. With the anti-gravs, two men would be able to guide the weapons with one hand each, leaving the other free to carry a phaser. Scott knew, though, that whoever was staffing the units would have their freedom of movement compromised.

"Mahmud," he said, "you and I will see to the torpedoes. Lindstrom and Ghrex will provide cover for us."

Pulling his phaser from his waist, Scott held the weapon up to inspect its setting and power level. "We have to get these into position and be ready to detonate on schedule. I dinna think we'll get another chance at this, so whatever happens, even if one of us gets hit or captured, the group keeps moving. Understood?"

The stark order had the effect of turning the expressions on the faces of al-Khaled and Lindstrom to those of grim determination. Seeing the reaction his words had on his two companions, Scott felt the sudden need to reassure them.

"Not to worry, we'll get through this," he offered with only slightly more confidence than he himself was feeling. With a mischievous grin he added, "After all, ye already did the hard part."

Al-Khaled made a show of rolling his eyes in mock exasperation. "Oh, sure. *Now* he gives the proper credit where it was so sorely overdue. Better late than never, I suppose."

As they emerged from the command center into an alley, their presence was almost immediately noticed.

Scott had to duck to avoid the brick that nearly took his head off, which smashed into the wall behind him and splintered into several pieces. Stone shrapnel peppered the team. Nearly losing his grip on the handle of the anti-gravity unit and its cargo of torpedoes, he instinctively dropped into a defensive crouch and turned to see where the brick had come from.

"Look out!" al-Khaled shouted, his own phaser already aiming at their attacker. It was a man, dressed in a smoke gray suit with a long black overcoat and top hat to complete the ensemble. The man's elegant manner of dress clashed with the expression of manic rage on his face. Dashing into the alley from the street, the assailant's eyes were wide and his mouth twisted into a sinister sneer as he wielded what looked to be a steel bar. The bar was held high, ready to strike at the first thing, or person, that presented a target.

Almost with a will of its own, Scott's weapon arm came up, aiming his phaser at the onrushing man as his finger pressed the firing stud. The phaser's cold blue-white energy beam washed over the man, halting his advance. As the glow of the beam faded, the attacker wobbled for a moment before crumpling to the ground, unconscious.

"Nice shooting," al-Khaled said as he adjusted his own grip on the anti-grav, taking a moment to ensure that the trio of torpedoes was still stable.

Scott nodded, exhaling audibly as he rose from his crouch after confirming that the man had been acting alone. "How much time do we have left?"

Lindstrom consulted his tricorder, which he

was also using to guide them to where they would plant the torpedoes. "About thirty minutes. We need to get moving."

"Let's do that, then." With Lindstrom leading the way, phaser in one hand and tricorder in the other, the Starfleet officers began moving in the direction of the street. Scott and al-Khaled maintained their positions in the middle of the group, with Ghrex bringing up the rear.

If Scott thought the greeting they had received in the alley was gruff, it was nothing compared to what was waiting for them as they emerged from the shadows of the buildings onto the sidewalk lining the street before them.

"Good lord," he whispered as they stopped just at the edge of the alley. Debris of all types—glass, wood, metal—littered the streets. People ran in all directions, some dashing frantically up and down the street while others attempted to force open doors leading into the various buildings. Still other citizens were fighting each other, as those who still retained their own self-control struggled to fend off those who had already succumbed once more to Landru's influence. The skirmishes in some cases were savage, with people using any and all means to overpower their opponents. Scott nearly recoiled in horror as one man slammed his assailant in the side of the head with a brick.

As his opponent fell to the ground, the man looked up and his eyes locked with Scott's. The engineer saw the look of abject terror on the face of someone fighting for his freedom if not his very life.

"Landru is coming for us all!" the man shouted. "He will find us and destroy us!" Then he pointed directly at Scott. "You are to blame for this! Landru is punishing us for your interference here!" Dropping the brick and allowing it to clatter to the street, the man abruptly turned and ran away, leaving Scott and his companions to stare after him in shock.

"Scotty, are you okay?" al-Khaled asked. Scott jerked his head in the direction of the voice and saw his friend's expression of concern. Swallowing hard, he nodded.

"Aye. He may be right, you know. If we can't stop that blasted contraption for good this time, there's no telling what fresh hell it's liable to unleash on these people." Pausing to take a deep breath in order to refocus himself, he added, "Let's get this done."

Once more they began to move, emerging from the tenuous protection of the alley. Lindstrom, one eye on his tricorder as he tried to watch all around him for other approaching threats, guided them up the street. Rather than risk getting caught out on the open street, the sociologist instead stayed close to the buildings, hugging the walls as he led them toward their target.

Phaser fire from behind him made Scott turn

to see Ghrex taking aim at another attacker, a woman this time, running at them while brandishing a club. The phaser beam cut her down, dropping her into an unconscious heap on the street. Almost immediately he heard al-Khaled's phaser whine as the engineer fired at another citizen. All around them people were beginning to take notice of the Starfleet officers.

"They are not of the Body!"

"Traitors! Kill them!"

"It is the will of Landru!"

Dropping his hold on the anti-gravity unit, Scott used his free hand to adjust the setting on his phaser. "Wide-field stun!" he called out. "It's the only way we'll be able to handle them all."

His companions reacted to the order, adjusting the power level on their own weapons as the first hail of stones, bricks, and whatever else the rapidly growing throng of attackers could find rained down on them. His free arm held protectively over his head, Scott had to dodge to his left to avoid an oil lamp hurled at him. The lamp's glass bulb exploded against the wall behind him as he danced away from the attack, his phaser already coming up to aim in on the man who had thrown it.

"Fire!" he yelled above the growing cacophony of yelled threats and cries of seething anger now being directed at them. The engineers each fired their own weapons, and the effect was that of a wall of blue energy erupting from the phasers. It expanded and enveloped the oncoming mob in an instant, rendering all of their attackers unconscious even before they collapsed to the ground.

The abrupt absence of near pandemonium surprised Scott for a moment. While he c? still hear sounds of chaos from elsewhere, area right in front of them was almost ser? now that nearly everyone in sight had been ne? tralized. Taking a second to ensure that none of the group was injured, Scott saw al-Khaled holding a free hand to the side of his head as he leaned against the wall of the nearby building. Blood flowed freely between the man's fingers and his face was screwed up in pain.

"Are ye all right, lad?"

Al-Khaled nodded. "I think I'll be all right. I zigged when I should have zagged."

Scott pulled his friend's hand back to inspect the wound. "Looks like ye got hit by a rock," he said. "We'll get ye fixed up."

"No time for that now, Scotty," al-Khaled said. "We have to get the torpedoes into position."

Knowing his friend was right, Scott turned and reached out for the anti-gravity unit. "Aye, and that's just what we're going to do. Mr. Lindstrom? How much time?"

"Less than fifteen minutes," Lindstrom reported. No further words were necessary as the engineers set out once again. Scott noted that al-Khaled had opted to retain his grip on his phaser while he carried his end of the anti-grav, leaving his head wound to bleed unabated. It was a nasty gash, and Scott suspected that it was all that his friend could do to simply remain conscious.

Moving quickly, they encountered no further resistance. Scott tried not to count off the seconds in his head as they jogged down the street, trying to stay close to the relative safety offered by the buildings. His eyes darted about, scanning each doorway, window, and gap between buildings for new threats, but no one appeared to challenge them.

"Over there," Lindstrom called out, pointing to the open area that Scott recognized as the Town Square. The vast courtyard, surrounded on all sides by buildings and dominated by the huge clock at the square's far end, was the first thing he had seen upon beaming down from the *Enterprise*.

The tension was palpable as they entered the square. Everyone in the group stepped up their level of alertness as they moved farther out into the open. Their vulnerability to attack was growing with every step, and as they hurried across the courtyard Scott's mind taunted him with visions of walking into a monstrous arena in order to do battle for the amusement of a crazed audience. However, what few people Scott did see on the street did not appear to be the least bit interested in the Starfleet officers.

"Let's get these beasties into position and find cover," Scott called out as they followed Lindstrom across the square. Finally the sociologist stopped and indicated a point on the ground with his tricorder.

"That's the spot."

With al-Khaled matching him step for step, Scott rushed across the last few meters and lowered his end of their precious package to the ground. Deactivating the unit's gravity-nullifying field, he disengaged it, leaving the torpedoes to settle under their own weight to the street.

"That's got it," he said. "They're not going anywhere now. Let's get the hell out of here."

"Scotty," al-Khaled said, his voice nearly a whisper.

When nothing else came, Scott looked up and saw that his friend was staring at something over his shoulder. He started to turn when movement several dozen meters away attracted his attention. It was a figure, standing at the end of the street.

A Lawgiver.

Another of Landru's enforcers was standing at the mouth of an alley. A third had appeared as if conjured by magic, standing in a doorway to Scott's right.

"They're coming out of the woodwork," Lindstrom said. Scott noted the anxiety in his friend's voice as he turned to see that another Lawgiver was standing in the street behind them, blocking the path that they had used to get there.

They were surrounded.

# CHAPTER
# 16

"They must think we're lonely."

Al-Khaled's quip did nothing to ease Scott's escalating tension as he regarded the four Lawgivers that had taken up stations around him and his companions.

"Whatever happens," he said, "we canna let them near the torpedoes. We only have to hold them off for a few more minutes."

"Less than five," Lindstrom offered, holding his tricorder up for emphasis. "We need to get away from here." Scott agreed. Though the torpedoes would not produce anything resembling their normal violent explosive force upon detonation, the electromagnetic pulse they would emit could still cause severe neurological damage to anyone standing too close. He had no intention of setting the weapons off until he and the others had found some form of cover.

"I don't think our friends are going to just let

us walk out of here," Ghrex said. Scott had to agree with the Denobulan's observation as he studied the Lawgivers, who had assumed nearly equidistant positions from one another, creating a circle with Scott and his companions in the center. The Starfleet officers quickly took up a defensive posture, facing outward with their backs to each other.

"You attack the Body," the Lawgiver in front of Scott said, pointing his staff at the engineer. "You will be absorbed."

Then he heard the whine, faint at first but growing in intensity with each passing second as, only a few meters in front of him, a pinpoint of light appeared. It stretched and elongated, taking on an unmistakable humanoid-like shape.

"Landru," Lindstrom said.

"A projection," Scott said, remembering Mr. Spock's report and its details of the holography Landru had demonstrated. Scott had hoped to study the mechanisms behind the incredible display of technology, provided enough time remained between the completion of his repair duties and the arrival of the *Enterprise* to pick him up.

*I know,* he chided himself. *Be careful what you wish for, and all that.*

"*You are the enemy,*" the projection said. "*The infection you carry is lethal, and your destruction is necessary to the continued health of the Body.*"

Scott shook his head. "I dinna think so." To the

rest of the group he said, "Time for us to leave, people." Taking aim once more at the Lawgiver nearest to him, Scott pressed the firing stud on his phaser.

*Click.*

Frowning, Scott tilted the weapon up to examine its power setting and, seeing that it still possessed most of its charge, attempted to aim and fire it again. Once more, the phaser refused to cooperate.

"Mine doesn't work, either," al-Khaled said, followed quickly by similar reports from Lindstrom and Ghrex.

*"Your weapons have been neutralized,"* Landru said, *"just as you shall be. You will become one with the ultimate good."*

As if in response to the computer's statement, the Lawgiver in front of Scott stepped forward and pointed once more to the engineer with his staff. "You will come."

"What do we do now?" al-Khaled asked.

Scott did not know. *After all, Captain Kirk's the one who knows how to talk to these blasted contraptions.* The engineer's expertise with computers was limited to the realm of keeping them operating at peak efficiency and diagnosing and repairing malfunctions.

He also knew that negotiating with Landru was out of the question. The computer was merely following the directives its creator had imparted to it thousands of years previously. So

too were the Lawgivers, each of them controlled
by the sliver of microcircuitry embedded within
their bodies. Their subservience to Landru was
absolute, and even if it was not, Scott had no
time to figure out how to circumvent their programming.

"Why don't they just kill us and get it over
with?" Ghrex asked.

"It would go against Landru's programming,"
Lindstrom said. "Violence is used as a last resort
when it senses that no other options are available. Its directive is to absorb its enemies and
stamp out the violence and hate it believes they
represent. Turning its enemies into allies of its
notion of good is a larger victory than simply
responding with violence in kind." Suddenly his
expression darkened. "Maybe that's it."

"What's it?" Scott asked.

Rather than replying, Lindstrom instead
returned his phaser to his hip. Then, raising his
hands to show that they were empty, he said to
the Lawgiver nearest to him, "We obey the will of
Landru."

Scott was aghast. "Chris, what are ye doin'?"

"Buying us some time," Lindstrom countered.

*"You will find peace and contentment within the
Body,"* the Landru projection said calmly, as if
responding to Lindstrom's act of surrender.

The Lawgiver pointed his staff at Lindstrom.
"You will come."

"This is crazy," al-Khaled said, and Scott had to

agree. What was Lindstrom thinking? He could applaud the man's bravery, and though the number of options open to them was rapidly dwindling, Scott had no intention of willingly handing himself over to these goons. Frantically he looked about the courtyard, searching for something that could be used as a weapon, anything that might give him some kind of advantage.

Then he saw the clock.

The giant clock at the end of the courtyard, its massive white face highlighted by the black numbers and hands denoting the time. He had not given it much thought in the past few minutes. As his eyes focused on it, however, he realized that the clock was all that really mattered now as it began to chime, sounding out across the courtyard and echoing off the brick facades of the surrounding buildings.

Six o'clock.

"It's time!" al-Khaled called out.

What had once been known here as "the Red Hour" was now the signal for Scott and his friends to put their plan into motion. In his mind's eye the engineer could see other members of the Starfleet contingent, stationed at key points across the city, carrying out their assigned tasks. Some of that work entailed disabling independent power control mechanisms that had already been installed by engineers from the *Lovell* to replace those systems that Landru had once oversaw. In some extreme cases, workers at this very moment were, if things were proceeding according to plan, even going so far as to physically cut power lines or destroy control consoles in various underground facilities where Landru had presided with total autonomy. Scott knew that actions, drastic as they may be, were the only methods to protect those critical systems that would be needed after Landru was deactivated once and for all.

*None of that'll matter though if we canna do anything.*

Apparently Lindstrom had not forgotten this, either.

Drawing abreast of one Lawgiver, the sociologist then flicked several switches on his tricorder. Suddenly several of the robed figures went into some kind of seizure, collapsing to the ground and shaking violently.

Lindstrom grabbed the Lawgiver's staff and wrenched the weapon free, then ran toward one of the Lawgivers who wasn't affected by whatever it was the sociologist did. Swinging the staff like a bat, Lindstrom struck the Lawgiver in the left shoulder, sending the man tumbling to the street.

"Watch out!" al-Khaled shouted even as he tried to take advantage of the distraction. He launched himself at another of the non-seizing Lawgivers as the enforcer aimed his staff at Lindstrom, tackling the robed figure and sending them both to the ground before the weapon discharged.

The projection of Landru, seemingly unfazed by the rapid turn of events, continued to speak in the same calm manner. *"You attempt to harm the Body. You must therefore be destroyed for the good of all."*

Scott called out to his friends, "Let's get out of here!" The four officers sprinted away from the torpedoes, heading for an alley that Scott had already seen and decided upon as the best place for cover in the limited time available to them. As they ran, Scott reached for his communicator, flipping the unit open and activating it.

*Almost there. Just another few seconds.*

Beside him, Lindstrom was trying to read the status display on his tricorder. "Hang on, Scotty. I don't know if everyone's ready for us or not."

"They bloody well better be," Scott replied as the group dodged into the alley. Throwing himself against one wall, he gave his communicator a final glance to ensure that it was set to the correct frequency before resting his thumb atop the transmit control. "Because we're out of time."

He pressed the switch.

The explosion was not nearly as loud as it would have been had the torpedoes' original payload been allowed to detonate. Still, it was impressive enough. Scott felt the shock wave hit the building they were hiding against as it buffeted the brick exterior, and the ground vibrated beneath his feet in response to the massive electromagnetic pulse the torpedoes unleashed.

*"You will be absorbed,"* were the last words of the Landru projection before it twisted and distorted, disappearing altogether as whatever source that had powered it fell in the face of the pulse.

Other effects became apparent immediately as well. First, Scott's communicator promptly went dead in his hand, the transtator circuitry offering no resistance to the pulse. Lindstrom's tricorder suffered a similar fate, as the sociologist was unable to deactivate the unit in time to protect it from the blast.

Within seconds the effects of the explosion began to dissipate, fading almost as quickly as they had appeared. Then there was only silence.

Poking his head around the corner of the building, Scott saw the four Lawgivers lying scattered across the courtyard near the casings of the three torpedoes. It was not hard to figure out what had happened to them, he realized grimly. The pulse would have overloaded the implants at the bases of their skulls as well. If the resulting shock had not killed them outright, the least it would have done is render them unconscious.

"Scotty," al-Khaled called out softly. As Scott turned to face his friend, the *Lovell* engineer held up his tricorder, which had been deactivated during the torpedo detonation. "According to my scans, most of the critical systems were shut down in time. We did lose some secondary power distribution relays, but nothing serious. Our plan worked."

Nodding, Scott said nothing at first. Instead he looked out again on the scene of the fallen Lawgivers, which to him illustrated profoundly the nature of what they had just done here. Once again they had cast off the oppressive hand of technology left to run rampant so that it could no longer control the free will of living beings.

Now what?

"Engineers. All you know how to do is fix machines."

Scott, al-Khaled, and Lindstrom walked down the sidewalk bordering one of the city's main streets. All around them, Betan citizens were going about the tasks of cleaning up the city in the aftermath of Landru's nearly successful bid to regain control over their lives. Various people offered smiles and warm gestures of greeting as they walked past. It was an altogether different scene from the one that had transpired here less than a day before.

"Are ye saying that this wasna an engineering problem, Mr. Lindstrom?" Scott asked. "Besides, that stunt you pulled on the Lawgivers looked like an engineering solution to me."

Lindstrom smiled sheepishly. "Well, I knew the high-level scan could induce that kind of seizure in some of the Lawgivers. It happened by accident before, so I thought it was worth a shot to do it on purpose this time."

Exchanging a wry grin with al-Khaled, Scott

said, "Well then, lad, perhaps you'll enlighten us as to where our thinking is wrong."

"It's not *wrong*," Lindstrom countered. "But where your expertise is in the machinery, mine is in the people those machines were built to serve. Landru wasn't out to kill us, merely to negate us as a threat. If we had continued to resist him and the Lawgivers, however, he would have eventually ordered his men to kill us, to protect himself if nothing else."

"But if we cooperated," al-Khaled added, "then his programming dictated that the Lawgivers take us to their absorption chambers. In other words, we should have just let them escort us far enough from the torpedoes so we could set them off anyway?"

Lindstrom nodded. "Exactly."

"A mighty bold idea, lad," Scott said. "So tell me, why didn't ye stick to it?"

The sociologist could only smile sheepishly. "When the clock sounded, I wasn't sure what the Lawgivers would do. I remembered about the scans, and I just reacted."

"Ah," Scott replied. "Spoken like a man after Captain Kirk's own heart. He'll love the report ye'll surely be filin' once all the dust settles here."

"That could be a while," al-Khaled said. "It will take some time to acclimate these people to their new situation. Some of them will not believe that Landru is gone forever, and still others will actually miss the control he once possessed. I do not envy you your task here, Mr. Lindstrom."

"It's a once-in-a-lifetime opportunity," Lindstrom said. "With help from Starfleet and the Federation, these people will have everything they'll need to make a better life for themselves. Even with Landru permanently disabled, the automated network he controlled is more than enough to keep essential services operational. It'll also provide a nice foundation for bringing in more advanced equipment to help with the transition. The Betan people have all the skills they need to work and thrive; they simply need a guiding hand to help them evolve socially and culturally."

Al-Khaled said, "Early reports indicate that Starfleet wants permission to use Beta III as a starship maintenance facility. It will take years to work out solutions to problems these people do not even know they are going to face yet, but who knows? One day, this could be one of the premier planets in the Federation. I almost regret that I will not be around to see it."

Scott almost agreed with his friend, though he knew that neither al-Khaled, nor himself for that matter, would ever have as much passion for such an endeavor as Lindstrom obviously possessed. The challenges the engineers sought lay elsewhere, after all.

"But that's why we're glad for experts like you," al-Khaled added. "While you want to meet new races of people and learn about their culture and maybe help to improve their lives, we just want to take apart all of their toys."

"Fair enough," Lindstrom said, "but suppose you and that shipload of engineers of yours are the first ones to come across a newly discovered race. You'll be able to figure out their hardware, of that I'm sure. But who's going to talk to the people who own it?"

It was an interesting question, one for which neither Scott nor al-Khaled had a ready answer.

At least, not today.

# CHAPTER
# 17

"I'm hungry," Bart Faulwell said as his stomach growled for the third time in ten minutes.

Involved as he was with his work at the main computer station of the Senuta ship's compact command deck, Soloman nevertheless paused to regard his companion. "I have noted the indicative sounds emanating from within your torso."

Faulwell chuckled at the perfect deadpan delivery of the statement. In his experience, the Bynars as a species weren't normally given to frivolous wordplay. They preferred instead to concentrate on ensuring that any communication was restricted only to what was essential to the accomplishment of a given task. This was especially true with verbal interaction, which was typically employed only when dealing with other species that did not possess the Bynars' fantastic ability to communicate at speeds rivaling the most advanced computer processors. Like other members of his race, Soloman much preferred interacting with machines instead of living beings, as it freed him of the need to slow down the process of giving and receiving information.

However, he had been taking infrequent, tentative steps of late to engage various members of the *da Vinci* crew in verbal discussion when it related to the assignment at hand or, more recently, in more casual conversation. Faulwell wouldn't categorize Soloman's attempts as "banter" or "chit chat," but it was a departure, and a most welcome one at that, from what had once characterized the Bynar's normal behavior.

"Well, if you know what it means," Faulwell said as he continued to study the array of computer display screens dominating the rear wall of the command deck, "then you also know that it's not something I'm going to want to ignore for too much longer."

Despite his teasing comment, he knew he had only himself to blame for being hungry. There had been plenty of time to grab something to eat prior to beaming over from the *da Vinci*, but Faulwell had elected to spend that time writing a quick note to Anthony. He'd spent thirty minutes painstakingly updating his partner on their current mission, composing his thoughts on paper by hand as he always did before transcribing the missive for transmission via subspace communication. The handwritten letter, like all of the others that he wrote to Anthony, would be saved until such time as Faulwell could deliver them in person. The intimate ritual was one of his few private pleasures, and he had become so engrossed in it that he had nearly lost track of time. When the reminder to report to the transporter room came from his computer terminal, Faulwell had been forced to leave the note unfinished until he returned from the Senuta ship.

*And after I get something to eat,* he reminded himself. *Sorry, Anthony.*

Looking up from his console, Soloman said, "You will be pleased to know that I have nearly completed restructuring the interface to the operating system and providing a simpler means for the Senuta crew to interact with the computer. It will not give them the entire range of capabilities the original interface possessed, but it will be sufficient to make up for the loss of the ship's computer technicians." His brow furrowing slightly, the Bynar added, "There is a great deal of security integrated into the various applications software, not unexpected for a vessel originally constructed for military use. In order to effect the interface, it was necessary to deactivate or bypass much of those protection schemes. I am preparing to run a final diagnostic to ensure the interface functions properly before instructing the Senuta on its operation."

"Sounds great," Faulwell replied as he glanced about the command deck. "I'd be lying if I said I wasn't more than ready to get back to the *da Vinci*." Once again he had to shake off the feeling that the room's bulkheads were closing in around him.

*I think it's going to be a while before I complain about how cramped my quarters are again.*

This room, like everything else on the ship, had been constructed to conform to the physiology of the comparatively smaller Senuta crewmembers. It had taken Faulwell more than a few minutes to adjust to the smaller-scaled equipment, which had been designed for a more diminutive body type. In contrast, Soloman had found the accommodations as comfortable as the furnishings of his own quarters on the *da Vinci*.

From behind them, a soft voice asked, "Have your repair efforts been successful?"

Faulwell turned to the two Senuta crewmembers. Each regarded him with what the linguist had come to recognize as their typical wide-eyed, expectant expression. Ircoral and Tkellan, as the two female Senuta had introduced themselves earlier, were part of the Senuta ship's engineering staff and had been assigned to assist Faulwell and Soloman by providing information about the systems overseeing the vessel's propulsion systems. Their expertise had allowed Soloman to craft the new interface to the ship's computer, giving the crewmembers more direct control of the automated systems than they had previously enjoyed. Though Ircoral and Tkellan had been intensely curious in the beginning, peppering the *da Vinci* engineers with a myriad of questions, once Soloman had gotten down to the serious work of reprogramming the computer they had been content to remain quiet, working at other stations, until they were needed again.

"Yes, Ircoral," Faulwell replied. "It looks as though we're almost done here. Thanks to your help, Soloman is nearly finished repairing the damage the storm caused to your computer and its software."

Soloman had been working steadily for the past two hours, his attention only rarely wavering from the bank of computer displays. Most of his attention had been focused on the subsystems overseeing the ship's engines and propulsion, which had borne the brunt of the storm's effects. It had been slow going at first, with the Bynar encountering more than a bit of difficulty in understanding the computer languages responsible for the software running the Senuta computers. That's where Faulwell had been able to help.

As a linguist and cryptographic specialist, Bart Faulwell had not set out to become anything resembling a computer expert. Called upon to perform more demanding assignments as his experience grew, such as deciphering enemy communications codes and encryption schemes, it soon became apparent to him that understanding the nuances of discourse used by living beings was not enough. Therefore, Faulwell had expanded his knowledge into the world of computers and the languages used to transform instructions into the actions carried out by machines.

In this case the work he had already done to translate the Senuta's spoken and written language had allowed him to assist Soloman in understanding the alien ship's computer system. Once the language barrier had been broken, the Bynar was able to interface with the Senuta computer easily. The only remaining obstacle was the level of technology itself, which Soloman had likened to that used by the Federation during the early to mid-twenty-third century.

"This degree of self-sufficiency is comparable to that of modern starships in several respects," Soloman said as he continued to work. "The major difference of course is that the Senuta are more easily inclined to entrust themselves to their computers than many of the humanoid species I have encountered."

Noting a quality in his companion's voice that didn't seem to be a ring of approval, Faulwell glanced momentarily in the direction of the two Senuta engineers. Neither of the aliens appeared to have heard the Bynar's words, though. "Is there something wrong with that?" he asked. "I figured that if anyone would appreciate the

Senuta's reliance on technology, it would be you."

The Bynar regarded him with an almost amused expression on his pale features. "My people have fashioned a society that embraces an interdependence on computers, yes, but the idea that we are slaves to automation is a misconception shared by many who do not understand us."

"Fair enough," Faulwell replied, now even more relieved that the Senuta had not overheard their conversation. After all, it would not do to offend these people so soon after establishing first contact. Though such initial meetings with new races usually caused Faulwell no small amount of concern, he still undertook the inherent responsibilities during such momentous occasions with all the seriousness they deserved.

*Besides, Carol will kill us if we find a way to screw this up.*

The lights on the bridge flickered around him and Faulwell became aware of a steady thrum resonating through the deck beneath his feet. The engines had come back online, he realized, thanks no doubt to the efforts of Kieran Duffy and his repair team from the *da Vinci*.

Turning in his seat, he saw the two Senuta engineers watching him again, anticipation dominating their features. Smiling, he nodded in their direction. "I think you're back in business."

Nodding excitedly, Tkellan replied, "Yes, it appears as though your companions have succeeded in helping our technicians. Your crew is very skilled."

Faulwell began to offer a response but was cut off by a voice from his combadge.

*"Duffy to Faulwell."*

"Go ahead, Commander."

*"As you may have noticed, Bart, we've finished our repairs on the engines. She'll run well enough to get them home. All that's missing is the link to the propulsion management subprocesses in their main computer. How are you coming up there?"*

The fatigue was evident in Duffy's voice. No doubt the repairs to the damaged engines had been extensive, as they had begun their work hours before Faulwell and Soloman had started their investigations of the Senuta's computer.

"We're almost finished, sir," he replied. "Soloman is preparing a final test of his reprogramming before we hand things over to the Senuta."

*"Outstanding. I don't know about you, but I'm ready to get back to the* da Vinci *and stretch out in my luxurious, oversized bed in my luxurious, oversized room."*

Faulwell laughed at that, looking around once again at the bland, cramped confines of the Senuta ship's command deck. "I hear you, Commander. I'd estimate another ten minutes and we'll be done here. See you back on the *da Vinci*. Faulwell out."

Severing the connection, he returned his attention to the two Senuta engineers. "With the engines fixed, all that's left is the computer, and we'll be ready to return control of it back to you."

"I do not know how we will be able to repay your generosity," Ircoral replied.

Shrugging, Faulwell tried to smile humbly as he thought of how Carol would want him to handle this. "Perhaps if our two peoples spend time together after this, we can learn more about each other and you'll be able to better understand our motivations for helping you."

Ircoral considered that for several moments. "A most excellent idea. I will be sure to pass it on to Daltren when he returns from your ship."

Nodding in approval, Faulwell turned his attention back to Soloman. "Anything else I can do to help?"

"No," the Bynar replied simply. "I've finished my preparations and I'm ready to begin my diagnostics." He tapped a final series of commands into the workstation's oddly configured manual interface. In response to his instructions, graphics on the array of computer displays began to shift and scroll information, almost too fast for Faulwell to follow.

And then the alarm sounded.

It did not have the droning, piercing wail of a red alert klaxon, but it nevertheless echoed across the compact command deck. Harsh red illumination promptly replaced the more normal soft lighting, and flashers began blinking frantically near the two doors providing exits from the room.

An audio message also began to play from the internal communications system. The message was spoken in the Senuta's native language, so it took Faulwell a second to understand the words.

*"Intruder alert. Activating countermeasures."*

"What's happening?" he called out over the alarms as his attention was drawn to the wall of computer displays. One by one, the monitors were blinking out, the various graphics and information being replaced with a single line of Senuta text.

*This station is deactivated.*

His fingers almost a blur on the consoles, Soloman did not look up as he answered. "My diagnostics have triggered some type of security protocol. The computer is closing out access to systems all across the ship."

Trying to keep his growing apprehension under control, Faulwell swallowed the lump that had risen in his throat. "I thought you said you disabled or bypassed the security protocols."

"I apparently missed at least one."

At any other time, Faulwell might have thought the straight delivery of the simple statement humorous, but this was rapidly becoming anything but one of those occasions. Rising from his chair, he turned to face the Senuta engineers. "Ircoral, what sort of countermeasures is the computer activating?"

Already studying their own display monitors, the Senuta did not immediately reply. After several seconds that seemed like an eternity to Faulwell, Tkellan turned to look at him.

"Our computer is proceeding as if combatting an unauthorized access by an enemy during wartime. There are a number of security procedures that were installed to prevent such an occurrence, as this was once a military vessel. Though onboard offensive weapons were removed years ago, the computer protocols were simply deactivated, as it had proven too expensive and time-consuming to completely remove those components from the computer system."

Ircoral added, "The protocol that has been activated was only intended for use if the crew is incapacitated and the ship has been boarded by enemy invaders."

His sense of dread continuing to worsen, Faulwell asked, "So what happens then?"

Ircoral turned to face Faulwell, her own expression one of near horror. "The computer's instructions are to prevent access to its systems at all costs, to include destroying the ship if necessary."

Pausing only long enough to look at Soloman, who was still working feverishly to salvage any kind of access to the Senuta computer system, Faulwell did the only thing that made sense to him at that moment.

He tapped his combadge.

"Faulwell to *da Vinci*. We've got a big problem here."

# CHAPTER
# 18

"Da Vinci *here. What's the problem, Faulwell?*"

Casting a worried look at Soloman, who was still engrossed in his attempts to override the computer, Faulwell replied, "We seem to have triggered some kind of booby trap, Captain. The computer is locking down access and has activated a self-destruct protocol."

"*What?*" There was no mistaking the shock in Gold's voice, something that happened only on rare occasions. Faulwell knew that the captain, like everyone else involved in the effort to assist the Senuta, had believed this to be a rather simple if time-consuming mission with few or no difficulties expected to be encountered. This latest revelation had shattered the peace of what should have been a routine set of tasks for the crew of the *da Vinci*.

*It's just not the S.C.E. if something doesn't go wrong,* he reminded himself.

*"Can you override the computer?"* Gold asked, his voice having returned to the measured delivery that made the captain the calm in the center of any storm.

Turning back to Soloman, Faulwell saw that the Bynar had abandoned his attempts to access the computer and was now looking at him with no small amount of worry.

"I have been locked out of the computer," the Bynar said as he reached for his tricorder. "There is nothing more I can do."

That was most definitely what Faulwell did not want to hear. "Are you saying the ship is going to blow itself up?"

"That is correct. I suggest we leave as soon as possible."

*"I heard that, Faulwell,"* Gold said over the communicator. *"I've already got Feliciano preparing to evacuate that ship. How much time do we have?"*

Soloman was working again, holding his tricorder in one hand while the other tapped a few tentative commands to the computer console. "I estimate that we have less than five minutes."

*"Stand by for beam-out,"* Gold ordered. *"Sensors are detecting a massive power buildup in the engines. I want to be out of here before she blows."*

Faulwell nodded at that, though the captain could not see him. "Soloman, it's time to leave," he called out to his friend who was still hard at work, seemingly oblivious to everything around him.

"One moment, Bart," the Bynar responded. "I am scanning and attempting to record as much information from the computer's central data banks as time will permit. I will need an additional few minutes to complete the task."

It was Faulwell's turn to be shocked again. "Soloman, I really don't think we have time for this."

"I am reasonably certain that the download will take slightly less time than we have remaining before the engines overload."

Reasonably certain? Was that supposed to make him feel better? Looking about the command deck, he tried to remember: How much did they have? How much time had passed? What if Soloman's estimate was wrong?

He noticed Ircoral and Tkellan regarding him, their faces masks of concern. "Are we leaving?" Tkellan asked, nervousness evident in her voice. Faulwell did not blame her. After all, it was not as if he wanted to be here, either.

Nodding to the Senuta engineer, he replied, "Yes, we're leaving in just a moment." Looking to Soloman he added, "We *are* leaving, right?"

"I'm nearly finished," the Bynar responded, not looking up from his tricorder.

*"Gold to Faulwell,"* the captain's voice called out again. *"Our sensors are saying that the engines are approaching the overload point. Stand by for transport."*

"Not yet," Soloman said.

*"What's that?"* Gold asked, his tone suddenly quite frosty. *"What does he mean, 'Not yet'?"*

Rolling his eyes, Faulwell offered a silent plea to any deity who might be paying attention to this particular dark comedy in the making: *Please let me live long enough to regret what I'm about to say.*

"Soloman is trying to retrieve as much information from the Senuta computer as he can, sir. He's almost finished, but he needs a bit more time."

He felt an abrupt rumbling beneath his feet, a rattling that shook the deck plates and the bulkheads. The ship shuddered around him, already gripped in the beginning of its death throes.

*"You're out of time, Faulwell,"* Gold said over the communicator. *"We're pulling you out of there right now."*

Another tremor shook the ship, more violent this time, nearly throwing Faulwell off his feet. He could feel the explosion somewhere beneath him and his mind envisioned the force of the blast tearing through the interior of the ship's engineering section, ripping it apart as the engines succumbed to the effects of the overload. He reached for a nearby console to retain his balance, seeing as he did so that Soloman and the two Senuta engineers were doing the same thing to avoid being tossed to the deck.

The first tendrils of a transporter beam reached out for him just as another shock wave enveloped the ship. As he felt his body start to dissolve, an insane thought gripped him: *If I survive this, it'll make a great finish to Anthony's letter.*

As he rematerialized in the *da Vinci's* transporter room and saw the expression on Kieran Duffy's face, however, Faulwell wondered if he should have just stayed on the Senuta ship.

Duffy came around from behind the transporter console, where he'd been standing next to Transporter Chief Diego Feliciano. As the latter shut the transporter down, Duffy asked, "Are you all right? The bridge reported that there was some kind of computer problem over there."

"You could say that," Faulwell replied as he looked around him on the transporter platform, relieved to see that Soloman as well as Ircoral and Tkellan had made the transport safely. Turning to Duffy he asked, "Everyone else was evacuated, right?"

Duffy nodded. "And we went to warp as soon as we had you aboard." Noticing the expectant yet resigned looks on the faces of Ircoral and Tkellan, his expression turned somber. "The engines reached overload and exploded. Your ship has been destroyed. I'm truly sorry."

Ircoral and Tkellan regarded Duffy with horrified expressions. "That means that we are stranded here, with no way to get home," Ircoral said. "What will we do now?"

"You're not stranded," Faulwell replied, stepping down from the transporter platform and turning to face the Senuta engineers. "We, and Starfleet, will see to it that you and the rest of your crew are returned to your homeworld."

Her brow furrowing, Tkellan said, "But without the navigational systems aboard our ship, we will not be able to plot a course to our planet."

In response to that, Soloman stepped forward. "I was able to record a great deal of information from your computer's memory banks, including what I believe to be your navigational databases. If that is the case, then it will allow our navigators to assist in locating your home and determining the most efficient route to get there."

Faulwell nodded in agreement. If Soloman had indeed managed to get that information from the Senuta's onboard computer, then the heart attack the Bynar had nearly given him by demanding to remain on the doomed vessel until the last possible second would be worth it.

Almost.

"That is very kind of you," Ircoral said. "I do not believe that we have ever encountered a race of people so willing to help others in need." Turning to Soloman, she amended, "Or, as I should have said, races of people."

Faulwell smiled reassuringly at her. Seeing Ircoral and Soloman together, he was reminded once again of how similar in physique and demeanor the Senuta were to the Bynars. "It's like I was telling you before, Ircoral. It's what we do. I guess that if there's a positive effect of what's happened, it's that you'll have more time to get to know us better." His smile faltering a bit, he added, "Besides, it's the least we can do. It was our trying to help that put you in this situation."

An exaggerated coughing sound interrupted him, and he turned to see Duffy looking at him, a mildly amused expression mixed with irritation on his face.

"Yeah, and about that," the engineer said with mock annoyance in his voice, "you couldn't blow up the ship *before* I spent all day fixing it?"

Before he could actually say anything, Faulwell's stomach replied for him, the noises it made echoing softly in the transporter room and causing Duffy's eyebrows to shoot skyward.

"Is that all you've got to say?" Duffy asked.

Shrugging, Faulwell replied, "At least until after dinner." He regretted the flippant words as soon they left his mouth and as he saw the expectant, almost helpless expressions on the faces of Ircoral and Tkellan. They were looking to him, and by extension the rest of the *da Vinci* crew, for help. This was no time for jokes.

*What the hell are we supposed to do now?*

Carol Abramowitz could feel a prize-winning headache coming on.

"*Are ye all right, lass?*" Captain Montgomery Scott asked, looking out at her from the conference lounge viewscreen. Hearing the concern in his voice, Abramowitz realized for the first time that she was rubbing her temples, trying without success to relieve the pressure steadily building behind her eyeballs.

"Abramowitz?" Captain Gold leaned forward in his seat, his expression also one of concern. "Is something wrong?"

Shaking her head, she replied, "I'm fine, sir. Thank you." Forcing herself back to the situation at hand, she directed her attention to the padd she had brought with her to the meeting. The text on the unit's display comprised the sum total of the report she had fashioned, both for Gold and for Captain Scott back at Starfleet Headquarters on Earth. Somehow, she decided, the words themselves were woefully inadequate. No matter what flowery language she used to describe their current situation, it did not change the simple fact: Despite the best of intentions, the actions of the *da Vinci*'s crew had trapped the Senuta here. Because of that, the Senuta were, at least for the time being, a people without a home.

However, after conversing with Daltren, the commander of the Senuta ship, Abramowitz had been unable to find any indication that the aliens harbored anything even resembling resentment or bitterness about the situation. During her meetings with the alien ship captain, he had shown nothing but gratitude for the *da Vinci* crew since first coming aboard. Even faced with the loss of his own vessel, his support for the Starfleet engineers had not wavered.

"Ensign Wong is continuing his attempts to extrapolate a reverse course to the Senuta homeworld," she said, reading more of the cold facts from her padd, "based on the route their ship was taking when we answered their distress signal. Additionally, Soloman is searching through the data he downloaded from their computer, looking for their navigational charts. He's not sure if he managed to retrieve those or not." Pausing, she winced involuntarily as another spasm stabbed at her brain.

Having only partially allowed himself to relax in his chair, Gold said, "You look like you could use a breather, Abramowitz, not that I'm surprised. You've been working as hard as anyone on this mission, and it shows. This is a sticky situation, but we'd be a lot worse off if not for you."

On the viewscreen, Scott added, "*Aye, yer captain's right. I for one am grateful to have ye on the job.*"

Though she was seldom comfortable with compliments directed at her, Abramowitz could not help but smile at the praise these two veteran officers had conferred upon her. She knew from past experience that neither Gold nor Scott offered such accolades lightly, yet that did not stop her from believing she was unworthy of them.

"I have to admit to feeling a bit out of my

depth, sirs," she said. "I've spent years training in a wide variety of subjects that allow me to interact with hundreds of cultures the Federation has encountered. But that's just it. All of my training and experience revolves around races and cultures we've already met. I'm nowhere close to being an expert when it comes to first contact situations."

"*Dr. Abramowitz,*" Scott replied, "*in my experience, there's no such thing as a first contact expert. After all, it's a mighty rare thing for one first contact to be like another. Life just doesn't work that way, I'm afraid. The best thing that can be done is to have people like you on hand for such eventualities.*"

Smiling at that, Abramowitz replied, "On any other day, I'd be tempted to argue that point. Truth be told, though, I'm really just too tired right now." She shrugged. "Sometimes I wonder if I should have just taken that research posting on Memory Alpha."

"And deprive us of your talents, to say nothing of your unflappable good nature?" Gold asked, amusement tugging at the corners of his mouth. "That would be criminal in the extreme, I think."

Adopting a more serious expression, the *da Vinci* captain leaned forward in his chair once more, clasping his hands atop the conference table. "Look, Carol, I know you think you're in over your head, but we all know that this isn't a normal mission, even by first contact standards.

The Senuta have been thrown for a loop to be sure, but they're confident that we'll do whatever it takes to get them home. The vast portion of that faith is due to you."

"*And that, more than anything else, is why we have cultural liaisons aboard our ships,*" Scott added. "*Even our S.C.E. ships.*" On the screen, the Starfleet legend shook his head. "*In fact, this whole thing reminds me of another time when a ship was lost far from home and came into contact with another species.*"

"Uh oh," Gold said, looking to Abramowitz with a mischievous glint in his eye. "I feel another story coming on."

Abramowitz could not help laughing at the captain's deadpan delivery. It was fascinating how Scott could be counted on to have a timely anecdote for whatever crisis the *da Vinci* crew happened to encounter. Then again, that quality was only part of what made Captain Montgomery Scott the unique individual he was.

"*Aye, but I think Dr. Abramowitz will appreciate this tale. For one thing, on this occasion it was one of our ships that was the lost little lamb, dependent on the goodwill of a previously unknown people to get them home. . . .*"

# CHAPTER
# 19

"What do ye call déjà vu the second time ye get it?"

As had happened three days earlier upon boarding the starship that had ferried him here, Montgomery Scott was struck by the familiarity of the transporter room in which he had just materialized. It, like its counterpart on the transport ship, was a near match for the *Enterprise*'s transporter room before his own ship's extensive refit. Here the higher level of lighting served to intensify the already vibrant colors and give the room a pulse, a certain zest that he occasionally admitted to missing aboard the *Enterprise*. He knew that the heart of his beloved ship still beat proudly from beneath newer and stronger hull plating, faster engines, and more advanced onboard systems. However, while his engineer's mind had long since embraced and even relished the improvements bestowed on his vessel, the romantic in him had refused to dismiss the sense that something had been lost in the *Enterprise*'s redesign.

One major difference, however, was that this ship's transporter console was missing most of its components. The transport ship had performed the beam-in procedure all by its lonesome. This vessel was no longer on active duty, and many components had been removed, including the transporter.

"You're not going to pine over the tune-up your ship got again, are you?" Commander Mahmud al-Khaled asked as he stood before the gutted transporter console with a wide grin on his face, moving forward to greet Scott as the latter stepped from the platform. "I've told you before and I'll tell you again: If you're looking for sympathy from me, you're wasting your time. You starship types are spoiled compared to the rest of us real engineers, so quit complaining every time they give you new toys to play with."

Ignoring Scott's outstretched hand, al-Khaled instead embraced his friend. Drawing back, he cast the *Enterprise* chief engineer an amused look.

"I thought you said you only grew that mustache on a dare and you were going to shave it off. How long ago was that?"

Smiling, Scott replied, "A few lassies convinced me to keep it."

Al-Khaled chuckled at that. "Well, mustache or no, welcome to the *Chandley*. I'm glad you could make the trip."

"I had to come," Scott said. "It was either this or Risa. Dr. McCoy has been champin' at the bit for me to take shore leave." His last conversation with the *Enterprise*'s chief medical officer prior to leaving the ship had been amusing, with McCoy shaking his head in disbelief that the engineer would choose to spend time with other engineers instead of immersing himself in the pleasures offered on the legendary resort planet.

Scott followed as al-Khaled led the way from the transporter room. "You know, you were right the other day about Alhena's knack for our line of work," al-Khaled said. "Her mother sent some images over subspace of her tearing into an old food processor. She almost got it put back together, too."

Scott smiled at that. Though he had never had the opportunity to meet al-Khaled's wife and daughter, he had heard all about them through his own irregular subspace correspondence with his friend. "What is she now, five?"

"Just turned," al-Khaled replied. "It's way too soon for this dad to wish for it, but if she wants to be an engineer when she grows up, I'm certainly not going to stand in her way. There are plenty of worse careers she could choose." Laughing mischievously he added, "I only hope I can convince her to join the Corps and avoid that cushy starship duty."

As they continued down the corridor, Scott could discern more signs that the *Chandley* was not a starship on active duty. Panels that had once provided access to circuitry overseeing many of the ship's key systems had been taken out, showing only dark maws where control mechanisms had once been. Defensive systems as well as most of the more powerful onboard sensor and computer components had been removed upon the vessel's decommissioning.

"They dinna leave much, did they?"

"Enough for the Kelvans," al-Khaled replied as they approached a turbolift. "When you see what they've been working on these last couple of years, I think you'll agree that the trip was worth it."

"I have to admit to bein' a wee bit intrigued at the offer," Scott replied. "I haven't been here in years, you know." How long had it been since his first visit to New Kelva? For that matter, what was the planet's original name? Tau Delta III, Delta Tau III, something else? The names of many worlds that Scott had visited during his service aboard the *Enterprise* had long since blended together, and the planet they were currently orbiting was not one he had ever regarded as a likely candidate for a return visit.

They stepped into the turbolift and al-Khaled ordered it to proceed to the engineering deck.

"The *Enterprise* crew is held in high esteem by Rojan and the others," he said. "After all, if not for you, New Kelva would not have been founded, and the Kelvans would not be in a position to unveil their little surprise today."

Scott frowned, uncomfortable with such praise. After all, his first and only encounter with the Kelvans had been a trying one. The aliens had hijacked the *Enterprise* after their own vessel had been damaged during passage through the powerful energy barrier at the edge of the galaxy. Part of an advance scouting party from their planet in the Andromeda galaxy, they had been sent to find a new home for their empire when Kelvan scientists discovered that radiation harmful to their life-forms was rising toward lethal levels. Projections called for the extinction of all life in their galaxy within ten thousand years.

Ships had been dispatched from the Kelvan Empire, traversing the void between their own area of space and the nearest neighboring galaxy, a journey that had taken generations to complete. In order to return with their report, the scouting party that had captured the *Enterprise* had intended to use the vessel to replace their own for the three-hundred-year voyage back to the Andromeda galaxy.

Scott suppressed an involuntary shudder at the memory of how the Kelvans had asserted their control over the *Enterprise* crew. Using the awesome power at their command, the aliens had transformed the bulk of the ship's crew into small, brittle duodecahredons, each containing the essential chemical components of the person it represented. He recalled walking the starship's corridors, mindful of each step around the seemingly innocuous geometric shapes that had littered the decks. An errant footfall would have crushed one of the blocks, and brought instant death to the crewmember whose essence it contained.

Despite the obstacles before him, however, Captain Kirk had naturally been unwilling to stand by and allow his ship to be taken from him.

"It was Captain Kirk who was the real motivator," he said. "Of course, he practically had to knock their leader through a bulkhead before he convinced the man that the Federation would rather welcome them than battle them."

Laughing, al-Khaled nodded. "Rojan told me the whole story over dinner last night. An inauspicious first contact to be sure, but one that could ultimately provide many positive ramifications for the Federation. They have been most generous in sharing their scientific and engineering knowledge, which as you may remember was very advanced in many areas, especially with regard to engine design."

"Aye, that's a fact," Scott replied. "I dinna know how they did it, but they rigged up the *Enterprise* to fly at a speed I've seen bested only once."

The turbolift slowed to a halt and the doors opened again. Here, on the *Chandley*'s engineering deck, the evidence of the ship's new status was even more apparent, though this time it was because of what was present rather than what might be missing. The corridor was littered with all manner of equipment, some of it undoubtedly Kelvan in origin and unfamiliar to Scott.

"You haven't seen anything yet, my friend," al-Khaled said as they proceeded down the passageway. "I've been here long enough to dig into what the Kelvans are going to show the Federation tomorrow. In a word, it's staggering."

Scott's brow furrowed. "What?"

"They may very well let the genie out of the bottle."

What did that mean? Scott knew from subspace correspondence with his friend that al-Khaled had been dispatched by Starfleet to report on the progress of the engine design project initiated by the Kelvans several years ago. What had he found here? Was Kelvan propulsion technology even more advanced than Scott had believed based on his previous encounter with the aliens?

He did not have time to ask any more questions before they arrived at the main engineering section. A glance around the room revealed a host of technicians, of whom almost none were dressed in any kind of Starfleet uniform. That made sense, of course, as most of the people currently aboard the ship were Kelvans. He had read in al-Khaled's last message that only thirty-six Kelvans lived on the planet below, most of those having been discovered nearly seven years ago marooned on a small planetoid several light-years from here. The castaways turned out to be from the same ship as the Kelvans encountered by the *Enterprise* crew, and after their rescue they had been brought here to join their ship-mates.

*No doubt they're anxious to find more of their people,* Scott thought before his eyes locked on the grouping of silver cylinders standing silently in the center of the engineering room.

"Will ye just look at that," he said as he regarded the odd object occupying the space where the matter/antimatter reaction chamber would normally have been situated. Appraising the construct, Scott realized it was not unfamiliar. After all, he had seen something very similar once before: the energy projector that Rojan and his group had installed aboard the *Enterprise.*

But this, Scott could plainly see, was something altogether different.

"Ah, yes," al-Khaled said as they crossed the floor to the unusual equipment, "the Kelvan version of an intermix chamber. I personally cannot wait to see this beauty in action."

Venturing forward to more closely inspect the device, Scott reached out to touch it and was a bit taken aback at the cool sensations on his fingertips. He could also feel the pulse of power from within its chambers. "Is this supposed to be the bottle yer genie is hidin' in, lad?"

A voice behind him said, "If you are asking whether or not this is the central component of our engine design, you are correct, Commander."

Scott was surprised to realize that he recognized the voice, although it had been many years since last hearing it. He turned to see a tall, black-haired man dressed in a utilitarian jumpsuit. His complexion was not pallid as Scott remembered it, his skin instead sporting a healthy tan no doubt cultivated beneath the warm rays of the New Kelvan sun.

"I believe you know Tomar," al-Khaled said to Scott. "From what I understand, you two are old drinking buddies."

Unable to stifle the laugh his friend's deadpan comment had provoked, Scott merely shook his head. It had been years since he had last thought about his unorthodox strategy to aid in overpowering the Kelvans who had taken over the *Enterprise*. He had managed to incapacitate Tomar, but it had taken several hours and nearly the entire contents of his liquor cabinet.

"Aye, I remember," he said as he extended his hand in greeting. "I certainly hope that you haven't held a grudge against me all these years."

Smiling slightly as he shook Scott's hand, Tomar nodded formally. "Neither I nor any of my people carry ill will toward you or your shipmates, Commander. I am grateful that you have chosen to join us for our tests, as your invitation was extended at my request."

"Mahmud here tells me that this project has been years in the making," Scott said. "If it's as successful as he says it should be, it'll be quite an achievement for all of ye."

Tomar turned to survey the drive structure. "We are proud of the accomplishments that have come about due to our cooperation with the Federation. As you already know, before we arrived in your galaxy our way was that of the conqueror. While in transit aboard our generational craft, we were taught only how to overpower and rule other worlds. Now, with your help, we are ready to venture out, possibly to unite with our fellow travelers or at least prepare for their ultimate arrival. This is far removed from what might have been."

"That's not to say you didn't have your share of settling-in adjustments," al-Khaled said. Scott recalled that al-Khaled and his ship, the *Lovell*, had been among the Starfleet detachment assigned to New Kelva to help establish the initial colony for Tomar and his companions.

Scott nodded. "As ye said, all of that is behind ye. But now I canna wait to learn more about these engines of yours."

"There is no need to trouble yourself with such details now, Commander."

Scott turned at the new voice and saw a young Andorian standing at al-Khaled's side, wearing a Starfleet uniform with insignia designating her as a lieutenant and an engineer. What Scott noticed most of all, however, was the hint of a smug grin on her soft blue face.

"There will be plenty of time to discuss specifications once we're on our way," she continued. "Before we can do that, however, I need to review some calibration data with Tomar."

Scott felt his jaw go nearly slack as Tomar excused himself and joined the Andorian, both of them stepping away to consult one of the computer monitors lining the bulkhead in this room. He had not been so smartly brushed aside by someone that . . . that young before.

"Well, that was a fine how-do-ye-do."

Al-Khaled leaned toward his friend. "Scotty, meet Lieutenant Talev zh'Thren, one of Starfleet's latest additions to the S.C.E. Though she's assigned to the *Tucker*, she's been on temporary duty here, helping with the *Chandley*'s refit. She knows her way around the computer system overseeing the new engines better than the Kelvans who designed it."

"Aye, but apparently she knows it," Scott replied, not bothering to keep his first impression of the young officer from his friend.

Chuckling at that, al-Khaled said, "I'll admit that she needs to refine her interpersonal skills, but don't let that close your mind to her abilities."

Scott frowned. *We'll have to see what we'll see, I guess.*

Dismissing the haughty young lieutenant for the time being, Scott instead looked about the engineering room. "You know, ye could have told me before that the *Chandley* had been selected for this project."

Al-Khaled exhaled sharply before saying anything. "Well, it has been a long time, and I wasn't sure that you would make the connection."

"That this was J'lenn's ship?" he asked, recalling the young Alpha Centauran whom he had known all too briefly before her tragic death so many years ago, during his first mission with al-Khaled. "She's always been hard to forget, I'm afraid."

One of the few things Scott had learned about J'lenn prior to her death was that a previous assignment had been aboard this very ship, which had been tasked with patrolling the area of space separating the Federation and the Klingon Empire.

"I think of her sometimes, Scotty," al-Khaled said. "She's always been a reminder to me that our work is dangerous. It hurts me any time one of my shipmates dies, but each one makes me think of J'lenn, and then it hurts worse."

"J'lenn was a fine engineer, Mahmud," Scott

said, sensing his friend's pain. It was al-Khaled who had assigned J'lenn to the detail that resulted in her death. "And 'twas your leadership that made that mission a success. Just like this one will be."

Frowning, al-Khaled replied, "I don't know about that. There are several hundred people involved with this project, many of them volunteers, but Rojan is still very much the leader here. He figures that more members of his race are out there, on their way from their home planet, and neither he nor the other Kelvans are content to simply sit and wait for them to arrive. They know that the clock is ticking for their people back home, and that if billions of migrating Kelvans show up without warning, there'll be no room for them. New Kelva can't sustain that many people, so Rojan and the others want to start looking for other suitable planets."

"So why not set up a contingency plan with the Federation?" Scott asked. "There are a legion of researchers and bureaucrats ready to place new settlements on planets of one sort or another."

"Because in spite of everything that's happened since they settled here, they're still Kelvans, Scotty. They want to do this, and they want to do it on their terms."

Gesturing for Scott to follow him, al-Khaled began a slow walking circuit of the engineering room, pausing every so often to inspect a computer display or a control console. Scott regarded his friend quizzically as he worked, shaking his head in mild amusement.

"Speaking of doing things on one's own terms, Mahmud, tell me something. You enjoyed being out on assignment, so why did you settle for a long-term job at Headquarters?"

Before replying, al-Khaled stopped to tap a series of diagnostic commands into one nearby console, nodding in satisfaction at the results the monitor displayed.

"Call it payback," he said. "After we pushed like hell to get the Corps into official standing with Starfleet, things changed. Instead of three old tubs, we had S.C.E. teams assigned to ten active starships, to say nothing of special assignments like this one. For the concept to truly work, it made sense to break up the original three teams in order to spread experienced crewmembers across all of the ships. Not everyone from the *Lovell* left me high and dry, though. Can you believe that O'Halloran and Anderson still want to take orders from me?"

Scott laughed. "Of course I can. What I canna believe, though, is that you're done givin' orders."

"I wouldn't exactly say that."

*Now what does that mean?* Once again Scott was left to consider his friend's cryptic words as al-Khaled completed his inspection tour of the engine room and returned to where Talev and Tomar were still reviewing data on one of the control consoles.

"Lieutenant," he said, "let's have a look at what you've come up with."

As Talev looked up from her computer station, Scott noted the not-quite-suppressed expression of irritation on her face. It seemed to him that the Andorian did not appreciate being interrupted, regardless of who might be doing the interrupting.

"We've identified a few minor fluctuations in the intermix chamber," she said, and Scott could almost hear her jaw tightening as she spoke. "However, at the speeds we're going to approach, these fluctuations are likely to cause no noticeable effect."

Scott chuckled. "Lieutenant, it's the little things that usually get ye into trouble. We had 'minor fluctuations' in the Enterprise's warp engines the first time we took her out after her refit, and we ended up in a wormhole and almost got ourselves killed."

Talev stood silently for a moment, and Scott got the distinct impression that he was being sized up by the younger officer. "Mr. Scott, the Enterprise's intermix formulas are remedial mathematics when compared to the technology we're working with here. We will manage just fine. I would like you to just sit back and enjoy your ride today, and to be prepared for a potential redefinition of warp speed as we understand it."

Neither convinced by nor impressed with the

Andorian's assertions, Scott nevertheless held back voicing his doubts when he saw the cautioning look on al-Khaled's face. For his friend's sake, he attempted a small smile as he regarded Talev zh'Thren.

"Well, in that case, Lieutenant, best of luck to ye. As they say, fortune favors the bold."

Just as he thought he might get away before his desire to throttle the young officer got the best of him, Talev decided to say one more thing.

"This is hardly a matter of luck or fortune, sir. We are here because of attention to research and application of our skill. Confidence, Mr. Scott. That's what they're teaching in the Academy these days."

Al-Khaled must have sensed his rising ire, because Scott quickly felt his friend's hand on his shoulder before he asked, "Do they also teach patronizing behavior toward superior officers, Lieutenant?"

"No, sir," Talev said, stiffening at the rebuke and shaking her head quickly. Pausing for a moment, she finally asked, "Permission to return to my departure preparations, sir?"

Nodding assent, al-Khaled waited until the Andorian was out of earshot before turning his attention back to an almost seething Scott.

"She certainly paid attention to her Academy cockiness course," Scott said.

"Scotty, she's young and full of herself," al-Khaled replied. "For her, this is like being in the locker room before the big game. I'll talk to her about it later, but right now I need her focused on her prelaunch duties."

Shaking his head, Scott sighed in exasperation as he cast a final look about the bustling engineering room. "Why do I get the sudden feeling that this is going to be a very long day?"

# CHAPTER
# 20

Montgomery Scott had always believed that the very atmosphere of a starship's bridge demanded action from its occupants. The constant barrage of sound, the flashing of indicators and switches, the flurry of personnel either at their posts or moving from station to station lent an almost palpable charge to the air.

Therefore, it did not seem right that he would be idly occupying a chair hugging the perimeter of the *Chandley*'s upper bridge deck, crammed out of the way at the edge of the turbolift alcove.

"I feel like I'm sittin' on my hands here, Mahmud," he said as he swiveled to his left, moving his legs from the path of a passing Kelvan engineer. "You know this is killin' me."

Al-Khaled smiled as he proffered the padd that had been resting in his lap. "You want something to do? You can write my report to Starfleet." When Scott shook his head at the offer, al-Khaled shrugged, returning the padd to his lap. "You're supposed to be a guest here, Scotty. Enjoy yourself, and let somebody else worry about the small stuff for once."

"Aye, just a wee shakedown, as ye said." But was it as simple as that? According to al-Khaled, Starfleet was most interested in the results of this test. If the Kelvans truly were on the cusp of some important advance in propulsion technology, such an accomplishment stood to benefit not only the Kelvans, who were now poised to take the next step in their quest for identity within their adopted family, but the Federation as well.

"I guess you could slide over there and eavesdrop," al-Khaled said, indicating the engineering station where Talev and Tomar were consulting the array of display monitors. "We're well enough away from New Kelva by now to engage the drive. I wonder if there's a problem."

"Now you're just goadin' me," Scott said, a smile creasing his features. "I'll stay put, if ye don't mind." He let his eyes wander over the other bridge stations, several of which were unmanned. Still others, such as the weapons control alcove just to the left of the main viewer, had been removed entirely, the gaping holes in the consoles where keypads and monitors had once been were now covered with plastisteel plating. It was yet another stark reminder to Scott that this vessel's days as an active ship in service to Starfleet were behind her.

"They might find something for us to do yet," al-Khaled said. "With only a skeleton crew aboard, anything's possible. I was surprised when Tomar said that only eighteen people would be onboard for this test. That's not even a tenth of this ship's normal complement."

Scott understood his friend's concern. This was not his first run-in with extreme shipboard automation, after all. The mishaps of Richard Daystrom's failed M-5 computer test on the *Enterprise* were still fodder for much debate, especially in the Starfleet engineering community, and had provided lessons that Scott himself would never forget.

He watched as Talev and Tomar stepped down into the bridge's command well and began to speak in quiet tones to the occupant of the captain's chair, Hanar. Scott recognized the dark-haired, slightly built man as another of the Kelvans who had hijacked the *Enterprise*. For that matter, the woman seated at the helm position was also familiar to him. He could not remember her name, but he was sure that she had also been part of that small group who had caused so much trouble for him and his shipmates.

"I'd have thought the Kelvans would have given up their humanoid appearance by now," Scott noted quietly as he watched the aliens at work.

"Interesting, isn't it?" al-Khaled replied. "I've

read Captain—I mean *Admiral* Kirk's report about how the Kelvans had encased themselves in a type of 'shell' in order to appear human and better interact with our technology during their voyage to the Andromeda galaxy on the *Enterprise*. I guess the same mindset is what led them to retain their humanoid appearance even after all these years." He shrugged. "Too bad, really. So far as I know, no one has ever seen any Kelvans in their natural form."

Scott's attention was drawn to Talev as the young Andorian returned to the engineering station, spending several moments examining the information on the console's displays. "Shipboard energy readings are optimal. Everything is in line with our computer simulations. I would say we're ready."

Nodding at the report, Hanar toggled a switch on the arm of the command chair. "This is Hanar. We are preparing to engage the primary drive. All personnel mind your stations and report any anomalies to the bridge immediately."

Apparently realizing that she was being watched, Talev turned in her seat to face Scott and al-Khaled. "Everything is proceeding according to plan, gentlemen. There's nothing to be concerned about."

"But an engineer is always concerned, Lieutenant," Scott replied. "And even if everything does happen as planned, an engineer is still concerned because there's always next time."

To Scott's surprise, Talev seemed to ponder his words rather than arrogantly discard them out of hand as he had expected. If she was going to respond to him, however, her opportunity was lost as Hanar spoke once again, this time to the female Kelvan seated at the helm.

"Drea, lay in the course for Starbase 22." Turning to face the communications station he added, "Jahn, please alert them that we are ready to commence our test." Scott knew that sensors on the starbase would record the *Chandley*'s passage, as well as provide a marker for the distance and speed portions of the test.

Waiting patiently for confirmation that his instructions had been carried out, Hanar calmly relayed his next order. "Engage the drive and accelerate to warp three." The order was as much a formality as anything else. The computer system designed and installed aboard the *Chandley* by the Kelvans would oversee the engines' operation, including monitoring of acceleration and performance once the desired speed was reached. The parameters of the test run had already been programmed by Talev, so Drea's duties in this regard would be limited to simply ordering the computer to carry out its predetermined instructions.

As the command was initiated, Scott sensed a quiver in the soles of his feet and the pit of his stomach. It was a feeling familiar to the engineer, yet tinged with a hint of uncertainty as, in his mind's eye, he saw the warp field created by the *Chandley*'s engines flare into existence. Scott imagined himself being pressed back in his chair as the ship entered subspace, a sensation he knew was wholly artificial thanks to the effectiveness of inertial dampers.

"Warp one," Drea reported, issuing updates as the ship continued to accelerate. Taking his eyes from the main viewer and its almost hypnotic field of streaking stars, Scott noted Tomar studying one of the monitors at the science station and wondered why the Kelvan had not issued any sort of status report since the ship had gone into warp.

Then the hairs on the back of his neck stood up at the precise instant a concerned frown crossed Tomar's features, and a full three seconds before Drea called out in alarm.

"Hanar! We're at warp four and continuing to accelerate!"

Without conscious thought Scott bolted from his chair, noting as he did so that al-Khaled had done the same thing. "What's the problem?" Scott asked.

"The computer doesn't appear to be following the test instructions," Drea replied, her brow furrowed as she hunched over the helm. "And it isn't responding to abort commands."

Talev rose from her chair and moved toward the science station. Scott turned to follow but felt al-Khaled's hand on his arm.

"This is their test, Scotty," al-Khaled said in a quiet voice. "Let them work."

His jaw torqued in growing annoyance, Scott heard Hanar call for Jahn to contact Starbase 22 as Talev and Tomar conferred at their console. He watched Tomar shake his head while Talev raised a hand as if to calm him.

*Now what's that about?*

As if in response, the young Andorian turned to Hanar. "We believe this is an anticipated effect of the new automated oversight system."

"How d'ye figure that?" The question exploded from Scott's mouth before he could do anything to suppress it, and he heard al-Khaled sigh in resignation. Despite that, he continued, "Y'expected the computer to deviate from its programming?"

"Of course not," Talev replied, and for a moment Scott detected a trace of the annoying demeanor the Andorian had displayed at their first meeting. "This is not a deviation." Turning back to Hanar, and effectively disregarding Scott in the process, she added, "The automation protocols are operating perfectly, and the computer is allowing the warp drive to operate at faster speeds because it knows the engines can accommodate the increased demands in a safe manner." She paused to look at the viewscreen and the streaking starfield displayed upon it. "Let it work, Hanar. I promise you that the computer will initiate safety protocols to avoid exceeding tolerance levels."

Much to Scott's dismay, Hanar appeared to consider the proposition. "Drea, what is our current speed?"

The Kelvan's voice quavered only slightly, but Scott noticed it nevertheless. "Warp seven-point-eight and continuing to accelerate."

"Ye dinna think that's approachin' tolerance levels?" Scott asked. "This ship isn't built for this kind of speed."

"Scotty," al-Khaled hissed, but Scott ignored him.

For the first time since the test had begun, Tomar turned from his station. "The ship is perfectly safe, Commander. We have not yet reached even the speed at which your vessel was traveling when we attempted to return to Andromeda."

*Of course, this would make sense,* Scott admitted. The Kelvans had obviously outfitted the *Chandley* with a similar form of reinforcement to the ship's structural integrity system that they had used on the *Enterprise* during their attempt to hijack her. The ship had reached speeds far in excess of its supposed limits, and according to Tomar had not even attained its maximum velocity before the hijacking had been thwarted.

"Commander," Talev said to him, "what you must understand is that this new drive generates a warp field unlike that of our Starfleet ships. In a sense, the field itself provides more protection for the vessel than would result from our current level of Federation technology. This turn of events is precisely what we need to study in our tests!"

*This youngster is startin' to irritate me,* Scott mused, tiring of the Andorian's condescending attitude but electing to say nothing about it for the time being. Once the situation was under control, however, he would have his say.

Swiveling in his seat, Hanar regarded al-Khaled. "Commander, you've not weighed in on this issue. What's your opinion?"

Frowning, al-Khaled studied Talev for a few seconds before responding. Finally, though, he nodded. "It seems that all systems appear to be functioning normally or *as expected.*" Scott caught the hard glare his friend leveled on the young Andorian as he spoke. It eased his discomfort, if only slightly, that al-Khaled appeared to have the same concerns that he did. With that in mind, the engineer in him found he could not disagree with him when al-Khaled finished with, "Since we are on a test mission, I recommend we see where this takes us."

Nodding in approval, Hanar exchanged looks with the rest of the bridge staff before he said, "Very well, then. We shall continue."

Personnel turned to their respective tasks, and Scott only partially listened as Drea continued to report on the *Chandley*'s acceleration. His attention was instead focused on the engineering station where Talev was standing, having resumed her study of the warp drive diagnostic displays.

He could not tell whether she failed to notice his approach or simply chose not to acknowledge it.

*Easy,* he reminded himself. *Let's keep things professional, eh?*

"Lieutenant," he began as he stepped closer, "I don't wanna believe ye knew this would happen, but I'm havin' a hard time of it."

Looking up at Scott, the Andorian smiled slightly in response. "We've known all along that this could be the next big step, that we could be opening the door to transwarp drive."

Transwarp. Of course. Supposedly the next big step in interstellar travel, engineers throughout the Federation had been carrying on about transwarp for years. Starfleet designers were at this very moment developing a prototype transwarp drive, and a whole new class of starship was being created to accommodate the new propulsion system. Scott himself was skeptical about the concept, but had the Kelvans developed the equivalent to transwarp, or even something superior? Was Talev merely consumed with ambition at the idea of being involved in such a staggering achievement? That would go a long way toward explaining her attitude, he decided.

"Ye knew that, did ye? Well, here's something that ye better learn quick," Scott said. "Engineers don't keep secrets. They don't hide tricks up their sleeves for their own amusement, and they don't keep a damn thing from their captains, even if the person playin' captain is a civilian overseein' a test run. This may be a great feather in your cap, but don't be so quick to smile. Ye've got nothin' to be proud of just yet."

Talev's smile faded and her posture stiffened in response to the comment. "And why is that?"

"Because ye've not got us home yet."

Several seconds passed as Scott held the young engineer's gaze. Talev did not flinch from his scrutiny, but he could see that his words had struck some sort of chord in her. That was good, he decided. His gut told him that she was a good officer, intelligent and full of passion. All that was really needed to fully tap her potential was experience, both practical and personal. Time would bring that, he knew, so long as she was receptive to the occasionally harsh lessons that experience would bring. Judging by what he had read in her eyes, he believed that would not be a problem.

A voice cut above the rest of the bridge noise, begging for his attention. It was Drea.

"Hanar, we have accelerated beyond our instruments' ability to measure."

Scott turned from Talev and moved toward the bridge railing as Hanar leaned forward in the center seat. "That's at least warp fifteen." Turning to Tomar he asked, "Engine status?"

Consulting the science displays, Tomar replied, "Engines are operating within tolerance levels, Hanar."

"What's our current position?" al-Khaled

asked as he stepped down into the command well.

Drea tapped a series of controls on her console. "We are traversing Sector 68H now." Scott frowned at the reference. So far as he knew, this sector of space had been charted but never explored. Life was believed to exist here but nothing substantial had ever been detected with the probes sent into this region.

"I think we should rein her in, Hanar," Scott said. "I dinna like the idea of stampedin' into an unknown region of space."

"Agreed," Hanar replied. "Drea, bring us to a full stop."

Several seconds passed as the Kelvan attempted to do just that. "The helm is not responding."

Hanar turned to Talev. "Lieutenant?"

Moving to the science station, the Andorian engineer's fingers were nearly a blur as she entered several strings of commands. Scott's apprehension grew as he watched her pause before repeating the sequence. Shaking her head, she turned back to Hanar. "The automation protocols refuse to abort the test."

A familiar knot tightened in Scott's gut, just like the one he had felt years ago when it had become apparent that Richard Daystrom's M-5 computer had seized control of his beloved *Enterprise* and refused to let go. "Where's the override?"

To her credit, Talev was obviously thinking in

that direction herself as she thumbed the inter-com switch on her console. "Engineering, this is zh'Thren. The computer won't let us slow the ship down. Initiate emergency override."

*"Stand by, Lieutenant,"* a disembodied voice answered. A few moments later, however, the voice returned with the words that Scott had dreaded but still expected. *"Overrides are not responsive."*

"What?" Talev exclaimed, clearly startled by the report. "That's impossible."

Exchanging looks with al-Khaled, Scott felt his pulse beginning to quicken. "Apparently not, Lieutenant," he said, hating the way the words sounded as he spoke them.

*This is no time for "I told you so."*

"If we can't override it," al-Khaled said as he moved to stand next to Scott, "then we have to deactivate it altogether."

Hanar nodded at the assessment. To Talev he said, "Go to engineering and see to it, please." He indicated Scott and al-Khaled. "I'm sure the com-manders would be most helpful, as well."

Though he bristled at the thought of being directed by the cocksure young engineer, Scott decided it would be best to bury such feelings belowdecks for the moment. "We'll have ye fixed in no time."

Scott let his head hang over the circuitry panel exposed before him as he brought a hand laser to bear over a small relay grid. What he and al-Khaled were about to try was a last resort after nearly fifteen minutes of attempting to reprogram the Kelvan computer system by conventional means and another twenty minutes of trying to understand the vast network of circuitry that formed the backbone of the new computer.

"A few shocks to the system should get us the hard reboot ye're lookin' for here," he said to Talev as he steadied the laser in two hands. "One or two jolts and we should have control back in no time."

Talev moved closer to get a better look at the junction that Scott had selected as the focus of his efforts. "I am trying to protect the integrity of this system, Commander," she said with no small amount of alarm in her voice. "Disabling it in this manner may compromise its ability to perform once we have regained command of the warp drive."

At the moment Scott only cared about arresting the *Chandley*'s headlong flight through space. Data gathered by the engines' automated oversight system indicated that its speed had peaked, though there was no way to be certain what that velocity might be. For all anyone knew, they could be traveling at warp twenty or better. With that sense of urgency propelling them, he and al-Khaled had practically taken over main engineering in the process of conducting their repair efforts.

"There's enough of us onboard to get the ship home on our own," Scott said as he used his thumb to tune the laser's beam width before firing. "And most of us are engineers, to boot. We're miracle workers, don't ye know." Calling out in a louder voice, he said, "Mahmud, I'm ready to try this if you are."

From the master control console in the rear of the engineering compartment, al-Khaled answered, "Standing by."

Taking one last look at the circuit junction he had selected, Scott fired the laser. The effect was immediate as he heard the Kelvan computer unit stutter momentarily before resuming its otherwise constant hum. He thought he also detected a telltale flicker in the room's lighting as the massive processor reset itself.

"Aye, that's got it," he said, nodding to himself. His suspicion was confirmed a second later as al-Khaled called out from the master console.

"Warp drive protocols have been released." Tapping a series of commands to the console he added, "Disengaging warp drive now."

In response to al-Khaled's instructions, the engines of the *Chandley* almost immediately changed as their former high-pitched whine began to deepen and lower in volume. Scott felt himself pulled to one side as the ship's inertial dampers struggled with the abrupt deceleration.

*That's a clue all by itself as to how much power those beasties must have been puttin' out.*

Several moments passed as the engines continued to power down. While al-Khaled was monitoring the engine status, Talev was busying herself with a hasty diagnostic of the Kelvan computer system.

"It appears that the remaining protocols for the drive are intact. Very nice work, Mr. Scott. Thank you for taking such care."

"So now what?" al-Khaled asked. "Do we make the necessary adjustments to the computer and set a course for home, or do we want to spring back into warp just long enough so we know we still can do it?"

Scott's reply was cut off by Hanar's voice over the ship's intercom system. "We have come to a full stop. Excellent work. However, it appears that we may have another problem. A vessel has entered sensor range."

"That didn't take long," al-Khaled said.

"It seems to have detected our passage through this region," Hanar continued, "and began following us as we decelerated. They are closing fast, and our sensors indicate that its weapons systems are armed."

# CHAPTER
# 21

As he regarded the image of the approaching alien spacecraft displayed on the main bridge viewer, Scott could not suppress an appreciative feeling for the ship's design. Unlike those of the Federation or other races that he had encountered in his travels, this vessel was flat and narrow, trading width and height for length. He saw no nacelles or any other structures indicating faster-than-light propulsion that he was familiar with, even though the craft had to be equipped with such technology for it to have intercepted the *Chandley* so quickly. The ship's dark metallic exterior was difficult to make out against the starfield even with the assistance of the viewer's computerized resolution. Scott saw no external illumination of any kind. To the naked eye the ship could almost certainly be missed if one did not know to look for it.

"That is one mean-looking ship," al-Khaled

said from the science station as he consulted the sensor displays. "Weapons are similar to disruptor cannons we've seen on the newer Klingon cruisers, and their shield generators are more powerful than anything on our ships. Their engines are matter/antimatter, but they're using something other than dilithium to regulate the reaction. I can't even tell you what the mineral is." Shaking his head, he added, "I'd love to take a walk around that engine room."

Standing next to his friend, Scott asked, "How soon will she be here?"

"Five minutes, twenty seconds."

Seated in the command chair, Hanar swiveled around to face the communications station. "Jahn? Any progress?"

"We are continuing to broadcast universal greetings on all frequencies. They've responded, but the translator is still deciphering their message."

Jahn toggled a switch and Scott winced at the cacophony of guttural noise that erupted from the intercom, a mishmash of barking animals and belching drunkards that drowned out the ambient noise on the bridge.

"They dinna sound very happy, do they?" Scott asked. The voice in the message, alien as it was to his ears, did indeed sound agitated. If the approaching craft was a threat, the *Chandley* was in no condition to defend itself. Without the weapons and deflector shield generators that had been removed following its decommission, the frigate would have no chance if the current situation turned hostile.

"The translator is making some progress," Jahn reported. Scott noted the Kelvan's narrowed eyes as Jahn listened to the information being relayed from the computer via the Feinberg receiver he held to his right ear. "It's just bits and pieces, but I think I can grasp the basic meaning of their message."

"Well?" al-Khaled prompted when several seconds elapsed without Jahn elaborating further.

"They're saying, 'Go away.'"

Despite the rising tension on the bridge, Scott could not help a small laugh at the report. "Ye canna put a thing past these universal translators nowadays."

From where she sat at the engineering station, Talev said, "If they want us to leave, then they'll almost certainly be upset when they arrive and we're still here."

It was a simple yet accurate observation, Scott conceded. Even though the *Chandley* had been broadcasting a standard greeting stating their affiliation with the Federation and their peaceful intentions, it was probable that the unknown aliens were suffering from the same lack of understanding toward a new language as the *Chandley*'s crew was.

"Let's just tell them what happened. Let them know that we're here by accident." Scott shrugged. "It certainly canna hurt."

Hanar rose from the center seat and turned to face Scott, a solemn expression on his face. "Commander, as this is a Kelvan mission, perhaps I should be the one to speak on our behalf."

"This might be a touchy situation, Hanar," al-Khaled said as he stepped to the bridge railing from the science station. "Have you ever conducted a first contact meeting with another race?"

Hanar nodded. "A few times, yes, though the circumstances were somewhat different." He cast a wry look at Scott. "Normally we were the aggressors." Turning back to the main viewer, he indicated for Jahn to open a hailing frequency.

"Greetings, fellow space travelers. I am Hanar, and I speak to you on behalf of the United Fed—"

An intense howling screech exploded from the intercom system, drowning out Hanar's greeting and every other sound on the bridge. Scott covered his ears with his hands in a vain attempt to block the jarring noise even as Jahn scrambled to reduce the volume. The shriek ended abruptly before he could do so, however, this time replaced with a translated voice that sounded very similar to the original guttural sounds they had heard earlier.

"... *addition to your flagrant intrusion into the sovereign territory of the Lutralian Hegemony, you have now compounded your insult by brazenly forcing visual communication upon us without our permission. These are not the actions of strangers seeking our friendship."*

"Cut the link!" Scott called out as the agitated alien speaker continued. Jahn immediately complied and the transmission ended, leaving only the normal background sounds of the bridge.

"I don't think that went very well," Talev said.

As if in response, the entire ship shuddered around them and the deck lurched violently beneath their feet. Alarm klaxons sounded as everyone on the bridge flailed for something to hold on to, and Scott barely managed to avoid being thrown to the deck as he grabbed for the bridge railing. From the corner of his eye he saw Talev fall from her chair as al-Khaled was tossed into a bulkhead. Though Drea was able to keep her seat at the helm, Hanar was thrown forward into the navigation console.

"Hang on!" Scott called out as, on the viewscreen, he saw the forward edge of the Lutralian craft flare crimson red and a pair of writhing energy bolts leap forward, crossing the space between the attacking vessel and the *Chandley.*

The ship groaned in protest under the force of the second assault but the bridge crew was better prepared this time, each of them able to maintain their grip on a console or chair to avoid being thrown about again. Instrumentation did not fare so well this time, though. The environmental control station, obviously the victim of an overload, exploded in a shower of sparks and shrapnel. Even as fire suppression systems activated, Scott gave silent thanks that the station hadn't been staffed. Anyone sitting at the console would surely have been injured, if not killed.

As the effects of the attack faded, al-Khaled dropped down into the command well to make sure that Hanar had not been injured before turning to Jahn at communications. "Get me a damage report, all stations."

Pulling himself upright, Scott looked to the viewscreen to see the alien vessel simply holding station, a dark spot amid the dim stars. Why had they not fired again? Why had they fired in the first place? Was the Lutralian ship without sensor technology and therefore unable to see that the *Chandley* was a defenseless target?

Scott hated tactical situations that were dictated by the whim of emotion rather than any of the measurable qualities in the realm of an engineer's influence. He understood command decisions influenced by a vessel's firepower, maneuverability, speed, or endurance, and he felt comfortable giving orders or carrying them out based on that understanding. Now, however, he and his companions were faced with predicting the actions and motives of a race of beings unknown to them, and to the Federation, mere minutes ago.

"Report from engineering," Jahn called out from the communications station. "We have hull breaches on several decks, but they're in unoccupied sections of the ship and those areas have been sealed off." Pausing for a moment to listen further he added, "Main life support is down but backups are functioning."

Listening to the reports, Scott continued to regard the Lutralian ship. What was its commander thinking? Was it sizing up the *Chandley* at this moment, determining the best avenue for a lethal final assault?

"Okay," al-Khaled said, "now for the big question: How are the engines?"

At the engineering station Tomar and Talev spent several seconds consulting the bank of monitors, all of which now displayed diagnostic information. "The engines themselves are fine," Talev reported, "but internal sensors are detecting a fluctuation in plasma levels."

Scott and al-Khaled crossed the bridge as Tomar tapped commands to his console. "We are venting plasma from our port nacelle," he said as the two veteran engineers moved to stand beside him. "A manifold has apparently sustained damage from the attack."

"If we don't close that off," al-Khaled said as he reviewed the computer graphic, "we'll lose all our plasma within two hours." Scott did not need his friend to complete the report. Without warp plasma, the engines would be all but useless, effectively stranding the *Chandley* and her crew here, in the sights of an alien ship's weapons.

Scott said, "Aye, somebody has to go outside and patch the rupture." He nodded in the direction of the viewer. "Of course, if our friends start shootin' again, it really won't matter." Without the means to defend itself, the *Chandley* could not withstand much more punishment at the hands of the Lutralians.

"They are hailing us," Jahn said, turning to face the group hovering near the engineering station.

"Are they asking for our surrender?" Talev asked.

Holding the Feinberg device to his ear, Jahn frowned in response to the message he was receiving. "There is no mention of that. They are, however, demanding visual communications be established."

"This should be interesting," al-Khaled said. "I suppose it's too late to pretend we're not home."

Scott cast a sardonic look at his friend before placing a hand on Hanar's shoulder. "Perhaps ye should let me take it this time, lad." The Kelvan agreed and Scott indicated for Jahn to open the channel.

On the main viewer the image of the Lutralian ship was replaced with that of a humanoid figure sitting ramrod straight in what looked to be a throne. Large and muscled, the alien had teal-colored skin that contrasted sharply with the highly polished, silver-colored armor chest plate it wore. Its head was devoid of hair and Scott could see what looked to be a large scar along the left side of its skull, and its eyes were two black pools set above a narrow nose and a mouth filled with even rows of sharp gleaming teeth. From the image on the screen it appeared as though the Lutralian was looking down at them, a sensation that put Scott immediately on edge. This was someone who was used to being perceived as an authority figure, he decided.

"*I am Nrech'lah, commander of the Lutralian warship* Durgejiin," the Lutralian said, its tone clipped and formal and confirming Scott's gut feeling.

"My name is Montgomery Scott, and I speak for this vessel. On behalf of my crew, I would like to thank ye for grantin' an audience with us."

Waving the attempted greeting away, Nrech'lah said, "*We have fired upon your vessel, and yet you are not roused to retaliation. You squandered an opportunity to strike. Why?*"

"It is not our way to declare those we do not know as enemies," Scott replied. "We came here by accident, having experienced technical malfunctions with our ship's drive systems. I respectfully request that we be allowed to make our repairs, and then we will leave your space in peace." He hoped the words were more convincing to Nrech'lah than they were to him, as he was certainly no diplomat. *Where's a poppinjay Federation ambassador when ye need one?*

On the screen, Nrech'lah's expression revealed

nothing. *"Interesting. You shirk the opportunity to engage us in combat. Are you unwilling or unable? I suspect the latter."*

Listening to the Lutralian captain, Scott thought his demeanor to be similar to that of Romulan ship commanders he had encountered over the years. Calm and composed, Nrech'lah affected an air of being in complete control, which of course was not far from the truth. Even without sophisticated sensor technology, it would not take long for him to figure out that the *Chandley* was incapable of mounting any kind of defense. The only decision Nrech'lah would have at that point would be whether or not to exploit his advantage. That he had not done so by now gave Scott a glimmer of hope that this situation could still be resolved peacefully.

"You are correct, Captain," he said. "Our ship possesses no weapons. To be truthful, we were testing a new engine design when we lost control. It brought us here, quite unintentionally, I assure you."

Nrech'lah appeared to consider this for several seconds before he nodded slowly. The smile on his face was anything but warm and welcoming, though.

*"Your candor is most reassuring, alien. As a gesture of goodwill, I will allow you a small amount of time to effect your repairs."*

Smiling himself, first at his companions and then at Nrech'lah, Scott nodded enthusiastically.

"That is most kind, Captain. Of course, we are in somewhat of a bind due to a shortage of personnel. We would certainly welcome any assistance you might lend to—"

A low menacing laugh echoed from the bridge's intercom as the Lutralian captain slowly shook his head. *"Are you attempting to insult us again?"*

*Careful, Scotty, don't blow it.*

"Not at all, sir," he replied, talking quickly to recover from his apparent misstep. "I merely thought you would like to help in the spirit of respect and friendship."

Again came the sinister laugh. *"We do not respect that which we can so easily brush aside, alien. This is not an issue of respect, at least, not yet. Attend to your repairs, but if you do not complete them in a timely manner, it will no longer be an issue. I trust you understand our position."*

With that Nrech'lah terminated the transmission, leaving only the image of the dark, silent Lutralian ship on the main viewer once more.

"I think I could have handled that a wee bit better," Scott said as he turned to his companions. These Lutralians, he decided, appeared to be even more hung up on protocol and the trappings of authority than Romulans or even Tholians, another race with which he had had some experience. He would have liked to spend more time figuring out why Nrech'lah appeared to view the *Chandley* and her crew with such disdain, but he had to remember that at present there were more critical priorities to worry about.

"The first order of business is repairin' that ruptured manifold," Scott said as he regarded the bridge personnel.

"Already on it," al-Khaled said from the engineering station. "I've got people assembling the gear we'll need. You and I are the best qualified to go outside, but one of us should stay here to coordinate the repair efforts if we're going to finish in anything resembling a short time. I have more hours in zero-g repair work than you do, so I should be the one to go."

Scott hated for al-Khaled to be right about this, but the fact was that with his years of service with the *Lovell* and the S.C.E., his friend had logged many more hours wearing an environmental suit. That decision, at least, was simple to make.

"Aye, when you're right, you're right. You need to take someone along with you as a backup, though."

"Don't worry, I have just the perfect volunteer for this job," al-Khaled replied, and Scott followed his gaze to the science station where Talev sat. So engrossed was the young Andorian in studying the rapid fire of information constantly being updated on the monitors that it took several seconds for her to realize that eyes were on her.

And why.

"Sir?" she asked, her expression one of shock and her tone possessing none of its former confidence.

*Well,* Scott thought, *at least I lived long enough to see that.*

*Left foot down. Right foot up. Right foot down. Left foot up . . .*

Talev kept pace silently as she made her way along the exterior of the *Chandley*'s port warp nacelle, peeling and lifting her magnetic-soled boots from the hull as she and Commander al-Khaled maneuvered toward the ship's leaking nacelle. Between them they carried a section of plating that, once secured over the hull rupture, would be large enough to contain the plasma leak.

She listened to the echoes of her own breathing in the bulbous helmet of her environmental suit. That she and al-Khaled were wearing an older model of suit, which had been retired from active service several years ago and apparently after the *Chandley*'s decommissioning, only added to her dismay at coming outside in the first place. The suits did not possess maneuvering thrusters, forcing the two engineers to be dependent on magnetic boots to grip the hull and safety tethers feeding out from the open hatchway at the base of the nacelle's support strut.

Though she did not suffer from claustrophobia or vertigo, as was the case with some people when they donned an environmental suit, Talev had never relished the idea of working outside a starship. She had dreaded the training classes at the Academy, always wishing for them to end as quickly as possible. Her assignments postgraduation had never called for her to work in such conditions, and she had gotten used to the idea that the chances of her being called to do so were minimal at best.

*And yet, here I am. Wonderful.*

They walked in silence for the most part, crossing the distance to the hull rupture where she could see the swirling cloud of gas leaking from the breach. It would be dangerous working near the released plasma, even with the low-level welding torch that al-Khaled had brought along for the task. She had disagreed with his and Scott's decision not to stop the plasma flow while they worked on the damaged nacelle, but she understood the reasoning: Doing so would have resulted in the shutdown of the warp drive, which would then require a cold restart. That would take at least another thirty minutes to accomplish, time they could not be sure the Lutralians would grant them. With that in mind, she and al-Khaled were faced with working in close proximity to the dangerous plasma as it vented freely from the damaged hull.

*"How are you doing, Lieutenant?"* al-Khaled asked through their commlink.

She nodded in reply before remembering that the commander could not see that. "I have been better, if you must know."

Al-Khaled laughed. *"A sense of humor. I love it. This really isn't that hard once you get a rhythm down, Lieutenant. Just shuffle along and don't hurry. You're doing fine."* Another few moments passed as they came upon the repair site, with al-Khaled directing where to step and how to angle the hull plate.

As they maneuvered the plate into the proper position, al-Khaled said, *"You know, this reminds me of why I got into the S.C.E. in the first place."*

Talev tried to take her mind off her apprehension as she stutter-stepped past al-Khaled and moved to where he wanted her to stand. Kneeling down and placing her hands on the hull plate, she asked, "The Corps of Engineers was not your first assignment?"

*"Not on your life,"* he replied. Between the two of them, it was simple work to move the replacement plate over the plasma leak. Taking a moment to judge their progress he said, *"This may look quick and dirty on the outside, but it'll do the job well enough."*

She watched as al-Khaled drew the welding laser he had brought with him and adjusted the tool's power setting before aiming it at one edge of the plate. An intense orange beam of energy lanced from the welder, beginning the process of joining the two hull sections. He had obviously done this many times before, she decided, as he made quick work, and Talev found herself caught up in watching wisps of plasma escape through the crack between the plate and the hull just before the phaser welded the seam closed.

*"My first assignment was at Starbase 2,"* al-Khaled said as he continued to work. *"I worked on everything imaginable there: ground craft, sub-orbital ships, even passing starships. It all came pretty quick to me, and at a starbase you learn to be resourceful. You don't think this is the first time I've used an all-purpose deckplate for an emergency repair, do you?"*

He talked as if the two of them were lounging in the mess hall rather than kneeling exposed on the surface of a starship hull. How did he do that? The answer was obvious, of course: because his experience gave him confidence. Talev had to admit that listening to his voice eased her own tension somewhat and she suspected that it was deliberate on al-Khaled's part. At any other time she might find such an attempt offensive and condescending, but not now. If it helped them to complete their task and get back inside the ship, then she welcomed the effort with open arms.

She shifted her position as al-Khaled moved in her direction with the welder. As she did so, she felt a vibration beneath her feet. Al-Khaled must have noticed it, too, because he deactivated the welder and turned to look at her.

*"Did you feel that?"*

Nodding, she looked down at the hull and saw tendrils of plasma seep from the weld line that al-Khaled had just created. How was that possible?

*"Mahmud,"* Scott's voice suddenly called out over the open communicator channel, *"we're registering spikes in the plasma flow. I'm shutting it down, but there's still a lot of released plasma. Be careful out—"*

The hull plate bucked upward sharply as vents of ignited plasma erupted from beneath it. Only partially secured to the nacelle's metallic exterior, the plate was wrenched away from the hull by the force of the explosion. Talev had but a heartbeat to throw her arms up in defense as the plate struck her. Then she was tumbling head over heels, and she realized she had been knocked free of the ship!

*"Talev!"* al-Khaled's voice rang in her helmet as she instinctively grabbed for her tether. Using both hands to pull on it as she twisted about in open space, Talev yanked but felt none of the resistance she had expected.

Her eyes followed the length of the tether to its abrupt end, where scorched metallic fibers bore mute testimony to where the intensely hot plasma had sliced through the line.

*"Commander!"*

# CHAPTER
## 22

As Talev zh'Thren fell away, al-Khaled exercised the only option open to him.

He jumped.

Arms stretched outward, al-Khaled kicked off from the *Chandley*'s hull, arcing away from the ship and into free space.

*"Commander!"* Talev called out again, her arms and legs thrashing about as she drifted farther from the ship. She was reaching out for anything that might arrest her motion, but of course there was nothing.

*"Hang on, Talev,"* al-Khaled said, speaking in as calm a voice as he could muster, all the while cursing whoever had dismantled the *Chandley*'s transporter. *"I'm coming."*

Drifting after her in the void, al-Khaled was helpless to do anything but listen to the echoes of his own breathing. His pulse raced and pounded in his ears as the distance between them shrank too damned slowly.

*"Mahmud,"* Scott's voice sounded in his helmet, *"what's wrong?"*

Not answering, al-Khaled's attention was instead focused on Talev, who was now close, so very close. Reaching out, al-Khaled's gloved fingers brushed against the side of the Andorian's boot. He missed the grab, the action serving to twist her body away from his hand, her body turning cartwheels in the vacuum. Her arm was swinging around, though, and al-Khaled angled to reach for it.

And then his tether line went taut.

"No!" he cried as his hand closed around nothing and he felt his body pulled back toward the ship. The gap between him and Talev, which had been mere millimeters an instant ago, started to widen again.

As her body turned about and the visor of her helmet became visible, Talev's expression was one of panic. *"Commander!"* She reached vainly in the direction of al-Khaled even as she continued to drift farther away from the *Chandley*. Al-Khaled flailed his arms in a desperate attempt to grab on to her, knowing even as he did so that the attempt was fruitless.

Then he saw movement in the corner of his eye.

Drifting past him was the remainder of Talev's tether, still attached to her environmental suit.

The severed safety line was arcing and twisting in response to the lieutenant's frantic motions, and now it was almost within al-Khaled's reach. But could he grab on to it?

*"Mahmud,"* Scott's voice repeated in his helmet, *"what the devil is goin' on out there?"*

*"I'm a little busy at the moment, Scotty,"* al-Khaled replied through clenched teeth. *"Stand by."*

He grabbed on to his own tether and, using it for the tenuous amount of leverage it possessed, al-Khaled twisted his body around and reached out one last time with his free hand. The material of Talev's safety line slid across his gloved fingers and he tightened his grip. His body curled around as the Andorian's momentum was transferred to him, and then he felt his own movement arrest as his own tether went taut once more. When he was jerked in the direction of the *Chandley* this time, however, it was with Talev's line still in his grip and the lieutenant now drifting along with him back toward the ship.

"Gotcha," he called out in triumph. *Easy there,* he cautioned himself. *You're not home free yet.*

As they drew nearer to the hull, he used his hold on his tether to bring himself around and plant his feet on the metal plating, letting the magnetic sensors in his boots secure him to the ship once again. Seconds later Talev was beside him, anchoring herself to the hull as well.

*"I can't take you anywhere, can I?"* al-Khaled

asked, breathing hard from the brief but intense exertion.

Shaking her head, Talev frowned behind her faceplate. *"I guess not. Thanks for coming after me."*

*"Save it until you get my bill,"* al-Khaled responded as he rechecked his boots' grip on the hull. He was sure he had detected a note of humility in the young Andorian's voice, a quality that had been notably absent in his previous dealings with her. *Interesting,* he thought.

Then Scott's exasperated voice was sounding in his helmet once more. *"Mahmud, so help me, if ye dinna answer I'm comin' out there and throttlin' the both of ye."*

As they began to make their way across the hull back to where the damaged manifold awaited the rest of their repairs, al-Khaled replied, *"Oh,* now *you offer to come outside and help. Your timing is impeccable as always, Commander."* Surveying the new damage to the ship's exterior from the plasma eruption he added, *"Bring me another hull plate while you're at it."*

*"He will probably want to kill you once we get back inside,"* Talev said.

Al-Khaled nodded. *"Probably. In that case, let's finish our work here. I do not want to die in vain, after all."*

Though the idea of killing al-Khaled did cross his mind, Scott decided that it would be best if he waited until they got home first.

"Repairs are spot on, Mahmud," he said as he studied a status display at the engineering station on the *Chandley*'s bridge. The decision not to shut down the plasma flow had been dangerous, even given their current situation, and they had nearly lost Talev because of it. For that he was furious with himself. *Sloppy engineers make dead engineers,* he reminded himself.

"Plasma levels are lower than I'd like, but they're holding steady. All we have to do now is bring those engines back online and let the computer run its start-up diagnostics. Once that's done, if we dinna give her too many bumps along the way, the old girl should get us home without too much trouble."

At the science station, Tomar turned in his seat, a frown creasing his features. "We may have another problem, Mr. Scott." As the trio of Starfleet engineers moved to join him, the Kelvan motioned for them to observe one of the monitors on the bulkhead above him. "The computer's diagnostics are reporting that the warp drive cannot be brought back online."

"What?" al-Khaled asked as he studied the display. "Is there something else wrong? Some other damage that we missed?"

Shaking his head, Tomar indicated a graphic in the computer screen's lower left corner. "We installed computer software that is dedicated to monitoring the warp drive systems. It uses a series of overlapping protocols that continuously recalibrate engine performance. Some of the adjustments it makes are so minute that most living beings can't even detect the change. The recalibrations are made much faster than flesh-and-blood engineers could accomplish them, as well."

Scott held up a hand. "Ye covered all of this at the briefing, Tomar, but what does that have to do with anything right now?"

From behind him, Talev replied, "Commander, what I believe Tomar is trying to say is that the computer will not allow the warp drive to be enabled because it views doing so with our drastically reduced plasma levels to be an inefficient if not outright unsafe operating condition."

Rolling his eyes, Scott forced himself to maintain his composure. Why was this so difficult? "So bypass the bloody thing."

"I wish it were that simple, my friend," Tomar replied, his expression almost one of embarrassment. "We designed the computer software to regulate the engines as close to standard technical specifications as possible, in order to ensure the best possible performance with the least required amount of interaction with our engineering staff. It was hoped that being able to rely on computers for such tasks would allow us to set out into space with smaller crews. We would then be able to distribute the limited number of experienced space travelers of our people more efficiently among our ships."

It was a laudable goal, Scott agreed. The Kelvans had always shown themselves to be self-reliant almost to a fault, dating back to the first time the *Enterprise* crew had encountered them. Naturally they would want to launch their new program of exploration with as little outside help as possible. Talev and the other Starfleet engineers temporarily assigned to New Kelva had been tolerated, to be sure, but only because of the opportunity to learn about Kelvan engineering techniques that had been part of the deal struck by Starfleet for the use of their ships.

Using automation to free up their limited number of personnel was a natural step to take. Though the duotronic computer components originally installed in the *Chandley* and other Federation starships were not ideally suited to complete automation, the Kelvans' expertise in software development rivaled their own engineering expertise. This, as much as the engine design that had been created and installed aboard the *Chandley*, had also piqued Starfleet's interest.

"It appears that we did our job too well," Tomar said. "The computer will not allow the engines to be brought online in their present state, I'm afraid."

Moving closer to the science station, Scott tapped a control on the console. "Computer, display a schematic of the automated warp drive oversight systems on Science Monitor 1."

*"Working,"* replied the stilted, feminine voice of the ship's computer. Several seconds passed before the image on the science station's leftmost viewscreen shifted to show the information Scott had ordered.

"What are you thinking?" al-Khaled asked.

Pointing to the monitor, Scott replied, "There has to be a way to bypass this thing. I'm not about to believe that we're beholden to a collection of circuits and computer programs. We'll find a way to trick this beastie, lad."

"You can't trick a computer, sir," Talev said.

Scott snorted. "Sure ye can. Talkin' a computer into doin' something it doesn't want to do is an art form, I'll give ye that much. But it can be done." Smiling at the Andorian, he added, "If ye dinna believe me, ye can just ask Admiral Kirk the next time ye see him."

"You mean if we see him," Talev said. Seeing the scowl her remark evoked from Scott, she quickly continued. "The software can be reprogrammed, yes, but we are talking about millions of lines of code."

"So why not simply craft a workaround?" Scott asked. "Surely ye can do that?"

Thinking about that a bit, Talev replied, "Perhaps, though it may take some time."

Nodding in the direction of the bridge's main viewer, al-Khaled said, "I wonder what our friends over there will think of that."

It was a valid question, Scott conceded. The

Lutralians had been patient to this point, allowing the *Chandley* crew to perform their repairs unobstructed. But Scott knew that their patience would not hold out forever. They had already expressed disdain over requests for their assistance, and there was no way to anticipate how a call for more time would be received.

What Scott also had to concede, though, was that he and his companions had no choice. If they were going to get home, then they would need more time to finish their work.

He shook his head, temporarily dismissing the concerns. "We'll cross that bridge when we come to it." He pointed to Talev. "Come, lassie. Let's see about convincin' this computer to do things our way."

Much to Scott's pleasant surprise, Talev's expertise as a computer specialist proved more than equal to the challenge of circumventing the warp drive oversight system.

"Fourteen minutes, twenty-six seconds," he said as he consulted a chronometer at the science station. "A very nice piece of work, Lieutenant. Very nice indeed." Though he himself was no expert in computer programming, Scott had spent enough time with such specialists in his career to appreciate their skill.

Like engineers of other disciplines, the best software developers understood the rules relating to their chosen field of endeavor, and by extension knew where those same rules could be bent, broken, or just plain ignored. Talev zh'Thren was obviously of this mold, Scott decided. Forgoing the verbal command set commonly used to interact with the computer, the Andorian had set to work in the customary manner of most programmers, working directly with the science station's primary interface console. Scott had been hard-pressed to keep up as he watched long strings of commands scroll past the edges of the display monitor in response to Talev's fingers moving in a near blur over the keyboard. Regardless of what he might think of her personality, there was no disputing her technical talents.

"Thank you, Commander," the lieutenant replied, and Scott noted more than a bit of pride in her voice. "I have to admit, I did not think such a workaround was possible, at least not in such a short time. The solution was rather simple when I started looking for it, however." Shaking her head, she added, "I almost looked past it completely."

Though she had not completely lost the arrogant streak that had dominated her personality at their first meeting, Scott thought he detected a distinct mellowing in the Andorian's attitude. Of course, having to be rescued from dying in space combined with being taught something about her chosen specialty by someone admittedly less skilled than herself would certainly contribute to such a shift in outlook. He could only hope that this mission, if they were successful and able to return home, had provided Talev with a valuable learning experience and an opportunity for growth as not only a Starfleet officer and an engineer, but also as just an ordinary person.

"The engines are free to activate," Tomar reported from the bridge's engineering station. "Engineering reports they are ready to begin the start-up sequence. Warp drive will be available in thirty-four minutes."

Indicating Talev with a nod, Scott replied, "Well, the good lieutenant has done her part, and we still have a bit o' work to tend to before we can think about leaving. Shall we see to it?"

# CHAPTER
# 23

Talev zh'Thren was sure of one thing: She did not want a command of her own.

Sitting in the center seat on the *Chandley*'s bridge, watching as others performed more meaningful tasks around her, she knew that she should feel pride at being given the conn. While Hanar, Tomar, and the others were down in engineering taking care of the final adjustments of the ship's distressed warp engines, she had been tasked with seeing to the welfare of the ship's overall operation. Everyone on the bridge, or on the entire ship for that matter, would turn to her for a decision so long as she occupied the captain's chair. Such power did have its allure, she had to admit. Besides, Hanar would not have placed her in this position were she incapable of carrying out her duties.

So why did she not embrace this responsibility?

Other Andorians had made fine Starfleet captains, she knew, some of them having served with distinction. The Andorian captain of a Federation science vessel had recently ordered her ship's destruction after a Klingon attack rather than allow the vessel to fall into enemy hands. Her actions had been in keeping with the highest standards of both Starfleet and her own people, and would almost certainly inspire many young people, of Andorian heritage as well as a myriad of other races, to pursue their own dreams of one day captaining a starship.

Many young people, yes, but not Talev zh'Thren.

She was reasonably sure she knew why, of course. Having never been comfortable around other people, the idea of being responsible for the actions of others was something that had never appealed to her. Talev much preferred the solace of machines, who only spoke the words programmed into them in response to situations as dictated to them by living beings. Machines did not have feelings or other personality quirks that served only to impede the efficiency of her work. She did not have to worry about offending a computer like she did with other officers, especially humans, who to her seemed able to take offense at the slightest provocation.

*Is it always them? Or is it you?*

Despite the way her initial meeting with Commander Scott had gone, the seasoned engineer had wasted no time calling on her technical expertise in solving their current problems. Any ill feelings he might have harbored toward her had been dismissed for the sake of the mission. Though Scott's computer skills were not as extensive as her own, he had still been able to devise a scheme to override the propulsion computer systems, systems she herself had played a hand in designing and implementing. A lesser person might have used that opportunity to gloat over her mistakes, but Scott had instead complimented her on her ability to improvise a workaround for the computer software.

The same had happened with Commander al-Khaled, who had chosen her to accompany him outside the ship for the repair operation. She knew that he had been at least partially motivated by a desire to perhaps humble her a bit. However, she also had to believe that the commander would not have placed himself at risk by undertaking a dangerous mission with someone he did not trust, and he had literally saved her life to boot.

After all that, Talev was certain of one thing: The past several hours had given her much to think about in regard to her interactions with fellow engineers and officers.

"Lieutenant zh'Thren," Jahn called from the communications station. "We are receiving an incoming hail from the Lutralian ship."

Feeling a knot tighten in the pit of her stomach, Talev acknowledged the order with a nod. There could be only one reason why the alien captain would be contacting them now, after all. She shifted in the command chair and straightened her posture, hoping that she appeared more confident than she actually felt.

"On screen."

As the intimidating features of the Lutralian commander again filled the main viewer she said, "Captain Nrech'lah, I am Lieutenant zh'Thren, temporarily in command. How may I help you?"

*"We have waited for you to complete your repairs, Lieutenant, but our patience wears thin."*

Talev's first instinct was to tell the Lutralian captain what he could do with his patience, thin or otherwise. However, she was sure that Commander Scott would most definitely not approve. Instead, she said, "I understand your concerns, sir, and I assure you that we are proceeding with all haste to finish our work."

*"Our Central Command has been notified of your presence here, and they have classified your vessel as a hazard to navigation. If you are unable to leave under your own power, my orders are to destroy your ship."*

Now what was she supposed to do? Talev was no diplomat, and if she had little patience for the niceties of regular social interaction, she had even less for the bloated flowery extensions of language normally employed by stuffy politicians. As difficult as such an admission might have been before today, she had no problem coming to terms with the fact that she was out of her depth right now.

To the viewscreen she said, "Captain, if you would grant me the necessary few moments, I need to consult with my superiors."

Nrech'lah considered the request for several seconds before nodding tersely. *"Very well, but do not take too long."*

Turning in her seat, Talev made a motion for Jahn to mute the signal before tapping a control on the arm of the command chair. "Zh'Thren to Commander Scott."

*"Go ahead, Lieutenant,"* Scott's voice said a second later, and Talev noted that the veteran engineer sounded harried, no doubt from his and the others' feverish attempts to finish the final repairs to the *Chandley*'s engines. With that in mind, she wasted little time bringing Scott up to speed on Captain Nrech'lah's latest ultimatum.

*"We need another fifteen minutes or so down here, lass. Ye'll just have to stall him until then."*

Talev would not have been more shocked if Scott had smacked her across the face. "Commander? Surely you don't mean that I should engage him in some sort of diplomatic dialogue."

*"I dinna care how ye do it, Lieutenant, but find me fifteen minutes."* As if sensing her uncertainty, the engineer added, *"Listen to me, Talev. Ye've already done everything ye can to get us out of here*

*with your hands, now use your head to get us the rest of the way. Just do me a favor and keep that famous Andorian ire in check, would ye?"*

"As humans are occasionally fond of saying, Commander, that is easier said than done. But I'll do my best, sir. Zh'Thren out." The connection was severed and she exhaled audibly.

*Fifteen minutes. He may as well have asked for fifteen years.*

She nodded to Jahn to reestablish connection with the Lutralian ship. "Captain, I have been informed by my superiors that we will be ready to depart in only a few of our minutes. You have my word that we will leave your space as soon as the repairs are complete."

When Nrech'lah did not reply, Talev considered what else she might say. How would a politician proceed at this point? Say something dull and sycophantic while using entirely too many words in the process, no doubt. Diplomats were experts at ingratiating themselves to others.

"Captain, as this is the first time our two peoples have encountered one another, we view this as an historic occasion. Perhaps there is something that we could take back to our leaders on your behalf, something that would give them a better understanding of your people and your culture?"

On the viewscreen, Nrech'lah smiled slightly. *"You stand before me with a defenseless vessel, knowing that I may destroy it and you as well, and yet you still manage to maintain your bearing. Bravery is a trait we admire. Tell me, alien, are you experienced in speaking as a representative of your people?"*

*Hardly,* Talev thought. To Nrech'lah, however, she said, "I must admit that it is not a specialty of mine. I suspect that you and I are alike in that we have little use for those who talk too much."

To her surprise, Nrech'lah laughed heartily at her statement. *"An excellent observation. I can appreciate the need for such skill, though I have no desire to cultivate it myself."*

Not daring to hope she might have made some kind of breakthrough with the Lutralian ship commander, Talev knew that at the very least she was buying Scott and the others a few precious minutes. Mindful of that, she decided to test the waters further.

"Perhaps we could discuss our mutual dislike of politicians, Captain," she said, making up the entreaty as she went. "It is a custom of many races in our Federation to share stories with friends, over a meal, for example. My commander is otherwise occupied at the moment, but I am sure he would have the time to meet with you, if you would accept my invitation to transport to our ship for dinner."

Nrech'lah laughed again, though this time he shook his head and the laugh was not as warm. *"It is an intriguing offer, but I am afraid I must decline. After all, I suspect you are not naïve enough to overlook the possible advantage of taking me hostage."* Regarding the Andorian for a few more seconds, though, he added, *"However, I will allow you to transfer over to the* Durgejiin.*"*

"Forgive me, Captain, but how do I know you won't take me hostage?"

Shrugging, Nrech'lah said, *"Capturing you would be a waste of time, alien, especially when my orders are to destroy you."* The smile returned, though this time it was the smile of someone who knew he was in command of the situation. *"I am committing a breach of those orders by delaying that action, however, so the least you could do is honor my request."*

How much more time did Scott need? Could she buy them the extra few minutes, and possibly more, by undertaking this risky scheme? Her gut told her that Nrech'lah was being truthful in telling her that she would be safe. The Lutralians could have destroyed the *Chandley* a dozen times over by now. Despite her misgivings, she had no choice but to explore the avenue that Nrech'lah was providing.

"When you put it that way, Captain, I feel obligated to accept."

Nodding, Nrech'lah replied, *"Then I await your arrival."* With that the communication was severed and the viewscreen image returned to that of the Lutralian ship.

"Are you really going over there?" Jahn asked.

"Do you want a weapon? You saw the looks he was giving you, Lieutenant. I don't think I'd trust him to act in the most honorable fashion."

Talev shook her head. "I can take care of myself." Shrugging, she added, "Besides, if he tries anything, I'll just bounce him off the bulkheads until Commander Scott is ready to leave."

"Not a very diplomatic solution," Jahn countered.

"Call it Andorian diplomacy."

As she stepped out of the small shuttlecraft that had taken her across space to the Lutralian ship, the first thing Talev saw was the two hulking figures, their body armor and weapons suggesting that they were the equivalent of a ship's security detail.

"You are to come with us," one of the guards said. Talev noted no malice in the order, though there was firmness behind the words that indicated the guards would not appreciate refusal. Their weapons were holstered, indicating that they did not consider her a threat. So far, it appeared that Nrech'lah was honoring his word not to harm her.

She nodded to the guards, who flanked her as they led her from the cargo hold into which she had piloted the shuttlecraft. The room itself was cluttered with containers and various equipment, most of it unrecognizable to her. Talev noted that although the chamber appeared to be utilitarian in purpose, the components and tools stored here seemed to be clean and well maintained. That suggested an orderliness and pride in work ethic to the young engineer, a notion that was strengthened as she was led into a corridor and deeper into the ship. The passageway itself was immaculate. Uniforms worn by the Lutralian crewmembers were meticulously tailored, with polished metal buttons, buckles, and other accessories. The military atmosphere of the *Durgejiin* was unmistakable.

Following the guards up a series of stairs, Talev wondered if she were being taken to the ship's command center. She found that unlikely. Perhaps a conference room or reception area, then. Her theory appeared to gain credence when the guards stopped before a pair of polished metal doors, both of which sported a multicolored ornamental crest unlike any of the markings she had seen elsewhere on the ship.

One of the guards reached out to a panel, which Talev recognized as a type of intercom control, set into the wall next to the door. "Captain, we have brought the alien as ordered."

*"Excellent, see her in,"* Nrech'lah's voice replied through the intercom. Seconds later the doors parted to reveal a dimly lit chamber beyond.

Talev paused before the threshold, allowing her eyes to adjust to the room's lower illumination. As she studied the room's interior, it became apparent that she had not been brought to a meeting room at all, but rather the captain's private quarters.

"Come in, Lieutenant," Nrech'lah called out from somewhere in the room. Stepping forward, Talev noted the ornate tapestries lining the walls and the eclectic collection of exotic weapons, art, and other decorative objects filling shelves and cabinets. The room's contents reflected an owner who had traveled extensively, most likely as part of a long and distinguished military career.

Following the sound of Nrech'lah's voice, she stepped deeper into the room. As she did so she became aware of a faint odor teasing her nostrils. Not completely unpleasant, the smell grew more pungent as she moved farther into the chamber. She noted steam coming from one doorway on her left, and guessed that the odor, whatever it might be, was coming from there.

*Tell me this isn't going where I think it's going.*

Stepping to the doorway, Talev looked in, her sense of dread growing as she beheld the room that lay beyond. Inside, a large tub dominated the chamber. Filled with a dark, thick liquid, it was undoubtedly the source of the odor. A trio of female Lutralians, each dressed in flimsy shifts hinting at the lithe forms only partially concealed beneath, moved about the room, either tending to the bath or to the person occupying it.

Captain Nrech'lah.

Seated in the tub, naked at least from the point that his chest rose above the surface of whatever it was that filled the tub, the Lutralian regarded Talev with a wide grin on his face.

"Please, come in, Lieutenant."

# CHAPTER
# 24

With a satisfying click, Scott felt the final retaining clip slide into place. The control panel immediately activated as power was restored, and its status displays illuminated as information began to once again transfer to it from the ship's computer.

"Aye, that's got it," Scott said as he tapped a series of test commands to the panel. The displays reacted to his requests, flashing diagnostic data about the *Chandley*'s warp drive. According to the readouts, the engines were operating as well as could be expected, given the damage they had sustained and the limited resources he, al-Khaled, and the team of engineers from New Kelva had at their disposal. Even with the lower-than-normal plasma levels, Scott was confident that the engines would function adequately enough to get them home.

*Assuming we can control them*, he reminded himself.

"All that's left now is to set the course and let the computer do the rest," al-Khaled said from a nearby control station. "I've been doing some computations based on the course we followed to get here, and I think that, with Talev's help, we can instruct the computer on how best to get us back to New Kelva."

From where he sat next to al-Khaled, Tomar pointed to one of the computer displays. "Without the computer overseeing propulsion, we will have to plot the navigation and set up the parameters for acceleration and braking ourselves. This of course invites the possibility of error."

Scott frowned at that. It was an incomplete grasp of the power harnessed by the Kelvan engine design that had gotten them here in the first place. Any modifications made to the navigational subsystems would be rushed, with no time for any sort of simulator testing. Whatever they did, it would have to be right the first time.

That meant they needed Talev to oversee the modifications.

"Scott to bridge," he called out as he tapped the console's intercom control. "Lieutenant zh'Thren, I'm gonna need ye one more time, lass."

Instead of the young Andorian, the uncertain voice of Jahn answered. *"Commander Scott? I'm afraid that the lieutenant is not here."*

"What do ye mean she's not there?" Scott replied, his brow furrowing in confusion. "Where the devil is she then?"

There was a pause of several seconds before Jahn spoke again. *"It was my understanding that she had informed you of her intention to go over to the Lutralian vessel."*

Scott's eyes went wide in shock. What had happened while he and the others had been finishing their repairs? "What in the name of hell is she doing over there?"

At the moment, Talev zh'Thren was standing in the doorway to Captain Nrech'lah's bathing chamber, hands on hips and with an annoyed expression on her face.

"The effects of the *doamjah* oil in the water are really quite therapeutic," Nrech'lah said as he drank from a large, polished goblet. Holding the vessel up for her to see, he added, "Especially when coupled with those of *elbbarcs* wine. You should do yourself a favor and try both."

Shaking her head slowly, Talev replied, "I appreciate the offer, Captain, but I'm afraid there really isn't time. With our repairs almost complete, we will be leaving shortly. I would like to take this opportunity to thank you for your generosity."

Nrech'lah made no attempt to hide his leering stares at her. "I note from the visual communications with your ship that you are different from your companions, and I do not simply mean the physical distinctions. There is a quality to you that seems to be lacking in the others, and I must confess that I find you most alluring, Lieutenant." Taking another drink, he added, "Therefore, if you wish to thank me you may do so by remaining here as my guest."

The first response to enter Talev's mind was to plant her boot squarely in the Lutralian captain's face. If he was operating under the assumption that she would offer herself to him in exchange for safe passage for the *Chandley*, then he was about to be very disappointed. He had made no indications of such an agenda during their previous communications. Had she misread him so completely? That, along with the fact that the captain appeared to be sincere in his desires only served to anger her further.

Even with an effort to remain calm and controlled as she straightened her posture, Talev could not keep a slight edge from her voice. "As I said, my ship will be leaving momentarily, and as much as your offer might flatter me, I must respectfully refuse."

She felt a hand on her shoulder just before one of the guards behind her said, "The captain does not take kindly to having his orders disobeyed."

Instinct took over as Talev reached for the hand on her shoulder, grabbing the guard's arm just above his wrist. Before the Lutralian could react she yanked on the arm and, using her own body for leverage, pulled the guard off his feet. She rolled the off-balance Lutralian over her hip, sending him crashing to the deck in a clumsy heap.

His partner also was reacting, drawing his weapon and bringing it up to aim at Talev. She turned to face the new threat, regretting for the first time that she had not elected to bring a phaser with her.

*You'll just have to make do with his.*

Before the guard could extend his weapon, Talev launched herself at him. Her left arm caught his hand and pushed the weapon up and away from her as she thrust the palm of her right hand up into the Lutralian's jaw. The guard's head snapped up as her other hand closed around the barrel of the weapon and yanked it from his grip. Pivoting on her heel, she spun clear and lashed out with her right foot, catching the Lutralian in the midsection and driving him back into the bulkhead. He struck the wall head-first before sliding stunned to the deck.

Light reflected from something metal and moving and she whirled to see the first guard coming at her, a large and ominous blade in his hand. With the Lutralian between her and the only known exit, there was time for only one course of action.

She shot him.

A thunderous crescendo filled the bathing chamber as she pulled the trigger. Unlike the phasers used by Starfleet personnel, the weapon she now held fired some kind of solid projectile that instantly crossed the space between her and her attacker and struck the guard square in the chest. As the Lutralian was thrown to the deck from the force of the impact, Talev was for a horrifying moment concerned that she may have killed him.

The guard was still moving, though he was holding a hand to the area of his chest armor where the projectile had hit. Talev realized that the armor had protected the Lutralian from the lethal force of the attack, but he did not appear to be making any attempt to regain his feet.

Exhaling in relief, she gave thanks for the hand-to-hand combat training the Academy had instilled in her, to say nothing of the personal fighting techniques that her sister had taught her during their formative years. Though she still exercised both disciplines regularly as a way to relax and relieve stress, she had never expected to make use of such skills in a real-life situation. Looking at the two incapacitated guards, it was nice to see that the time spent in practice had not been wasted. With neither guard posing a threat, she turned and aimed the weapon in the direction of the bath.

While his trio of servants had sought cover behind a waist-high partition at the rear of the room, Nrech'lah had remained seated in the tub, not even bothering to discard his wine goblet. His smile had not faded, either, even when she leveled the muzzle of the weapon at his bare chest. Talev found his reaction most disconcerting.

Then he set his wineglass down and began to clap.

"Very nicely done, Lieutenant."

Talev was sorely tempted to simply shoot him and be done with it. Part of her wanted to see what effect the weapon would have on soft tissue, bone, and muscle as the projectile tore into the Lutralian's chest.

"Would you mind explaining to me what the hell is going on here?"

Nrech'lah retrieved his goblet before answering. "As you indicated earlier, you are a poor diplomat. That much was obvious from our previous conversations. It is equally obvious from your crew's actions to this point that you are not our opponent, so the only question that remained was whether or not you are a worthy ally."

The words took a few seconds to register with Talev, but when realization dawned, it took a renewed effort on her part not to pull the trigger.

"Are you saying that this was a test of some kind?"

Laughing again, Nrech'lah replied, "Of a sort, yes. You showed great bravery on your ship by agreeing to come over here. I wanted to see if that courage was heartfelt or merely a bluff to buy time for your comrades."

It was now Talev's turn to laugh. "Well, I was buying time for them, actually." By her reckoning she had given Commander Scott and the others the time they needed to finish their repairs.

"Fair enough," Nrech'lah replied. "I would expect no less from either a worthy ally or enemy."

Indicating the bath chamber with her weapon, Talev asked, "So why all of this? This was all a setup? It was fake, just to test my reactions?"

Nrech'lah shrugged. "Not all of it, I confess. I was being truthful when I said I found you alluring." Placing a hand on his chest, presumably where his heart might be, he smiled again as he added, "I sincerely apologize if you are upset."

Frowning, Talev said, "It seems like a big waste of time to get information that you could have simply asked for."

"Ah, but then I would have been denied the exquisite look on your face." Nrech'lah's laughter nearly drowned out the sound of her communicator chirping for her attention. Reaching into a pocket of her uniform, she retrieved the unit and flipped it open.

"Zh'Thren here."

*"This is Scott. Do ye mind tellin' me just what the hell ye think yer doin', Lieutenant?"*

Regarding Nrech'lah for a moment, Talev finally lowered the weapon. "I am concluding negotiations with the Lutralian commander, Mr. Scott. Please stand by."

*"But—"*

The reply was cut off as she closed the communicator and returned her full attention to Nrech'lah.

"Captain," she began, "as we have already agreed, I am not a politician, and neither are any of my shipmates. It is obvious to me that you are not looking for a fight with us, and we are neither interested in nor capable of fighting you. Contact your leaders and tell them about us, and extend our offer to have a proper diplomatic envoy sent here from the Federation to meet with them. If you and I could find common ground here today, imagine what our governments might accomplish if given the opportunity."

Nrech'lah nodded in approval, a wry smile warming his features. "Spoken like a politician. You may have missed your calling, Lieutenant. I will pass on your request to our leadership. For now, though, perhaps you would honor me by agreeing to stay, for dinner at least. If you wanted to stay longer, that could certainly be arranged as well." He started to rise from the tub but froze in place as Talev aimed the weapon at him once more.

"Is this another test?" she asked with a wicked smile of her own. "Because if it is, I promise you I will fail this one."

Opting not to press their luck more than was absolutely necessary, Scott ordered the *Chandley* to warp speed as quickly as possible. With Talev proceeding directly to engineering from the shuttle bay, she had assisted al-Khaled in coaxing the ship's propulsion monitoring systems. The engines, despite their compromised condition, had operated almost flawlessly and in a short time Scott was once again looking at the blue-green hue of New Kelva on the main bridge viewer.

"We are home," Tomar said from the science station, more than a hint of relief in his voice. Turning in his seat, he nodded formally in Scott's direction. "My people will be most grateful for Starfleet's assistance in this matter, Commander. We could not have succeeded without you."

Scott indicated the bridge and, by extension the rest of the ship, with a nod of his head. "It was ye and yer friends on New Kelva who built the engines in the first place, Tomar. I think yer designs are a few years away from being widely accepted, but if ye can devise the system that will keep those beasties under control, we may be lookin' at a whole new generation of warp drive. Can ye imagine havin' to recalibrate the warp scale because of what's happened here today?" The very thought excited Scott. Until now, the scale had been thought to be absolute, but it was obvious that still faster speeds were obtainable. Perhaps in a few years, that scale would indeed be in need of revising.

He heard the hiss of turbolift doors opening

behind him and turned to see al-Khaled and Talev step out onto the bridge.

"Welcome back, Lieutenant," he said as the young Andorian moved from the turbolift alcove toward the command well. He started to extend his hand in greeting but stopped short as a foul odor abruptly assaulted his nostrils.

"What in God's name is that smell?"

Near the engineering station, al-Khaled regarded his friend with an annoyed expression. "What are you complaining about? You didn't have to ride in the turbolift with her."

"It's a long story," Talev said. "But suffice it to say that I was successful. The Lutralian government will be expecting a communiqué from the Federation. They are interested in establishing diplomatic ties in the interests of mutual cooperation."

Scott smiled in approval. "A very nice piece of work, Lieutenant. It seems that computer skills aren't the only talents ye're blessed with." His smile faded a bit, though, as he added, "Ye could have at least told me ye were goin' over there."

"I apologize for that, Commander," Talev said, and Scott easily detected the sincerity in the lieutenant's voice. "Given our situation at that time, I did not feel it appropriate to distract you any further than I already had. Your instructions were to stall Captain Nrech'lah long enough for you to complete repairs. Engaging him in a personal dialogue seemed to be the most effective course of action."

Rolling his eyes at that, Scott could not suppress a chuckle. He doubted that Talev was aware of just how much like Mr. Spock she had sounded just then.

"Well, I have to say ye did a fine job, all things considered. It might not have been the smoothest first contact mission ever made, but I know of several that have gone a lot worse. My hat's off to ye, Lieutenant."

Tomar added, "Congratulations, Lieutenant. I hope this does not mean you will give up your engineering duties to pursue a career in diplomacy. The successes we have enjoyed with our engine designs are as much a credit to you as to anyone else."

"I am not planning a career move, Tomar," Talev replied, smiling as she did so. "You and I still have a lot of work to do before this project is finished." Turning to al-Khaled she asked, "Isn't that right, Commander?"

"Right enough," al-Khaled said, rising from the engineering station and approaching the bridge railing. "But I will admit that this mission has given me something new to think about." Looking over at Scott he said, "Engineers in a first contact situation? Sounds like something we should be better prepared for in the future, don't you think?"

Scott frowned at the question. "If ye mean the

S.C.E., I'm not sure I follow. Even if this had been an S.C.E. mission, it wasn't exactly run-of-the-mill."

"No S.C.E. mission is run-of-the-mill," al-Khaled countered. "That's the whole point of the Corps in the first place." Pausing for a moment, the engineer began to pace the upper bridge deck. "Remember that mission we had on Beta III, and what Chris Lindstrom said?"

Nodding, Scott replied, "He said that engineers only know how to fix machines, and that it took specialists of a different sort to understand the people who construct them."

"Exactly," al-Khaled said. "And this mission was a perfect example of what he was talking about. The S.C.E. is being tasked with all manner of missions nowadays. Anytime an ancient alien ship is found, or one of our starships finds the remnants of a dead civilization, they're sending in S.C.E. teams to investigate and evaluate the technology." Indicating Tomar, he added, "What if an S.C.E. team had originally encountered the Kelvans? How might that first contact have gone?"

Tomar replied, "I suspect that the outcome would have been much different, and that we would not be having this conversation today."

"It's only a matter of time before our teams are the first to encounter a new alien species," Talev said. "If that happens, then the S.C.E. has to be ready."

Al-Khaled nodded. "Our teams should be augmented with cultural specialists and linguists, people who are trained to handle the rough spots when different species interact." Shrugging, he added, "Engineers can't be prepared for every type of alien technology they encounter. They can only draw from their previous experience when they encounter something new. But somebody who can deal with the people responsible for that technology should be present, too. I intend to see that our teams are prepared for that eventuality." Smiling, he added, "I told you I wasn't done giving orders, Scotty, and I intend to make this plan my first order of business when I get back to Earth."

Perking up at that, Scott cast a guarded look at his friend. Was this the part where al-Khaled finally clued him in as to his next assignment? "What have ye got in mind, Mahmud?"

"Starfleet has created a new staff position at Headquarters: liaison for the S.C.E. This person will be responsible for coordinating all of the missions the Corps undertakes, as well as ensuring that the teams get the personnel and logistical support they need." Pausing dramatically, he tapped himself on the chest. "You are looking at the first S.C.E. Liaison."

So this was the big mystery, Scott realized as Tomar and Talev offered their congratulations. This was what al-Khaled had hinted at when Scott had first come aboard the *Chandley*. His friend was getting back into the game, all right, and doing so in a big way. After all these years of faithful service, Starfleet had finally seen the value of the S.C.E. and had appointed one of its most talented members to ensure that the Corps continued to thrive and succeed.

There was only one thing wrong with the notion.

"A desk job?" he scoffed. "That's a fine waste of ye talent if ye ask me. I could never see myself trapped in some office. It's just not in my blood, Mahmud, and I dinna think it was in yers."

Chuckling at that, al-Khaled pointed a warning finger at Scott. "If I can be talked into such a job, anything's possible. Never say never, my friend."

Scott laughed at the idea. Him, sitting at a desk while there might be a ship out there in need of an engineer?

*Never, indeed.*

# CHAPTER
# 25

"Chicken broth, Abramowitz Recipe Number Five."

As the mess hall replicator processed her request and her drink appeared, Carol Abramowitz reached for the steaming mug, bringing it to her nose and savoring the aroma of its contents. The addition of the Cajun spices she preferred gave the broth a sharp, pleasing flavor that never failed to elicit a sigh of contentment from her as she took the first sip.

Settling herself at one of the tables in the rear of the mess hall, Abramowitz looked down at her padd for what seemed like the hundredth time today. The lines of text had long since begun to blur into a single indistinct mass, resisting her attempts to comprehend it. Somewhere amid that chaos was her latest report to Gabriel Marshall, the representative of the Federation Diplomatic Corps who had been assigned to this mission.

Perpetually gruff and irritable, the diplomat had no great love for anyone in a uniform who wavered from his idyllic notion of what a Starfleet officer should be: a drone who followed orders without question and avoided complicating the lives of diplomats. Dealing with him, as well as confronting the data she had been collecting, organizing, and reviewing all day, had finally conspired to leave Abramowitz exhausted and dejected. This, despite the pep talk Captain Gold had given her earlier and the combination story/history lesson she had received from Captain Scott. Worst of all, she still had the same headache that had plagued her these past several hours. She could get any one of a number of remedies from Dr. Lense, but Abramowitz had never been one to take medication for what she considered simple ailments. What she needed, she knew, was rest.

Rest, and a damned fine mug of chicken broth.

"How's it going?" a voice asked from near the replicators and Abramowitz looked up to see Kieran Duffy walking toward her with a glass in his hand. How had he entered the room without her noticing?

Shaking her head, Abramowitz took a sip from her mug. "Yet another report for Headquarters. I'm trying to find some way to make this one a little less traumatic. Marshall nearly had a stroke when he heard what happened to the Senuta ship."

Duffy laughed at that. "My best buddy Gabe? How's he doing, anyway? You should tell him I said hello."

The flippant remark brought a much-needed smile to Abramowitz's face. "Somehow I don't think that would go over very well."

Marshall had wanted Duffy's head on a pike several months ago during the *da Vinci*'s mission to recover the century-old *U.S.S. Defiant* from an interspatial rift deep in Tholian space. When the Starfleet engineers discovered incriminating evidence aboard the derelict vessel linking the Tholians to a devastating attack on a Klingon colony, the normally reclusive aliens had launched an assault on the *da Vinci* and the *Defiant*. While in temporary command of the *da Vinci*, Duffy had managed to defuse the situation, salvaging both the recovery operation and the tenuous peace between the Federation and the Tholian Assembly.

That, however, had done nothing to calm Gabriel Marshall's anger over how the mission, one he had not endorsed in the first place, had come dangerously close to becoming a full-blown interstellar incident. Since then, the diplomat had continued to publicly make clear his disdain for Starfleet in general, and Duffy and the *da Vinci* in particular. It had certainly served to make Abramowitz's subsequent interactions with the man that much more trying.

"He's going out of his skull trying to figure out what to do," she said. "Headquarters is hip-deep working out all the bugs to get the Senuta home, but they keep stumbling over the fact that no one knows where their home is." Smiling again she added, "They're not used to being in the dark like that. And on top of everything else, Marshall can't seem to get a grip on the idea that the Senuta aren't blaming us for stranding them here."

Duffy drank from his water glass before continuing. "It throws him off his rhythm. Diplomats need a balance of good things to take credit for and bad things to blame on enemies, or else the entire political fabric of the reality in which we live would be swallowed by entropy. They can't stand the simple idea of everyone just getting along and not trying to point fingers at each other all the time. Such a notion gives them ulcers."

"No dreams of serving on the Federation Council, I see," Abramowitz quipped as she raised her mug to her lips. "That's probably a good thing."

"I should announce my candidacy for the next elections," Duffy replied, "just to see how many shades of purple I can get out of Marshall."

As the pair shared a laugh at Duffy's irreverent view of politics, the mess hall doors parted to admit Bart Faulwell and the two Senuta engineers, Ircoral and Tkellan. The diminutive aliens wore their now familiar wide-eyed expressions of wonder as they followed the *da Vinci*'s linguistic expert into the ship's dining facility, their eyes taking in the room's every detail.

"Hello, you two," Faulwell said, a satisfied smile on his face as he crossed the room to join Abramowitz and Duffy.

His own features screwing into a suspicious frown, Duffy regarded Faulwell warily. "You look entirely too smug about something. What's the smile about?"

Faulwell took a seat at the table, followed almost immediately by Ircoral and Tkellan. "I bring good news," he said. "Soloman has found the navigational charts in the data he recovered from the Senuta ship. I've taken a look at them and they're pretty limited by our standards, but not unlike what our first deep exploration starships possessed a couple of centuries ago."

"Ensign Wong can probably make short work of those," Duffy replied.

Faulwell nodded. "Already has. He was able to cross-reference against our own navigational databases. It took some doing, though. The Senuta are from a star system deep in the Beta Quadrant, on the edge of explored Klingon space. Weeks away at high warp." Shaking his head, he added, "I'm amazed that the Klingons didn't intercept them."

"That's great," Abramowitz said. "Of course, this makes Marshall's job harder, as now he'll have to explain how an alien ship tore through Klingon space and how they'll be asked to allow these same trespassing aliens back through so they can get home."

"Lucky for us we have an ambassador who's friends with the Klingon chancellor," Duffy said. Worf, the first Klingon to serve in Starfleet, had resigned his commission the previous year in order to assume the role of Federation ambassador to the Klingon Empire. Abramowitz had not yet met Worf but his reputation preceded him, of course. She was sure that this situation would be concluded with little further difficulty with his assistance. It was Worf who had overseen talks among the Federation, the Klingons, and the Tholians in the wake of the *da Vinci*'s mission to recover the *Defiant*, with the Klingons and Tholians actually engaging in the first true peaceful negotiations ever attempted between those two peoples. If Worf could handle that, then getting safe passage for the wayward Senuta would be child's play for him.

"We will be going home soon," Ircoral said, her face beaming. "My only regret is that we will be forced to leave you while there is still so much to be learned."

Leaning forward in his chair, Duffy said, "Oh, I wouldn't worry too much about that. If there's one thing that you can count on when it comes to diplomacy, it's that it takes time. Then there's the matter of securing a ship to ferry you home. My guess is that we've still got a few days together, at least."

"What do we do now?" Tkellan asked. "If we are to be together for a while longer, then we should not waste the opportunity. Surely there is something more you can tell us."

Breathing a sigh of relief, Abramowitz settled back into her seat and allowed herself to relax for the first time since this mission had begun. The Senuta would be returned home, no doubt accompanied by Federation envoys eager to open a dialogue with the newly encountered people. While she of course would not be going along with the delegation, she could take satisfaction that she and her shipmates had set into motion the process that would allow that meeting to take place at all. Further, this entire mission had served as a reminder to her, and to her companions, just why there was a Starfleet Corps of Engineers, and just why she and others like her traveled with them.

Regarding the two Senuta engineers now, though, Abramowitz found herself with an uncustomary lack of ideas on what to do next. She did not want to disappoint Ircoral and Tkellan when they were so obviously expecting something from her and her companions. But all she really wanted to do was just finish her chicken broth, take a hot shower, and then crawl into bed for a decent night's sleep. Seeing the look in Faulwell's eyes, she figured that the linguist felt very much the same way.

Only Duffy appeared to have any measure of energy left, and suddenly she had her answer. She cast a wicked look at the engineer, who saw the evil smile on her face and swallowed nervously.

"What?" he asked.

Abramowitz turned her attention to the Senuta instead.

"Have you ever heard of a Tellarite?"

# ABOUT THE AUTHORS

DAYTON WARD got his start in professional writing by placing stories in each of the first three *Star Trek: Strange New Worlds* anthologies. He is the author of the *Star Trek* novel *In the Name of Honor*, the Calhoun short story in *Star Trek: New Frontier: No Limits*, and the science fiction novel *The Last World War*. With Kevin Dilmore, he has written several other *Star Trek: S.C.E.* adventures besides the one in your hands, a story for the summer 2004 *Star Trek: Tales of the Dominion War* anthology, and a pair of upcoming *Star Trek: The Next Generation* novels titled *A Time to Sow* and *A Time to Harvest*. Though he currently lives in Kansas City with his wife, Michi, Dayton is a Florida native and still maintains a torrid long-distance romance with his beloved Tampa Bay Buccaneers. You can contact Dayton and learn more about his writing at www.daytonward.com.

\*       \*       \*

After fifteen years as a newspaper reporter and editor, KEVIN DILMORE turned his full attention to his freelance writing career in 2003. Since 1997, he has been a contributing writer to *Star Trek Communicator*, writing news stories and personality profiles for the bimonthly publication of the Official *Star Trek* Fan Club. With Dayton Ward, he has written a story for this summer's *Star Trek: Tales of the Dominion War*, three other *Star Trek: S.C.E.* installments, and a forthcoming two-book *Star Trek: The Next Generation* tale, with more to come. His first foray into solo fiction was the story "The Road to Edos" in *Star Trek: New Frontier: No Limits*. Kevin also conducted interviews with some of *Star Trek*'s most popular authors in volumes of the *Star Trek* Signature Editions published by Pocket Books in the fall of 2003. A graduate of the University of Kansas, Kevin lives in Prairie Village, Kansas, with his wife, Michelle, and their three daughters.

# STAR TREK®

## STARGAZER: OBLIVION

### MICHAEL JAN FRIEDMAN

In 1893, A TIME-TRAVELING JEAN-LUC

PICARD ENCOUNTERED A LONG-LIVED ALIEN

NAMED GUINAN, WHO WAS POSING AS A

HUMAN TO LEARN EARTH'S CUSTOMS.

THIS IS THE STORY OF A GUINAN VERY DIF-

FERENT FROM THE WOMAN WE THINK WE

KNOW.

A GUINAN WHO YEARNS FOR

OBLIVION.

AVAILABLE NOW

STSO.01

# KNOW NO BOUNDARIES

# STAR TREK®

STAR TREK CROSSWORD SERIES